The Monkey King:

A Journey to a State of Presence

A novel by Amira Tchlyndria Kidd

Printed in the United States of America
First Printing, 2015
ISBN 978-0692438633

CreateSpace
4900 LaCross Road
North Charleston, SC 29406 USA

https://www.createspace.com/Help/Rights/TermsOfUse.jsp

Contents

PROLOGUE~

It's said that beauty is in the eye of the beholder, and material items such as the contour shape of a large sparkling diamond or the master paintings of the late Jean Michel Basquiat, no matter how beautiful are not always adored by all. But there are instances when beauty is just that, beauty. It can't be denied or ignored, and there is no finer example than in the breath taking creation of some human beings. Close your eyes and imagine lips that can make quenched soles, parch with lust to suck, only to be parched again by sheer desire. Now, open your eyes. I bet there are a few around you who can draw another in like a dry camel to cool water. But sooner or later this beauty must fade like the painted walls of an old building, and what then? For example take a beautiful porcelain piece that has been standing for years in some nameless museum, one day it is bound to crack, and what do you think will be found behind those cracked pieces, nothing. On the other hand there is more than beauty to a human being. Peel back the fleshy remains and what you have left is the core of the human, it's soul. This is where you get to know the true person, where hopefully there is beauty to be found, for if not, an ugliness that wasn't obvious before may rear its' nasty head. But the soul does not stand-alone. It must be nourished and it is this that lies behind the twinkling eyes of every human, the spirit. What the soul needs the spirit provides. A hungry stomach demands food, a tired body needs rest, and a lustful thirst needs quenching, while a shattered heart needs mending. The spirit is a free entity and because it nourishes the soul, it is like a wild animal stopping at nothing to please its' master. It can be flirtatious and playful, serious and conserved, demanding and cold, or just whimsical and silly. But when a spirit is broken, it causes friction with the soul, and a cycle of life is disturbed, put off balance. And how you may ask is a spirit broken, by the negative souls that happen to surround it. It is then that the spirit is confined, held in a tight grip of uncertainty, bound to the turmoil's of its soul, until it is freed. But who should free a spirit, and how? No one's true spirit should be hidden, because sooner or later the soul will push until the spirit fights hard enough to reveal itself to the world.

1~

FERTILIZATION OF AN IDEA

A tall, handsome, dark eyed Casanova stood on 42nd street staring into a retail window. Behind a male mannequin dressed in the latest Versace suit stood a petit beautiful young woman. She was American in posture, but French in her way of dress. Draped in a brown pencil skirt with buttons in the center that trailed just above her knees to the top of her waistline, it complimented the simple off white blouse with sleeves that came just pass the elbow. This casual look was dressed up with a short rope of small pearls that lay elegantly upon her neck. The dark eyes of the Casanova moved away from the pearls, up her neck, past the plush lips, and small nose to her slightly cut eyes. Like his the color was dark brown to go along with the eyebrows that lined them. Her lovely face was shaped with cheeks that rose high as mountaintops. Jet-black hair cropped just past the eyes hid the woman's full beauty from the sides, while her short bangs allowed her to view those daring enough to take a peak. He had seen her many times before, but this was the first time he had seen her out of her element. An assistant teacher at his university, she frequented the English department regularly. Never too much for his eyes to take, this unexpected encounter was a pleasurable treat. She was all he ever thought about, and at that moment the only thing that stood between them was a simple show room window.

"Salem, I know you like that suit, but now we don't

have time to look," Lamya said, as she stood behind her brother.

Lost in the beauty that stood before him he had completely forgotten about Lamya, whose reflection he could see in the window. Unlike the object of his affection her hair was covered by a dark brown hijab. She chose to wear it soon after returning home some years ago. It fit snug around her full face bringing out her big round eyes, pug nose and thin arched lips. Those features permanently replaced the beauty of her large loopy dark curls, often pushed back away from her forehead by pretty little flowery headbands. These locks were now only seen behind closed doors. He remembered his sister wore short skirts with white knee high socks, accented with colorful t-shirts and tennis shoes. Unfortunately these were replaced with long sleeve shirts and full-length skirts. In the west it left little to be desired. Turning around he grabbed his sister's hand. The family, were in the states for one month, and on the second evening of arriving it would be their mother's first time fixing a Moroccan meal on US soil. It had been a while since he had sat down with his family to eat. Looking back through the glass once more his beauty would have to wait.

A far cry from home Salem had long left the dorm life deciding instead to take a chance as a man in the big city. Though he loved the colorful people, walks in Greange village, and that casual run through central park, what he loved most was that feeling of being home without actually being there. Astoria was the area he chose, and for him it was perfect. The neighborhood gave him the taste of the familiar without him having to swallow a mouthful. He had the best of both worlds and as he walked with Lamya away from the main city towards Astoria, the thoughts of home forced him to close his eyes and take a deep imaginary breath of the ethnic scents that would soon fill

his nose. Not to spend too much money they grabbed a cab.

Betting on a short cut they took an alley- way, which led to

a side door straight to a lift. On the way up to the seventh

floor, as his stomach began to grumble he realized that he

couldn't think just about himself anymore. His apartment

had become like his childhood home, and at least for a

month it was family that would have to come first, no

matter what. Playing, he pushed his sister to the side racing

toward the door. On that day there would be no nanny to

meet them, but instead their mother happy to see her two

siblings together.

In less than two days his family had managed to turn a

two-bedroom New York flat into the likes of a villa in Abu

Dhabi, the new suburbs of the U.A.E. As they entered his

apartment facing the opposite end of the room were two

colorful Moroccan lamps placed strategically on each side

of his living room window greeting anyone who dared to visit. As he closed the door the smell of incense over took any food cooking on the stove. Happy to see her two children their mother's embrace seemed to last an eternity. Grabbing her son by the hand she led him straight to the dining room table. Different from when he left it that morning the table was dressed with a miniature marble water fountain that sat on top of a table runner decorated with tiny silk brocades. Though he loved his family the added additions to his place made him feel as if there was no room to breathe. To escape he gave the excuse of having to wash his hands.

Splashing his face with water he dried his hands while looking closely into the mirror. He hadn't done this in a while and attributed the habit resurfacing due to his families visit. It was definitely not one of his favorite past times, though he never truly understood why. Without a blemish on his face and too much hair to deal with, there was nothing he had to complain about. In-fact whoever set eyes on him: friend or foe had to agree that he was a hot item. With a nice body, sparkling white teeth and a face most magazine editors would die for who could ask for anything more. Yet each glimpse into any mirror gave Salem an empty feeling.

"Salem, Yala, Yala," his mother shouted from the living room.

Startled but relieved he took a deep breath and went back to the dining room table to try to enjoy the meal he had been waiting so long for.

It was big day for Salem. He would pick up his cap and gown for the last time. Just before noon he would finish his last exam, making him free of responsibility for at least the summer. Having little time to eat he stuffed himself as much as he could and then kissed his mother goodbye, pressed for his sister to hurry, he handed his father the cup of tea his mother had just made. Grabbing Lamya by the hand as she finished wrapping her hijab he rushed out the door. Listening for any sign of their parents, they leaned against the wall, both taking a deep breath and exhaling in relief. This was another habit that had resurfaced in him, another habit that he couldn't explain. It was understandable that Lamya kept it up, she had been staying with their parents, but for him, it was different, he had been away, on his own for eight years straight. That morning there was no time for him to sit back and think about his motives, there was only time to enjoy the external fruits of the day. As if they knew what the other was thinking brother and sister looked at each other, shrugged their shoulders and hurried to the elevator.

It was unusually hot for an April morning as they reached the university. It kind of reminded them of home. Waving good-bye they both went their separate ways. Lamya went to explore campus and the fit guys who populated it, while he headed to his classroom. Entering the classroom as if free money were awaiting him, he noticed for the first time in three months that the room was actually full. He took his usual seat in the back of the room, and though he considered himself a gentleman at that moment, the last three years of his college career was filled with more classroom pranks and plots than he could remember. He had a reputation; so sitting in the back of the class drew attention away from him. In the past year he had matured considerably, and on that final day he began to feel as if he had graduated into adulthood. As the exams were passed out he reclined in his seat confident, it only took him thirty minutes to finish. The professor graded it on the spot and handed it back to him with a peculiar look on his face.

"You know I couldn't have cheated. You create the exams at the last minute. Everyone knows that," Salem said.

The professor smiled, shook his hand, and pointed to the 95% at the top of his exam. Ecstatic he gave the professor a fare well pat on the back. The 95% assured him of a 4.0 graduating average. The long walk the library was well welcomed. Never again would he have to race across campus just to make it to class. In a month he would be an alumnus, and he was sucking up all the fresh air that went with it. By the time he reached the library the line for graduation robes extended to the front door. It seemed as if the whole university was graduating.

Waiting in line for at least fifteen minutes, a tap on the shoulder broke his boredom.

"Hey man what's up? It's all up hill from now on baby!

Just one week and it's on to bigger and better things," Mitch chanted.

Mitchell or Mitch as he preferred was his closest friend since stepping foot on campus. Salem was wondering where he had disappeared to the weekend before.

"Man, where have you been? I had to spend the whole weekend with my family," Salem rebutted.

Looking puzzled Mitch gives him a shove in the shoulder.

"Man what are you talking about? I was doing the same thing you were. I told you my family would be here too. Favorite son had to play catch up with all the family gossip," Mitch said pushing him forward in line.

"Damn, I'm sorry. I forgot too. You should have picked

up the phone. We need to talk. I told you I was serious about throwing that party. Are you in," he asked raising his eyebrow as he spoke.

Grinning from ear to ear Mitch raised his hand high in the air waiting to receive a high five.

"I'm all in. We might as well do it up and make it hot while we're at it," Mitch said pushing Salem forward once more.

Annoyed by his lack of attention and his continuous lack of notice to her, the attendant frowned. Freckled face, with a red bob, a short stature, and a wide physique she pushed her square shaped glasses high on her nose.

"Excuse me! Can I help you," she grumbled.

Startled Salem turned abruptly surprising her so much that she almost fell backwards out of her chair.

"Oh, I'm so sorry. I thought I still had a few people in front of me," he said as he reached to try to help her regain her posture.

As if the abrupt surprise shook her out of a trance her attitude quickly changed as she gave him a sheepish look.

"It's okay Salem, just give me your last name," she batting her eyes.

"Do I know you," he asked.

"I'm Liz. We started here at the same time," she replied as she rolled her eyes to what seemed like the back of her head.

As Liz spoke he noticed that there was also a line to the right of him. Looking down at the many feet that awaited for their turn at the head of the line, the attendants agitated voice caused him to look up and notice the first in line right next to him was the assistant teacher that he admired. Caught in her beauty he stood with his mouth wide open. Ignored once more Liz slammed her hand down on the counter.

"Salem, what is your last name," she nearly screamed.

Embarrassed Salem tried to give his full attention to her with a sheepish smile himself.

"I'm so sorry, it's Tamimi," he said pulling his wallet out of his pocket.

"Tamimi, where are you from," she asked taking a chance and batting her eyes again.

"It's Arabic," he replied.

Turning his head slightly towards the assistant teacher, she was too busy to even notice him. In return the attendant could only frown as she turned to search for the cap and gown with his name on it. He was focused on the assistant and smiled at her hoping she would. Assuming everyone was just happy to be in the cap and gown line she gave him a slight smile in return, picked up her package and walked away. Losing all hope the attendant slammed Salem's package on the counter and pushed him aside to help Mitch. Giving Mitch a shove he pointed at the assistant grabbed his package from the counter and inconspicuously followed her through the bookstore. Grasping the package close to his chest he realized that if he were ever going to speak with her it would have to be at that moment. Who knew what would happen after graduating day. In just the few minutes of following her, he learned that though she taught English as an assistant, she was a journalist for the universities paper. She talked a lot and seemed to have quit a few friends. The more he learned the more he needed to know. As she walked out the door, he grabbed her by the hand. The sun was still high as the doors opened, and even though he meant to touch her slightly, he held with a tight grip. Startled she turned and for the first time he stood speechless, that is until Mitch slapped him on the back as he was walking out.

"As soon as possible, as soon as possible" Mitch said as he took a quick glance at Salem's hand.

He let go of the assistant's hand as he watched Mitch leave, and not wanting to feel like a loser he spoke fast so Mitch wouldn't have anything to say later.

"Hi, I know you don't know me, but me and my friend

who just left, I believe are graduating with you. So, some buddies of mine, and the international club are holding a graduation party on the 29th. We would love if you and some of your friends could be gracious to volunteer some time to help us coordinate it. We want as much variety as possible and with you working with the paper," he said as he pointed at the paper she held in her hand. Putting her once confined hand on her hip she pretended not to be startled.

"How do you know I work for the paper? You're in one of my classes aren't you," she asked, as she looked him up and down.

"Yeah, English 235 with professor Chow, and I'm an avid reader of the schools news paper," he said in a confident tone.

Almost on his tiptoes he stood taller waiting for a letdown.

"Sure, I already have some friends that are in the club. I don't have my phone right now, but you can take my number," she said pulling a pen out of her purse.

With a sigh of relief and a smile that followed, he found it almost impossible to contain himself.

"It's Salem," he said while pulling the cap and gown receipt out of his pocket.

"Okay, Salem my name is Cherise Leflore. Look me up in the school directory. It's a busy day for me, so try me tomorrow," she replied writing down the information and quickly handing it back to him.

And that was it, after all that time he finally knew her name and had a possibility of meeting up with her again. It was a good day and walking out the door he couldn't help but marvel at the fact that he had his cap and gown in hand, had spoken to the assistant for the first time, and his sister was able to flounce around campus as she pleased free from the wondering eyes of her parents. He was ready for the new chapters to come in his life.

Searching for his sister around campus, he found her with a few other girls chatting in the cafeteria. They were rating the guys as they passed by. He watched his sister closely. He had never seen her flirt before. She never told him anything about her personal life, and he did the same, but now he wondered. Either way for him first things were first. He was never one to let a good opportunity pass him up. What he knew better than Mitch or any of his friends, was that having a sister younger or older had one big advantage. Opening the door to the cafeteria he made his way not only to his sister, but the gorgeous girls who stood talking with her. Approaching the women with his Casanova smile, he sneaked up behind his sister and put his hands over her eyes. Getting the attention he wanted as the other girls giggled, he weaved his charismatic ways around them. He was hoping to assure eye candy for the party.

"Hello ladies, I hope my sister is not bothering you too much," he said as he gave them all a big smile.

Lamya playfully pushed her brother to the side, shyly introducing the girls to him.

"I'm sorry this is my brother Salem," she said as he stepped in front of her.

The girls were mesmerized, and the look he received

from them was all too familiar.

"I didn't know my sister knew anyone at this school. She's here visiting from the U.A. E... But if you're interested you should get my sister's number. I'm having a graduation party and it would be great if you could come," he said giving his sister one of the most fake hugs of all time, as he signaled for her to pull out her cell phone.

Still giggling the girls gave him a nod. Salem was not an arrogant guy, but he knew how the girls loved him. He also knew that before they reached the cafeteria doors his sister would have each of the women's numbers. Outside under the sun he stretched his arms out while looking up towards the sky. He soaked up all the sun he could get, knowing that it would eventually be sucked out of him after reaching home. Rushing out of the cafeteria excited that she would get to meet her new friends again, Lamya grabbed her brother by the hand leading him down the sidewalk.

"I didn't know you were having a party, I have to go shopping," she said.

Pulling away from her Salem looked around to see if anyone was watching. Brother and sister holding hands may have been fine back home, but in the states it was a different story.

"Hey you can't tell mom or dad about this party or else you and me will find our-selves sitting at home that night," he said as he walked ahead of her.

Lamya agreed not wanting to lose a chance at experiencing probably the last American party in her life and there was no way their parents were going to interfere with that.

2~

BIRTH OF DEFIANCE

Leaving his sister to sleep in on a perfectly lazy

Saturday morning, Salem reluctantly grabbed his keys and

followed his parents into the streets of New York. Along

with finishing school he knew that whatever happened, the

most important item on his agenda was his career. If he

hadn't realized this, his parents would certainly not let him

forget. Going into a week of being with their son the

newness of the states was beginning to wear off, and all the

Tamimi's wanted to do was talk business. Family business

was always talked out over breakfast, and the Tamimis chose Jackson Hole Diner as their spot for negotiations. Salem took great thought in what he wanted to do with his future and was positive of what direction he would take. What Salem wasn't sure of was whether he wanted to go back home or not. Though he had great things to present to his parents, he was not looking forward to seeing their reactions. He even felt guilty about the choice of dress he wore that morning. The family would have loved for him to wear a djellaba or even a gandora, but he was more comfortable in his Reul shorts and white T-shirt. His father was especially excited that morning and like any Moroccan son he wanted to do all he could to keep a smile on his father's face. Walking behind his parents he almost cringed at the fact that his father looked like a stranger to him. Back home he worked, lounged and celebrated every moment of his life in a gandora. Because his son wasn't in traditional clothing, he too decided to go local in a pair of Levi jeans and a black and white stripped button down short sleeve shirt that were beginning to look like a perfect fit. Even his mother parted with tradition choosing to wear a light white shirt with a jean skirt, that just hit her ankles, and to top it all off a jean inspired hijab.

Jackson Hole Diner 69-35 Astoria Blvd was extremely busy. This made Salem feel at ease. He figured the more people that were present, the more unlikely that his father would refrain from causing a scene. It was a pancake morning for the Tamimis, and Salem's mother couldn't get enough of them. Her motto was "One taste of America's cakes was like taking that first step into heaven." Waiting for their order his father leaned across the table giving him a slap on the shoulder. His smile was broad, so much that his son had to return it with an embarrassing blush.

"So go ahead and tell us what your plans are. You have

been holding us in suspense for long enough," He asked leaning across the table he raised his eyebrows and waited for his son's response.

Nervously Salem palmed a cup of coffee being handed out by the waitress. Taking a sip he took he took a deep breath along with it. Reluctantly putting it down he began to spill the beans.

"Well, I've been searching and I actually found two good offers," he said nervously.

The eyes of his father widen with anticipation.

"So, don't leave us in suspense. Go ahead and talk," Mrs. Tamimi said copying her husband in his lean across the table.

Nervous, but proud of what he had accomplished, he

couldn't contain it any longer.

"I was offered a position with Raphael Vinoly Architects PC. It seems my three years of experience has gotten me just where I want to be. Dad both companies are offering me a start of 80,000 dollars. Can you imagine," he asked.

Though he wasn't in the country Mr. Tamimi happened upon a chance to get his son a job with a small architecture company in the city. Whenever he got the chance Salem would go to sites and even put some insight into whatever was going on. Four three years he did this and at that moment Mr. Tamimi was glad that he was able to help. The eyes of Mr. Tamimi began to twinkle as his mother took her hands and covered her mouth in astonishment. Tears ran down her face, as the excitement over the news and the appearance of her three stacks of pancakes were just too much to take at once. Giving his wife a hug Mr. Tamimi then looked over to his son in question.

"So why haven't you chose one," his father asked.

Taking a bite of his pancakes Salem collapsed back into his chair. Grinding his teeth he tried to hide his excitement.

"Because both of the jobs are here in the U.S., and I was hoping, inshallah that you would be happy for me," he said nervously dragging a piece of pancake around the plate with his fork.

Hearing the news both parents collapsed back into their chairs. They seemed shocked and Salem expected it.

"It's not like I haven't been looking at home, it's just that nothing has come up. Plus if I work here I can earn my PHD easier," he said taking a bite of his pancake.

His words didn't do much to cushion the news, and it never occurred to either of them that he might not return home.

"And what about your family Salem, what about us," Mrs. Tamimi whined as the tears seemed to fall no stop.

Though life was comfortable in Abu Dhabi, there was nothing like home. Because his mother knew how he felt, she always figured that after her son's graduation he would come home and help them out. Salem knew this and tried to ease their concerns.

"I know the goal for you is to get back home. I haven't forgotten, and with me making this type of money here, you can get back home quicker than what we originally thought. In fact if I take an offer now you can be back in Morocco looking for property in two months," he said as he opened his arms wide as if he had just given them the world.

"I know that you've been here for some time, but how much longer can you do without family around? Back home there are ways that you must live. Here anything is acceptable. Don't you think that this could be troubling?

To his father they were words of gold. Mr. Tamimi slowly left his wife's shoulders, resting his elbows on the table instead. He clutched his hands together resting his forehead upon them. After a moment of silence he began to speak.

"Habibti, does he look troubled? Has he been troubled? Maybe this is good, just what he needs. So, Salem, you're saying in two months after leaving here I can begin searching for some land in Morocco," his father asked.

Salem sat up in his chair. He loved his father's optimism even though he didn't always agree with it.

"Yes, dad, with either company I'm getting a sign on bonus of 85,000, just to get me settled," he said leaning across the table looking his father straight in the eyes.

A quiet but pleasing bellow came from his father. Ecstatic he grabbed his wife by the shoulders trying to shake some since into her. A smile gradually appeared and finally she gave him an approving nod. Reaching over the table she motioned for her son's hands. As he had done since he was boy she put her hands together and slid his in between hers. Holding his hands tightly, she looked him straight in the eyes. He had been away for a while and had forgotten about this habit of hers. It's true that no one knows themselves better than themselves, but it's usually the mother who discovers those inner layers of a child before the child himself has come into his own. She knew something and he knew that she knew. He just didn't know what exactly what it was that she knew. This is why between each ritual stare he would interrupt it by running to another room. The problem was there was know where to run that morning, so he reached over and gave her a strong hug. It distracted her for the moment, and Salem saw the breakfast as a success. The last business of the day was breaking the news to his sister. He wondered could she survive alone without him. He also wondered if she would feel portrayed. Having other things on his mind as well the rest of the morning began a world wind of phone calls and mall shopping. Knowing that their son could repay them for all the tuition money obviously well spent, they decided to celebrate by buying gifts for the family back home, along with some items for themselves. While they made calls to the family, Salem decided to make a special call to Andy Richmond, head designer for Raphael and Vindy Architect

PC. A dedicated employee Richmond frequented the architectural office many times on Saturdays, and it was this guy that Salem had to give his yes to. He had made his choice a few weeks ago and couldn't believe he was finally saying yes. As he talked with Andy the words came smooth from his mouth like melted butter on hot toast. It was a done deal. It had become the best weekend of his life. In the afternoon after shopping and sightseeing he decided that it would be nice to give them a little taste of home American style, and treated them to Little Morocco. Dinner would not have been complete without Lamya, and so giving her a call Mrs. Tamimi couldn't contain herself. She told Lamya she had a surprise, just as Salem had forgotten all about it. To soften the blow decided he'd order her favorite dish, lamb sausage tucked in French bread topped with green olive relish.

Two hours later dinner was being served and Lamya's

was the last to be set at the table. Sitting by her father he grabbed her head planting a kiss on his daughter's cheek. She thought that maybe they were going to bring up the husband subject or had found one as happy as they seemed, at least her parents; Salem on the other hand could hardly hold his head up. He knew his parents would spit out the news and again there was nowhere for him to run. Clasping his daughter's cheeks, Mr. Tamimi looked her straight in the eyes and broke the news.

"Oh habibi, before your father dies you will be able to live in your own home in Morocco," he said with wide eyes.

It was worse than she thought; Lamya shook her head, while Mrs. Tamimi gave her husband a disapproving stare wanting to explain more. Salem volunteered the news instead.

"I uh got a job here and I'm staying," he said folding his arms as he spoke.

Lamya too slumped back in her seat. The words that came from his mouth made her feel as if she had been punched in the stomach. It was blow to her perspective on her future in Abu Dhabi. She thought with her brother around, she would have some freedom again. With her mouth wide open staring into space, she searched for safe words.

"I thought you wanted to come home," she asked with a questionable face.

Salem's heart sunk. He knew how hard it was being a girl in the Middle East. And yes, a lot guys said this, but he was one who actually meant it. It was their connection.

"So, I guess I'll see you on holidays Uh," Lamya said finally sitting up in her chair.

Salem held his head low. Lamya had nothing else to say on the subject. During dinner each time her brother even thought about passing a smile her way she would give him and evil glance rolling her eyes, as she looked the other way. He didn't enjoy dinner like he thought he would, but as he took his last bite, something put a smile on his face. Coming down the isle with his girl friend on one arm and a shopping bag in another was his friend Mitch. Grinning from ear to ear after seeing Salem, he unlocked his right arm from his girl friend and raises it high in the air, while sliding down the aisle giving Salem a high five. "Hey call me tonight we have some people asking about the thing," he said as he took a glance over at what he figured had to be Salem's parents.

He knew about Salem's conservative family and caught himself just before saying another word. Salem took a deep breath and directed his smile toward Lamya. She didn't know Mitch, but she had a very good idea that she knew what he was talking about. She hated her brother right then and at that moment if she wanted to she could have relinquished any dreams of him holding or attending any party. It would be just like he had just surprisingly relinquished her dreams of freedom. She could feel her parents staring at her and if she were going to do anything, it would have been right then. Opening her mouth to say something the thought of such a devious move kept her from saying anything. She instead gave her brother a smile back and reclined in her chair. Salem exhaled as Mitch said only hello and quickly disappeared.

"That was a good friend of mine. You'll get to meet him a little later," he said wiping off his mouth with a napkin.

After dinner Salem lagged behind his parents who were now in a hurry to get home. Pulling his sister by the arm he spoke lightly in her hear.

"Hey, we'll spend as much time as possible here, no matter what is going on. That's the reason I wanted you at the party in the first place. Where I go you go. We'll figure something out,"

Lamya knew her brother meant well. She also knew that he was just living his life. Her cheeks grew a rosy red as she gave him a heartwarming smile. She also thought something had to be done. She just didn't know what.

3~

ONE OF 108 DEFILEMENTS OF PASSION

It would be two nights later that Salem would meet up with Mitch. He lived in Harlem, deciding also to push campus living to the curb. Salem enjoyed going to his place. There was just something about it that made him want to stay. He could never figure out what it was, but he just knew he never felt like leaving. He always took the same route going to Mitch's place. Living on the corner of 120th street close to Adam Clayton Park, he would catch the NW line to the number 7, finally hitting 125th street, where he would walk a mile just to enjoy the view. The walk was different this time around for him, because he suddenly realized from that point on he would call New York home. It was late afternoon when he arrived at Mitch's place and the sun was setting. He would have loved if his sister had joined him that day, but his parents insisted that she stay home to meet other family members from Detroit. Nothing like Salem when it came to living, Mitch was A VIP baseball player before transferring to Cambridge. He had all types of sports paraphernalia on his walls. Though the place was clean, it was definitely a bachelor's pad. After hurting his arm permanently in a game four years ago, Mitch switched from collecting sport items to buying high tech merchandise instead. He needed something to keep himself busy, so his pacifier became making his living room into the ultimate private theater. Music blasting from his Bang Olufsen speakers, while his twenty five inch flat screen showed the latest videos, Mitch sat at his dining room table finishing up some work for the week when Salem walked in. Unlike most of the future graduates Mitch started working at least three months before graduating. Having the right contacts due to his past baseball fame, he found a cushy job doing exactly what he had always wanted to do. He was a consultant for Nintendo of America Inc. In two months after training they would be sending him all over the world. He even managed to fix a deal where he could help create games. The funny thing was that Mitch would have died if anyone knew that the infamous lady's man was actually an undercover computer geek. Salem held back his grin as he shook his friend's hand.

"What's wrong? It looks like your holding in a bathroom run man," he said as he stared suspiciously at Salem.

Hiding his grin as he shook Mitch's hand he turned to

take another look at the room. He wanted to make sure Mitch hadn't invested in more equipment without him knowing.

"Nothing man. I just don't see how you can blast this stuff without worrying about walking in one day and finding it gone," he yelled over the music.

Turning the music down Mitch beckons him to the kitchen.

"I'm glad you made it man. I have my brother over here making us some snacks. He's goanna be our all around handy man now and during the party. I also have some people here who have volunteered to help us out. Sure enough as Salem entered the kitchen there was fifteen-year old Thomas wearing a white apron pouring coke and sprite for his brother's guest. The spitting image of his brother, he knew he was a good-looking kid. It was the reason why he was able to convince his girl friend to assist him in his brother's venture. Giving her his handed down genetic Casanova smile he pointed to Salem who stood in the kitchen door. Unlike his brother Thomas was a show off.

"Hey Salem, long time no see. This is Lizy, and Lizy this is Salem," he said.

The same age as Thomas, Salem had to admit that the girl was cute. If Mitch was the lady-killer, then he wondered what Thomas would have up his sleeve in another two years. Saying hello he didn't want to disturbed his little friends working flow so he left the kitchen and went into Mitch's guest room, which he had turned into a small social room. Looking around Mitch had recruited the right people. Ilana Moshki from the international club, Rodrick Clay a good friend of Mitch's, and Professor Chow of the International studies all stood talking about everyday things. Walking in further he realized sitting on the couch behind those people were two girls, one of which was Ms. Leflore. The casual charismatic mood of Salem changed. Wanting to hit himself upside the head, he realized that he had forgotten to call her. Timidly he walked up to her with a soft hello. In return she offered him a handshake. Not wanting him to forget his mistake, as they shook she raised her left eyebrow.

"You seemed so excited about this, what happened to your phone call," she asked abruptly letting go of his hand.

The high brow went away and she broke into laughter. Nudging his right arm it reassured him that she was okay.

"Hey, everyone is busy at this time of year. I had forgotten myself until Professor Chow here invited me to this meeting, and then your friend Mitch reminded me of you," she said as she looked across the room.

She was looking at Mitch, a look that made Salem nervous. Not having any words he watched as she walked towards the kitchen. She passed Mitch giving him a friendly smile and continued to the kitchen. Proceeding to follow her, Salem was stopped by Professor Chow.

"So Salem, what exactly are we in store for this graduation," the professor asked as he sat on the couch resting his drink on top of his very round stomach.

Forcing his body to turn towards the professor he reluctantly walked over and took a seat. The party was far from his mind at that moment, and all he wanted was to get a chance to talk with Leflore some more. Seeing that he wasn't going to get out of the situation any time soon, he decided to get the ball rolling and gestured for Mitch to join them.

"Well Mr. Chow, I was thinking that it would be great to bring not only international, but all of the students together and have what we call the Last Horrah," Mitch said taking a seat next to Salem.

With Professor Chow looking unconvinced Salem decided to speak up.

"What Mitch is trying to say is that we have all of these students that pass each other by in the halls, and the classroom, but they never get to know each other, most of the time because they only hang with their own click, usually an ethnic click, not because they have a problem with others, but because they feel more comfortable with those they are familiar with. So we thought this would be the last horrah within the walls of the university, but not life," he said taking a glance at Mitch; he wanted to pass the ball.

"We'll do a Columbia Forever booth. I'll create a database of all those who come to the party, where they can take part in exchanging numbers. Those people going into the same fields looking for jobs or already having jobs can keep in touch to help each other out, and I believe long after that graduation night we'll have new budding relationships that will last a life time," Mitch said wanting badly to laugh at his on bull, but decided to give the professor a smile any photographer would appreciate.

He had impressed everyone, including Leflore who stood in the kitchen door way smiling.

"Wow that's a great idea. I have a lot of friends

graduating that are literally pulling out their hairs, trying to get a lead on a job," she said as she looked intensely at Mitch.

Salem didn't like it. Gesturing for Mitch to meet him in the kitchen, he decided that maybe they should do some ordering out.

"Hey, I know you want that, but you better get to working on it or she just may be lost forever in my gorgeous eyes," Mitch told him even before his friend could start up on him.

Giving Mitch his sneaky smile, he yelled out to the others from the kitchen.

"Hey you guys let's eat up the snacks that Thomas has so graciously made us, and in the mean time I'll order some sushi and pizza. The best apart is that it's on me in celebration of accepting a position with Rafael Vindy Architects.

A huge firm Salem received applauses. For the occasion Mitch broke out not two but three glasses of wine. Still any conversation with Leflore seemed uneventful with the talk of his job and the party. She left earlier than the others and after a full stomach of sushi and pizza Salem headed home too.

The next morning he lay in bed looking at the ceiling. Now that the party was actually a reality, all he wanted was to get a chance to speak with Leflore for longer than fifteen minutes. He thought about asking Mitch's advice, but he knew any suggestion he had would include some type of sports bar. Nope, he thought it was better that he came up with his own plan. Unfortunately, any ideas that came to mind were lost when his sister tapped on the door. Not waiting for his answer she jumped on the bed laying next to her brother. She then proceeded to use his body like a punching bag.

"Salem, what am I suppose to do? I can't live with them by myself. I'll go crazy." she expressed as she shoved her elbow into his back.

Even though Lamya's smile seemed brighter than usual Salem knew the elbows to the back were his punishment for being selfish. Obviously the talk at the restaurant wasn't enough, and he couldn't blame her, he would probably react the same way. Turning around to face his prosecutor, he followed the ends of her smile to her deep dimples. Even though she was in hate mode, he couldn't ignore her.

"You know it wasn't like I planned this. They were the

companies who seemed to just fall into my lap. You've heard what's going to happen in two months. If I was going back home I could never do what I'm going to be able to do," he said turning on his back.

Explaining himself he still felt guilty. At the beginning of his college career not just him, but Lamya had her first taste of freedom. Their mother had taken ill, while their father was in between jobs. Salem was paid up for college for two years, but with Lamya the family felt it better that she was away from home in order not to be stressed out about all that was going on. The plan was for her to stay the summer, but summer slid into fall, fall slid into winter, and before they knew it she had been in the states for almost a year. At the time they had family in queens, Jackson heights to be exact, and while Lamya stayed with her aunt during the week, she would make her way to her brother's on the weekends. He was just nineteen at the time and lived with a female roommate. She was a regular partier and had got him in the habit of going out each and every weekend. With Lamya as their weekend roommate there was no way he could leave her alone.

"Salem, are you listening? What am I suppose to do back home," Lamya said shaking what seemed to be a lifeless body.

He had gone back to his U.S. beginnings forgetting the present. He said nothing and instead gave his sister a look of acknowledgement that he was at least thinking about the situation. Closing his eyes he went back to the past.

"Hey boy, get off that computer. Me and you have a party to get ready for," she said as she smiled with her mouth wide open.

It was the second weekend that his sister had stayed at

his place, but with Fatima around there was no way that Salem would be able to stay in on a Saturday night.

"Look at her. I can't go and just leave her sitting here alone on the couch. Plus if she knew where I was going I know she'd have something to say to dad," he said as he stood in the hallway looking into the living room.

Placing her hands on her lower back, she cocked her head to the side and gave him a look as if he wasn't supposed to make a decision at all. Fatima's family was originally from Ethiopia. First generation American, there was no mixed blood running through her veins. One look at her face made a person believe they were standing in front of ancient royalty. Most Ethiopian girls had this look and to Salem she was no exception. Her skin tone was not mocha, not quite light brown and or dark brown, but in between. Salem called her copper. Her eyes were round and black, and they sat nicely with in her thin oval shaped face. She wore her hair naturally curly, usually leaving a few strands on each side of her head to frame her gorgeous face. And though it seemed that Allah had blessed her generously with beauty, it wasn't the hair, eyes, tone, full-defined lips, or her high rounded cheekbones that gave her distinction. No, for Fatima it was the high arch of her nose. All of these attributes together made a stranger want to bow just in awe. She was magnificent, and if she had ever forgotten, Salem's stares would always remind her.

"Okay, so you're telling me you're willing to just sit at home tonight," she said walking around him waiting for an answer.

"What else would I do," he said heading back into his room.

Fatima all ready had a plan. Holding Salem by the back

of his t-shirt, she pulled him back towards her.

"Your sister telling on you, she wouldn't do that," Fatima said loudly making sure Lamia would hear her.

Walking into the living room giving Lamya a huge hug, she sat on the corner of the couch, where her magic began to work immediately. Curious Lamya looked back over the couch at her brother and Fatima.

"Won't tell what," she said raising an eyebrow.

Along with her looks Fatima was a firecracker, and not much could hold her back once she got started.

"What do you mean what? It's Saturday night girl. It's time to party! Want to come," she asked with what Salem believed was the sneakiest look he had seen in a long time.

Wandering what exactly was behind her madness, it took him a few moments to realize that she was serious. Even Lamya was puzzled at first. Her smile held a question mark as she looked anxiously for a response from her brother. Not knowing what else to say he rode with the fantasy trip of Fatima.

"Yea, the weekend is for a good time," he replied trying not to grind his teeth in frustration.

He feared that he didn't sound too confident. This must not have been the case for Lamya though, because before he could say another word, she was off the couch and in Fatima's room. As Lamya dug through her new club mate's wardrobe for her own club gear, Salem was whispering in Fatima's ear.

"What are you doing? She can't come with us. If the any

of the family saw her out, we would be over, done," he said folding his arms as he spoke.

Fatima never looked his way.

It's not like you're at home, I know, no one is going to know what you're doing here. Besides she'll wear something that covers most of her and that's that. Not liking the idea Salem collapsed on the bed.

"Okay, it's a campus thing whether she wears anything or not you have to be a student to get in, and she doesn't have an ID," he said sarcastically as Fatima thought.

"I'll get the ID from Layla. She's decided to go back home and she looks too much like your sister," she said watching Lamya closely.

Salem sat up. She was right. Layla was also Moroccan

and she and Lamya could have been sisters. The plan was set and after that night Lamya didn't stop partying until she left for the airport ten months later. He couldn't deny it. Lamya was use to her freedom, and it was all because of him.

Knocked back into the present by another punch in the shoulder, he soon learned that Lamya had come up with her own solution for keeping her freedom in check.

"You know you could sponsor me," she said.

She was right and he didn't know why he didn't think about it before. And then out of know where this feeling of fright came over him. There was no question that he wanted his sister near him, but how near. If he were to sponsor her she would be by his side day in and day out. This bothered him more than the fact that their parents may not want to speak to him ever again.

"Well, after two months I'm sure we could file the papers, but what about the rest of the family," he asked pointing towards the hall way.

She really hadn't given them any thought. Though she was an adult, a year older than her brother, her parents still treated her like a child. She had to think it through further, and in doing so she put her finger to her brother's lips, and then tip toed backwards out of his bedroom door.

4~

SUBMISSIVE UNIONS

The morning started out well for Salem, but the talk with Lamya put a sour taste in his mouth, well into the afternoon. Dress rehearsals would be coming up soon and along with the dress rehearsals would come more family, parties and other celebrations. He needed to take care of business, so it wouldn't get in the way later. Wanting to show a good impression he went to meet with Mr. Ricmond the man he would be working for.

"Mr. Tamimi right," the red head said with a smile any

sales man would kill for.

Salem nodded in agreement. It was an unusual name to remember and it surprised Salem at how easy the name seemed to roll off of his tongue. This made him feel comfortable for the moment, but he knew he was like any other employee there. His business was to do a job, and make sure that it was done well. Any other way and he figured the big smile Richmond held would shrink to little of nothing, or no smile at all. He liked this feeling, because if he kept it, one day he would be head designer, and Richmond could be looking for a job elsewhere. Salem didn't get this job just because of his looks, no he got it because even in the classroom when it was time to prove himself, he was like a lion on the prowl, and for him to finish last was like that same lion not getting his dinner for the evening. So Salem decided to spend half the day with Mr.Richmond.

"Tamimi we're a huge company and as a team we can make miracles happen, but when it comes to specifics we're all about the individual here," he said as he held his arms up towards the ceiling.

He could see that Richmond loved the company he worked for and expected everyone who joined the group to feel the same. Salem knew he would enjoy what he would be doing, but he wasn't so sure about the rest of it. He thought of himself more as an artist, not just a run of the mill architecture who made dreams come true for others. He considered himself the type of guy who would prefer working alone than with a group of wanna be big heads sitting in an office trying to brain storm on how to conceptualize someone else's ideas. In deep thought Salem followed Richmond through some double doors. In front of them stood a long cherry wood table accompanied by fifteen high back chairs on each side and one on each end. In the middle of the table sat a model of the future transportation hub in remembrance of the tragedy of 911, at ground zero. He would be working with Mr. Crick, on his U.S. partnership with the company to get the project on the roll. Though he didn't agree with the cost of the project, he felt as if it would be an honor to be a part of this project. He was Arab and what he wanted to do was show that not all Muslims had the same thoughts about America or American's. It had been eleven years since the tragedy, yet when he was applying for school in the states he remembered the persecution some of his family members were going through at the time. Over and over again after announcing that he would be heading to the states, the family tried their best to persuade him to go elsewhere. As the manager gave him a closer look at the model, all he could do was smile.

"So what do you think so far," Richmond asked as he

gestured for him to follow him into another room.

Walking into a room about half the size of the first one, he found another cherry wood desk half the size as the one in the conference room, but with just as much style. A desk top Mac as well as a PC sat on opposite sides of the desk, while a sketching table facing a huge office window sat a few feet across from it.

"Our fourth in design had some family problems that just couldn't wait, so we decided you could have the larger office and maybe even a bigger one if you could try and fill his shoes," Richmond smirked.

He knew he could fill his shoes, and they had just given him the opportunity. He didn't just have one foot in the door, now he had two and with the second foot he planned on kicking Richmond to the curb.

"Well, come on give me something," he said giving him a pat on the shoulder.

Salem was doing all he could to hold back his grin. He was a humble guy, but sometimes being humble left a lot to be desired.

"Everything looks great and I can't wait to fill those shoes for you," he replied giving Richmond a handshake in return for the pat on his back.

"Great, so I'll just go ahead and get back to work. There are some files in the desk draw. I know you have another month, but if you'd like you can go ahead and get acquainted with the work ahead. There's also some more paper work for you to fill out before you leave. So make yourself comfortable and get use to your new surroundings," he said as he waved good-bye a shut the door behind him.

Enjoying the work he was studying, talking with other employees and taking a personal tour of the building, he realized that he had spent over four hours at the company. He didn't want to start work right away, and decided that it was better for him to enjoy the last month of freedom he would have for quite a while. Not wanting to go back home right away he decided to go into Manhattan close to SoHo. The busy streets of Manhattan were like food for his soul and always made a brighter day even better. There was a diner behind the SoHo Boutique Hotel called Tick Tock Diner. Even though it was busy he loved the place. He could always see new faces there, and the best thing about it was that he could get in and out without having to always hold a polite conversation with everyone he met. The partiers from the night before were just dragging in. He stood in line behind them starring at their messy hair and wrinkled clothes. Mostly guys they went on and on about the girls they had met the night before and the ones they woke up with that morning. The girls seemed absent from the group so Salem figured it was just all talk.

Deciding to keep his distance from the group, he took a seat near the back by a window. Three men sat behind him watching the rest of the crowd precariously. A male waiter around the same age as him took his order. Deciding on an omlet, hash browns and a fruit cup, he noticed the waiter looking at the guys sitting behind him, from the corner of his eyes. Out of curiosity he took a look back as well. Dressed in blue, grey and beige bugatchi sleeveless sweaters over white short sleeve T-shirts, it wouldn't have surprised him if they all had black skinny jeans to match. They were like walking magazine ads. As he looked back they gave him a smile that made him feel uneasy. Giving them a nod he sheepishly turned back to his table. The waiter stepped away to fetch his drink and upon returning began to say something, that is until he was totally ignored by the sight of someone who looked familiar to Salem. It was Leflore with one of the most beautiful smiles he had seen from her yet. She noticed him right away and waved for him to come over. He felt special, but he wasn't alone. Two friends accompanied her.

"Hurry up," she yelled.

Salem grabbed his drink and motioned for the waiter to bring the rest of his order to a larger table. Usually dressed somewhat more along the lines of contemporary preppy, he realized real quick that this was a girl who knew how to have fun. She looked relaxed, and sexy in dark blue, wide leg Armani jeans. To match them she wore an aqua blue, black and gold sleeveless hoodie shirt that surprisingly had part of the back cut out of it.

"So, how did you find my secret diner," he said as he welcomed everyone to take a seat.

"Hey, I've been coming to this diner since I started school. I wanted the whole SOHO experience so I rented a room right there across the street and spent a few days in this area," she replied.

"So you've been around the whole time and I had no clue," he said making room for the food the waiter bought.

"The question is what are you doing here," she said reaching over to steal one of his has browns.

"I uhm, start work a month after graduating so I went into the office to make myself look good you know," he said nervously taking a bite out of his omelet.

He didn't want to seem like he was all work and no play.

"That's it? Last week for five hours Monday through Thursday I was still working on my internship. Shoot, I'm hoping it gets me a position before graduation day," she said stuffing the last piece of hash brown into her mouth.

"Hey, I hope you get it," he said.

"Oh well, we'll see. Anyway these are my friends Kenji and Sprints; they're still searching too. That's why we're so excited about your party. We're gonna help you out as much as possible. That's why we're out actually. We're going to do a little shopping for the party. Mitch gave me a call and asked if I could pick up some office supplies," she said motioning for the waiter to come over.

He wanted to choke Mitch, and bothered him more was

how did Mitch have time to even get Leflore's number? Mitch seemed to be holding out on him.

"When did this come about," he asked.

"Just this morning," she said as she eyed another one of Salem's hash browns.

With his cell phone vibrating, he knew it was his mother. Since he hadn't shown up for lunch and she would expect him for dinner, along with items to pick up from the market.

"It's family. I'm sure they want me to run some sort errands for dinner, so I better head out," he said.

She hardly noticed him as he slid his remaining hash browns over to her. She was too busy looking over the menu, but aware enough to reach down and pick up the hash brown. She waved good-bye without looking up as he left the restaurant. Outside of the diner he received a phone call from Mitch.

"Hey what's up," he happily shouted through the phone.

"Not a thing unless you want to mention the fact that Leflore is running errands," he shouted back.

"Yeah, it just hit me we needed a few things for our booth, so I asked Mr. Chow for Cherise's number," he said.

"Cherise, now you're calling her by her first name," he questioned

"Mr. Chow calls her Cherise. I didn't think anything of it," he replied.

"Alright man, what else is going on," he replied.

"I'm glad you asked, because I need you to set up something to arrange the music and food. I can't deal with it right now because I had more family than I expected just arrive," he said almost whining over the phone.

"It's my turn to make a move anyway, in more ways than one, but where in the world am I goanna find out anything about music," he said scratching his head in dismay.

"Ask Cherise she seems to have a lot of contacts. Hopefully she can point us in the right direction," he said rushing his girlfriend out of the house and paying for some well-deserved fast food delivery.

Mitch's question struck Salem's heart like a dagger

through a vampire.

"I don't think I still have her number," holding his breath desperately waiting for Mitch to save him.

"I'll text it to you as soon as I get off the phone. You're goanna stay angry at me if you don't ever make a play," he replied shaking his head and clicking the phone off.

As he had guessed his mother called for him to run some errands. It took him at least two hours to pick up what she wanted and another hour to reach home. By the time he hit the door he was starving again. It was unusually quiet for the afternoon and there were movers blocking the hallway. Taking the side escape stairs he entered through his bedroom. Smelling the food he headed straight to the kitchen where he found no one, that is until he started getting items out of the bag.

"Lamya, mom," he yelled looking up to see his family and some strangers staring back at him from the living room. His mother and sister were sitting on the couch in abbyas, while his father sat in traditional clothing on one of the foot cushions, they were accompanied by two men who sat across from the ladies on the shorter couch. The older one was the first to stand up and shake his hand, while the younger one followed suit. They were Moroccan as well and looking the younger guy up and down he almost stopped breathing.

"Salem I'd like you to meet the Awads," he said smiling gleefully.

He knew the deal. Last year before he had even graduated his parents had already set him up for marriage.

"Dad I thought we agreed that all of us would have an

input on this decision," he asked looking at his farther crossly.

His father motioned for him to take a seat next to him.

"You do have some say, but you're my son and I'm the parent," he replied.

Though Mr. Tamimi smiled he noticed that his son's eyes looked crazed. Perspiring he loosened his tie.

"As I was saying these are the Awads and I believe that they would be the perfect family for Lamya to marry into," he said.

Right then he wished that he had gotten the paper work that day to sponsor his sister. In fear he had held his breath for what seemed to be like five minutes, until a lump had

grown where the air should have been swallowed. Being
diplomatic he shook the hands of both men. He could feel
Lamya's eyes burning a hole through his head forehead. He
chose not to look her way and instead gave a long hard
stare at his father.

"When did this happen," Salem asked still in shock.

"After visiting some of the family in Detroit, your
mother made a few phone calls," Mr. Tamimi replied.

To him the most natural freedom in life was put in the
hands of their parents, because it's believed that parents
know best. Thinking to him-self if they knew best, then
what happen to them dealing with their children's feelings.
He looked over at the young man sitting with a great big
smile on his face. He knew who he was. They were friends
at one time. He was just a couple of years older than Salem.

Sadeeq was his name and though he knew right away that he was from a good family, the only memory that came to him was watching thirteen-year old Sadeeq sit on the steps of Marina mall, and when he thought know one was looking he dug deep into his nose putting whatever he retrieved into his mouth. If his sister were going to marry anybody, it sure wouldn't be Sadeeq. It was then that he looked directly into his sister's eyes, though there were no tears, he could see that she was red with anger.

"Did she know about this," he asked.

"We told her we were looking into it," his father rebutted shamefully.

In frustration Salem clinched his teeth. He couldn't say anything in front of the guest so he gestured for his father to follow him into the kitchen.

Mr. Tamimi knew that he was getting ready to be given a hard time. He asked the guest to excuse him and the rest of the family for a few moments. Upon walking out of the room, the smile vanished from his face.

"What's wrong," Mr. Tamimi asked with folded arms.

"What's wrong is that do you really think she's prepared to get married," he asked.

Mr. Tamimi looked over at his wife. He knew she wasn't ready, but Mrs. Tamimi was beginning to think that leaving her in the states had made her lose some of her cultural values. She thought that marriage would bring Lamya back to reality.

"No, but she has enough freedom as there is to have. It

has to be done sooner or later. She'll be twenty seven soon," Mrs. Tamimi replied.

Lamya didn't say a word. Instead she held her head down refusing to even look at her parents.

"If that's the case then why not take the time out and find her someone westernized someone she could at least like. This guy is okay, but his family is too traditional. You aren't even that traditional. You really want that for Lamya," he asked starring at his parents intensely.

Mr. Tamimi looked at his daughter and then his wife. "That sounds fair," his father exclaimed.

No one said a word; they kind of just looked down at the floor. Lamya had no problem with an arranged marriage, but she wanted to at least be pleased with who she married, besides she thought, she could have sworn that once or twice she had seen Sadeeq eat his own mucus. Still looking at the floor she gently grabbed her father's hand, but as she felt his prickly hairs that were so familiar to her she couldn't help but to grip even tighter, so tight that his hand turned red.

"You know he has an older brother who lives here to, Maybe he can introduce us to something a little more your type," he said as he watched his wife roll her eyes at his words.

Holding a big grin on his face he forced his wife to smile back. She would have rather seen the engagement go ahead as planned, but as long as it happened with someone, what was the harm. Grabbing his family and huddling together, they gave each other one big hug. They then brained stormed on how to get the Awads out of the house.

5~

DECEPTION IS SOMETIMES KEY

The house was a little different after the marriage

ordeal. Lamya seemed to talk nonstop with her parents

about who she thought would be a good match for her. Mr.

Tamimi liked the fact that his daughter was speaking

openly about the subject. He prided himself in believing

that he was more of an open minded individual than many

fathers he knew. While the graduation visit was the first

time he had visited the states, as children his parents spent

quite a while in the U.S. and upon their return to Morocco

bought with them new traditions and ideas. He had always

liked the balance of east and west in theory, and didn't mind experimenting with it on his own family in subtle ways. So he thought to himself and only himself what better way to bring east and west together, but through marriage.

On the other hand Mrs. Tamimi had different ideas. She was bought up in an eastern family with all the culture and authority that came with it. Though she truly wanted her daughter to have the utmost freedom, she needed for her to respect where she came from. She looked down at the bubbles in the sink. It wasn't cheap to have a maid in the states. She was washing dishes, and hated doing it. Back home maids were cheap labor, and she hardly even thought about the dishes after a meal. To take herself away from what she was actually doing, he liked to think back, and hearing her husband and daughter talk she went back to when she was only nineteen. She and her family were celebrating her late entrance into college. A year and a half

earlier she decided to stay with her cousins in Turkey and

figured if she had stayed six months, why would another

six really matter. It was gorgeous night for the celebration.

Under beige Moroccan tents cousins, aunts and uncles

adorned her with gifts and kisses. It was one of the happiest

nights of her life at least that's what she thought. Led into a

caidal, designed in a rich pallet of gold, red and splashes of

blue, those happy thoughts began to leave her. She failed to

recognize anyone. Unlike the others this group didn't

dance, instead they sat talking. A table was placed in the

middle of the tent and food was laid out for them all to

enjoy. Her mother pushed her in the front of the group,

making her sit at the center of the table. Taking a deep

breath she understood that the situation was a serious one.

She had heard of these types of meetings before, and knew

that they all had something to do with marriage. Any smile

that she had left her face and was replaced with a mood and

look of suspicion, which grew stronger each, extra moment that she remained seated. The people were Darija Arab. She knew this because most of the guest dressed in her traditional clothing, but there were others, men who sat next to her adorned in darshdasha clothing, white garbs mostly with a red and white head dress to match. She was hoping that in no way were they in-laws. Obviously not from Arabia these people stared at her through eyes that should have been as round and as large as dirham's, but instead were small, not too much larger than an American dime. They looked her up and down while she spent time looking up and down the table for the one man who considered himself sort of lucky that night. For thirty minutes she answered questions about how much she loved her family, life, and so on, even though at that moment she was wondering why she was even born. She answered them all, with each added question making her feel as if she were on trial. It was definitely a marriage set up, and she didn't want anything to do with it. She walked out of the tent never meeting the one they intended for her to marry. She didn't care about the arranged marriage; she just wanted it done with her not being surprised. She could have waited another eternity, but two years later, and thirty years to date her parents introduced her to Mr. Tamimi.

Though she wasn't in love with the states, there were a few things that she liked about it, such as the great pancake breakfast that she seemed to desire almost every morning and the large amount of freedom American girls were afforded. For a second she questioned who she was, and wondered if things were different and Lamya was not only able to choose whom she married, but was also allowed to date. This thought scared her and she decided that it was better to focus on washing the dishes.

Salem could hear Lamya and his father talking as well.

He knew for a fact that if Lamya could wait to get married until she was forty she would do it. What puzzled him was why in the world now would she rant on and on about something that she openly dreaded. After walking into the potential proposal, Salem thought that it was best if he stayed close by home for a couple of days, just in case. Anyway he had a strong urge to get his sister alone to knock some since into her head. A few hours later their parents decided to make a run to the market. As soon as the door shut Salem raced to the living room, as Lamya switched on the television to catch up on some MTV.

"You've been smoking something right, because what other reason would the Lamya I know want to talk about marriage until her tongue falls out," he asked standing over her.

Spread out on the couch she smiled up at her brother

who he decided to hop across the couch on to the floor.

"It's not like I don't want to get married anytime in my life, but if I make it look like I'm only against it they may try the same stunt again. I can't go through with that again," she said hitting her brother in the back of his head.

Grabbing the remote from her neither of the siblings realized that just as they spoke on the matter, so did their parents.

"Would you really allow Lamya to marry a western man," Mrs. Tamimi asked as she watched the cars pass.

Taking a step across the street Mr. Tamimi grabbed his wife and scurried across the rest of the way.

"Why not, I think it would be good for Lamya and the

man she marries. You know she can be a hand full. The men here have more patients. What eastern man would deal with her sarcasm for long," he asked looking over at his wife and a young Arab man passing by.

His wife was hopping on to the curb as he spoke. She wore loose fitting boot cut jeans with an attractive black long sleeve blouse. Wearing a black scarf wrapped loosely around her head the ends flapped loosely in the wind she didn't realize hair was exposed. Mr. Tamimi didn't say a word. It made him think back to the first day that he met her.

Tamimi's family lived in Dubai at the time, though he himself had never been to the states, he was reminded everyday of the western ways. Moving away from Morocco half a year earlier he missed the continuous tourist traffic. At that time a lot of people who landed in Dubai stayed in

Dubai. They were a part of that group. They weren't locals, but they weren't tourist either so it took a little time getting use to. He didn't mind the situation much. The new place gave him a new since of freedom. He was turning twenty-six and like his father he would become a professor of architecture, and like his father he believed that Dubai was a city worth looking into for future studies. The Arab world, at least in the U.A.E. was changing and like his father he loved it. Morocco had already been explored and would be until the end of time he guessed, but Dubai was different. It was possible that Dubai could take him around the world. It was Ramadan as he randomly thought about his situation. He was going to meet his bride to be and he was ready. At a certain age there was no reason for him to do otherwise. Besides he had partied harder than anyone he knew. He secretly dated Arab girls, European and American girls, but like many in the U.A.E., they were just passing through. His parents had found a girl for him year earlier in Morocco. The girl was his mother's choice. He had requested that the girl have some western traditions, but that fell through. Instead his mother promised that the girl would be pretty easy for him to mold into what he was looking for. Later that evening entering the Ramadan gathering the girl was the first thing he saw. Surrounded by family she wore a magnificent Cafta, white with embedded gold leaf designed into flowers on silk fabric. Her head was wrapped in a white and gold trimmed Scarf; at least he was able to see her face. She was beautiful, and he thought maybe, just maybe his mother was right. Maybe it was possible that they could explore the world together. Thirty years later and years of pushing, he was finally triumphant in getting her to tour the west, even if it was only for their son's graduation.

Snapping her fingers in his face, Mr. Tamimi was regrettably bought back to the present. He found it hard to smile for a moment, but then he realized he was standing on a busy corner in the middle of New York, some things in life were still good.

"And what happens if both of the only two children we have, decide to marry westerners, then what," she complained as she pulled him back from walking ahead.

Mr. Tamimi stopped, looked up at the sky for a moment and then gave his wife a smile.

"Then we'll just be extra cultured," he said pulling her hand close and continuing toward the market.

Back at the apartment as she reached for the remote from Salem another thought came to her.

"Besides I think dad doesn't care so much who I marry

as much as mom may," she said quite sure of herself.

"What, why do you think that," he said releasing the grip on the remote.

Jamming from MTV to VH1, Lamya made her claim.

"One she wanted me to get engaged. If you hadn't of walked in the deal would have went through. Two every time we talk about the subject dad is open and ready to talk, but she always stays quiet. Now what do you think is going on in that head of hers," she asked.

While the siblings continued to talk at home, the Tamimi's had finally reached the market. Looking over some fresh eggplant another thought had crossed Mrs. Tamimi's mind. Running towards her husband who was looking through a magazine, she put her hand on top of the page slowly pushing it out of his view.

"What if she doesn't get married at all? If Salem doesn't want to get married its okay, but not Lamya. She has never talked about marriage so much in her life, so why now? What is she's just lying to you?

Mr. Tamimi removed his wife's hand from the magazine, lifting it once more for his viewing.

Frowning at no response she headed back to her eggplants, but not without a last word.

"What you have nothing to say? I know why, because I know that if you could have, you would have married a western girl," she said stumping away.

There was no reaction from Mr.Tamimi; instead he just

focused on the magazine. He could hear her walking away and thinking about her comment, he had to be true to himself. If the right girl had come around, she would have been western. But how could he blame his wife who had no idea about her past? To him and her it was only a story that supposedly began in 1420 when Zang He of the Ming Dynasty sailed into Somalia. During his stop he ordered the great Buddhist monk Yuan Zang to take a smaller crew from the Indian Ocean into the Atlantic. Accompanied by his servant Xing Zhe formerly Sun Wukong or the Monkey King. Belonging to the Tang dynasty, they realized enlightenment centuries before, and as reward for their good deeds, their lights were dimmed shortly so they could witness and enjoy first hand how their good deeds eventually influenced the world. The Ming dynasty respected them fiercely and the voyage through the Atlantic was a gift from Hen as their first solo voyage into the new world alone. Finding the port of Casablanca intriguing,

Zang ordered his crew to rest sail; they traveled the rest of the way by foot. Finding an abundance of vegetables and fish like the Nile perch sunfish leaping mullet and rainbow trout. Their mouths were spoiled with the flavors of Anise, ginger, olive oil, and preserved lemons, that seemed to linger on their pallets until the night they left Morocco's port. Zang believed that he'd found a jewel. The land was laid out well. The city of Rabat, the soul of government shined like an unclean pearl, while the gates of Tangier welcomed strange men of pale skin from the north, but nothing attracted Zang more than the city of Fes el Bali or the old walled city. This complex, but majestic city led to dark winding streets filled with shops and homes that sat so close to each other Zhe wondered how the people could breathe. Stone fountains decorated the city's squares, and the city squares were filled with educated scholars entering what seemed to be an impressive place of study. Not allowed to enter Zang peered intensely from the entrance at a curious family that sat talking by a fountain. A welcoming demeanor as they left the court yard, the father welcomed the new strangers to their home for a meal. Devouring the meal as if they had never eaten before, the offering of tea by the family's oldest daughter made Zang hungry for affection. Her name was Amina, a close descendant of Tariq Ibn Ziyad, and like her ancestor she had such fire in her eyes that it was hard for Zang to look away. Turning his back on his Buddhist pillars. It would be a mistake that he would regret. His punishment would not only affect him, but his faithful assistant. Enlightenment would be taken away from Zang and taken and given away to Xing Zhe for eternity. Attempting to stop, but not stopping Zang's situation was Zhe's failed deed. Every male child born into the Ziyad's family after Amina would poses a piece of Xing Zhe's soul, the deep depths of his soul where Sun Wunkong, the pretentious monkey king was laid to rest. A mischievous monkey that loved the idea of causing havoc even if I t were at his on expense. The first son born to the first female of the eighth generation of the Ziyad family would force Xing Zhe to return to the state of the unknowing empty soul of the monkey king. Zhe's continued transformation to enlightenment would depend on the first-born son's self-realization. Whenever realized Xing Zhe would regain the title of Dou-Zansheng-Fo or victorious fighting Buddha, his eight and final title in his path to enlightenment.

Zang and Zhe were not the only culprits in this deed, Amina was also, and to lay unwed with any man especially a holy man was considered a great sin. Unlike her accomplices, her punishment came swift. The more satisfaction she received from the enlightened one, the more her appearance changed. Her toasty caramel color turned a rigid pearl white and her eyes a cold watery blue. Her deed welcomed the Djin into her realm. A creature the

Moroccans called the Jinn, these delinquent twins of the other realm mirrored their human counter parts. Amina would watch first hand for eternity their dirty deeds. For as they entered her world she would be forever trapped in theirs, forced to watch as the Jinn would take hold of the third piece of the first born's soul. What would be left of each child was a shattered soul held together only by it's central core of energy, controlled by the boy born with it.

Mr. Tamimi looked up from his magazine, and watched as others passed him by. He never believed in the tale, but the birth of his son made him think different. At first sight of his son Mr. Tamimi prayed for piece and called his first-born Salem.

Back at the apartment Salem had come to his own realization.

"You know if they're looking for you to get married,

they may not let me sponsor you at all," he said.

Sitting up she looked at her brother intensely.

"I know, that's why I'm applying on line for jobs as we speak," she said with the wink of an eye.

Sitting up Salem grabs his head in shock.

"Are you serious," he asked.

He knew she was serious; she was the smarter of the two. She graduated at fifteen and used her free time before college volunteering in other Muslim countries helping those in need. In fact most of her friends joked about her being the princess mother Teresa. A year earlier she graduated from an American sister school in astrological physics. It was almost a given that she could easily get a job in the states.

"Come on, I'm a physicist. We don't come around every day you know. I'd get to stay here, live my life and hopefully find my own husband," she said lying down on the couch.

This was a brave move even for Lamya. It wasn't like it was a new concept, but no one in their family had ever tried it before. He just hoped that it ended positive for her.

6~

A MOUNTAIN MUST BE DISCOVERED BEFORE

MOVED

Waking up on what seemed to be a very quiet morning,

the first thought that came to his head was the next move

his sister was about to make. It had been a day or so since

he last talked with Leflore and thought she was the perfect

distraction from Lamya. Looking down at his phone he

wasn't the only one who thought so. Opening a text

message from Mitch, it simply read, "Call her!" Mitch

definitely knew something was up. Texting him back

Salem typed, "I'm calling her now. Talk to you later."
Though his text made him sound gong ho about the whole
situation, he knew he wasn't fooling anyone especially
himself. Locating an older text from Mitch he dialed her
number. It rang once, twice, three times, going towards the
fourth ring he seriously considered hanging up, that is until
he remembered voice mail, and then finally on the fifth ring
someone answered.

"Whoo, hello," she said struggling to keep a toddler on
her hip.

Startled Salem stuttered over her name.

"May I speak to Le - Leflore please," he said gripping
the phone tighter.

He felt like an idiot finally spitting out her name.

"Well, yea that's me I think," she sarcastically responded.

He kind of felt nervous to even have to say his name. Any other girl would have remembered him.

"It's Salem, Mitch's friend," he replied.

He wouldn't have been so nervous if he had known that she was on the other end of the phone with not just a kid on her hip, but another pulling at her pants leg.

"Oh, I'm so sorry. Sometimes these kids don't give you even a second to take a breath. How are you doing," she said struggling to put the child down.

The word kids stuck in his head like gum to the bottom of a table. He hoped that he was hearing wrong.

"I'm sorry; I didn't realize you were busy. I could call you back later," he said rolling his eyes waiting for more than one answer.

Putting one child down just to pick another one up she switched ears with the phone.

"Well, that won't do you any good, because I'm here for another two hours, and I don't know if I ever told you, but my first name is Cherise," she said just a bit annoyed.

He wanted to ask where she was, but at the same time he was really embarrassed, he never did ask her first name, but she knew his. He had to think fast.

"You know I'm so sorry. I'm so used to hearing you being called by your last name that I didn't think it would be gentlemen of men to do any different," he could help to say with a sly smile on his face.

"Okay, well my name is Cherise, S-a-l-e-m.

If it weren't for her laughing after the remark Salem wouldn't have known what to do.

"Nice to meet you again Cherise, I was hoping that we could get together to talk about our next step for this party we have going on," he wasn't that sure of himself, but he was calm.

"Okay, but, I'm far ahead of you smart mouth. Believe it or not I have someone who is willing to DJ. If you'd like we can go by his place later on if you're free. I'm only working half a day today. We can meet around two and that will give me a chance to go home for a few," she suggested hoping to get a yes.

The job had to do something with babysitting he

thought. He couldn't see Cherise with kids; she seemed just a little to in to herself to have anyone else to care for.

"Alright, that will give me enough time to reach you. Where do you want to meet," he asked jumping up from bed.

"Why not meet me at 218 Bedford Avenue. There is a record shop their called Sick Sounds," she said putting the other child down and rushing to grab a bottle.

Salem was ecstatic. He was goanna finally learn what Cherise was all about.

"Alright, then I'll see you there," he said with a big grin.

Hanging up the phone he tried to imagine what the day would be like. He couldn't phantom anything, and jumping out of bed he scurried to the closet deciding on what to wear. He didn't want to make the mistake of out dressing her. One thing about Salem was that he might have been a guy, but a guy who loved clothes. He always felt that the clothes on his back completed who he was as a person. If he were going to a game it was either Sean Jean or Ruel. If he were going out to dinner it had to be Guess or Dolce and Gabbana. But if he were going on a date, which was far in between, he delved into some funky Versace. But this wasn't a date, dinner or sporting event. They would probably end up in someone's apartment, or somewhere else. He had made up his mind, Sean jean off white slacks and a straight out black T-shirt that read N.E.R.D. Pulling out some Puma sneakers to complete the look; he paused before closing the closet door. Focusing on a single box hid behind his hanging clothes, he had a strong urge to open it, and would have if his father hadn't knocked on the door.

"Sali, Sali are you up," he sang as he knocked

repeatedly.

Salem quickly closed the closet door and grabbed his towel as if he were going to shave.

"Come in dad," he said reaching to open the door.

Before he could reach the knob his father opened the door and was reaching awkwardly for a hug. Salem dreaded moments like this with his father, and refused to try and figure out why. Moments such as that moment were always the same and even though Salem hated them he did appreciate his father trying. Releasing his hug his father's shoulders were still broad, almost massive, and at age sixty his biceps were the pillar of a man of strength and good health. Salem let his arms fall to his side as his father took a grip onto his shoulders. They almost stood eye to eye. Mr. Tamimi was six-one and Salem was five - ten. Some people say that it's the eyes that tell it all, and maybe that's what Salem dreaded. Like his mother his father also had the habit of looking him straight in the eyes. With his mother eye contact was easier to avoid, but with his father, it was different, he just wanted to please him. There was always something missing between them and all he really wanted was to be his father's golden boy.

"So my son you have been in the house longer than usual since we have been here. Is something wrong," he said trying not to seem so nosey.

"Nothing is wrong, actually today I have some where to be around three," he could honestly say with a smile.

"Well Sali I have some where to be at two. Do you mind walking with me on your way," he said letting go of his son's shoulders.

His father had adapted the habit of going to Eastern Light Cafe on Steinway Street almost every morning for a dose of Shesha and a little Arab talk.

"I know dad Eastern Lights. We'll grab a sandwich and walk, and then I'll catch the train from there," he said reluctantly.

"So where are you off to," he asked.

"Going to visit some friends at a record shop," he said abruptly.

Slinging his towel over his shoulder he headed toward the bathroom leaving his father in the room. He was already clean-shaven and just acted as if he had to freshen up to stop his father from asking more questions.

Blue skies, a light breeze and plenty of sunshine made

walking in the city a pure delight. Back home even with the tourism and expatriates the majority of what you saw at least in Abu Dhabi were Arabs to the right of you and Arabs to the left of you. Of course you could go down into Dubai, but who wanted to do that each weekend. New York was different and you could feel it when you walked down the streets of Astoria. On one corner you could see a Puerto Rican woman shouting up at the window of their ex's apartment, while on another corner you could see a thirteen year old skate boarder with a fly fro and army fatigues, hawking down a Japanese female DJ who's storing her equipment away until the next night. This was New York, always fresh, always new and Salem just knew he was meant to be a permanent fixture in its backdrop.

"Sali, have you thought any more about marriage," he asked with no shame.

Any oneness that Salem had with the city came to a

screeching halt. He began walking faster.

"I thought we talked about this. Let me get settled in my job and then we can think about that," he said refusing to give his father any eye contact.

"Slow down," Mr. Tamimi puffed finding it hard to keep up with his son.

Slowing down Salem was forced to give his father at least a glance.

"I'm bringing this up because sometimes we men have urges stronger than women and not having a partner can sometimes be a struggle to stay decent," he said glad that his son had stopped walking.

Salem stopped in his tracks as well. He had no idea what

his dad had up his sleeves.

"What do you mean," he asked suspiciously.

Mr. Tamimi put his right arm on his son's shoulder. With his left arm he reached into his pocket and pulled out a pink braw. Salem's eyes widened, his heart beat uncontrollably, and his mouth just hung wide open. His first reaction was to grab the braw but he thought that it would be rude, plus it didn't look like his father was ready to let it go.

"Dad please give that too me, he said.

Not embarrassed at all his father smiled putting the hand with the braw behind his back, while pointing his finger at his son's face with his other hand.

"Ha, ha, you see even now you can't resist being excited

by this," he said hardly being able to control his laughter.

Looking to see if anyone was watching the situation, Salem had never been so embarrassed in his life.

"Where did you get that from and why did you bring it here," he said angrily while grinding his teeth.

"You know how I am, you went take a shower and I lied on your bed just to see how comfy it was. I sat up pulling myself by the mattress, and as I stood the braw came with me. Glad it was just me and not your mother around," he laughed briefly holding the braw out in the open.

Salem had some quick explaining to do.

"Well, it's not mine. I had a party just before you came. I guess one of my friends had more fun than I thought," he explained.

His father didn't believe a word he said, and even it was

true he would rather it not be. He began to laugh patting his son on the back and urging him to continue walking.

"Whatever the story it seems that you like healthy girls, and that's good because your wife will be able to bare children easier," he said smiling.

Salem rolled his eyes in aggravation. How could he forget and leave something like that around? Passing by a trashcan Mr. Tamimi calmly walked up and threw it away. Salem held his breath in anger. He should have been the one who decided whether to throw it away or not.

"So are you sure you're not ready to get married because of the job, or because your still having too much fun," he asked walking pass his son.

Grinding his teeth and rolling his eyes, again he reassured his father that work was his only concern at the moment. Seeming proud of the moment that they spent together, Mr. Tamimi patted Salem on the back once more, and crossed the street towards Eastern Lights Cafe.

The sky was still blue, but his father had torn down any defenses that he held up between them. He wondered if his father really just slipped up and found the bra or was he snooping around when he shouldn't have been. His mood had changed, but someone was waiting on him, and didn't want to leave them hanging. Catching the NW line to the G line he wound up in Brooklyn at three on the dot. He didn't want to seem to anxious so he decided to walk around the corner, and not a second later did he turn the corner that he saw Cherice entering the shop. He took his time, but followed behind her. She always kept herself interesting, and Salem liked it. On that occasion she wore satin green army fatigues that fell just below her naval. Above the naval she wore a short sleeve black military jacket trimmed in gold, with just a touch of red. It buttoned up straight to her chin. It all fit well with her black-heeled slip ons. He didn't know whether to continue following her or grabbing her in a passionate embrace.

Like Cherise the record shop was also interesting. The walls were painted psychedelic colors of green, orange, yellow and black. In the main room was a collection of used albums, cds, and tapes. A basic square room in design, in the center of each wall was another door, which led to a smaller room. Above each smaller door covered with hypnotic beads were the headings rock, pop, hip-hop and alternative. The designs made a person focus on what it sold and nothing else. Forced to take his eyes off the walls and doors he noticed Cherise lingering in the center of the room focusing on some Michael Jackson albums. It seemed liked she wanted to pick one up, but he figured she wouldn't since after his death the prices on his items went through the roof. Stepping back from the shelf she walked over to the counter, and shook the hand of the attendant. Salem pretended to browse some music as they talked. It seemed to him that the attendant could have been some sort of competition. The guy had a different look, Jewish, African American, Lebanese, or something of the sort he thought. He may not have known what he was, but the vibe he had going on was mack daddy in full mode. The guy was high yellow. He wore beattle shades, and had a fro most guys in the U.A.E. would die for. Salem was getting jealous. Along with his natural fro, the guy sported a throwback of Reggie Bush's number twenty-five that some guys would kill for. Along with the throw back he wore skinny leg white jeans, a style that Salem wasn't exactly feeling. Even though he wore skinny jeans the guy had confidence, more confidence than Salem ever had. He'd had enough, and trying to take his focus off of the guy he proceeded to rest his back side on an album shelf that stood behind him, causing a seen as the shelf began to fall backwards.

"Hey watch out," the attendant yelled as he ran to support the shelf.

Salem didn't seem the wiser and as soon as the attendant left the counter all he could focus on was Cherish.

"Ah Cherish there you are," he shouted walking toward her.

Though she worried about the attendant she put her hand up and gave him a big wave along with a corky grin, not sure if it was Salem or someone else who caused the disturbance in the first place.

"I didn't know you were here already," he said hoping she hadn't seen him earlier.

Giving her a huge, hug hoping she would forget whatever the attendant was doing, the scent of Viva la Juicy tantalized his senses, while the hug gave him satisfaction. He could have held her forever, but the crowd demanding help behind him wouldn't allow it. The attendant reached the counter again and rolling his eyes in the process pushed the two aside.

"And I thought I was goanna be late," she said playfully.

Almost blushing Salem had his excuse ready, which was partly true.

"I'm sorry for taking so long, but I had to run an errand before coming here," he quickly answered.

Okay with his reply Cherise turned toward one of the smaller rooms gesturing for him to follow behind her.

"Right now we have to wait for Joint to get the crowd down then he'll join us later, as soon as Ced takes his place," she said.

They were in the room of rock and roll where posters of AC DC and Metallica plastered the walls. Salem didn't care too much for that type of music unless it was wrapped around a little hip-hop. In this room across from the collection of music was a smaller door. Walking in ducking his head as he went, the new room was dimmer than the one they left. There was nothing to focus on in the room but themselves. Cherise didn't go any further.

"I know this seems strange, but it's the quickest way to get to his place," she said.

Another opportunity to speak with Cherise was again

interrupted by the attendant.

"I'm sorry shorty, but the crowd just kept rising," he said with a big smile on his face.

Pulling a light switch he unlocked a third door while giving a smirk to Salem. Even though he wore dark shades Salem could feel that he was sizing him up. Hearing the click of the lock he decided to introduce himself to Salem.

"By the way my name is Joint my man. What's yours," he asked.

He then signaled for the two to follow him. Walking up a narrow case of stairs Salem introduced himself while avoiding Joint's backside as they climbed.

"Salem," he replied.

Unlocking another door Joint burst into laughter.

"Say who," he asked.

Having gone through the same scenario more times than he thought Joint could count, he played it cool.

"It's Salem. If that's too difficult for you then just call me Sal," he replied.

"Chill man I just wasn't sure if I was hearing Sal, Salem, or salami. You know how it is," he replied.

It was obvious that this Joint hadn't let the shelf situation go, but as Salem entered the next room any bad vibes he had seemed to melt away. It may be true that most people fall in love with New York, but what was also true is that New York was the ultimate concrete jungle. The only green a New Yorker was liable to see was a make shift garden in an alley way or through a nice view of central park. Salem thought that he had seen everything that is until his feet touched what felt like grass. He thought he was entering a simple room; instead he had walked into an atrium on top of a record shop. As he looked up a white wall to the right of him lead his eyes to a rectangular glass seal slanted at a ninety-degree angle where the glass and wall met. To the left he could follow the glass to the edge of the roof and see what seemed to be all of Harlem. Beneath his feet was a patch of grass that lead to a brick walk way. On each side of the walk way was a flat landscape of more greenery lined with short round shrubs perfectly shaped which lead to a house door in the white wall? The scene was so serene that he couldn't understand why the other two would have wanted to take a step any further. Opening the door Joint gave Salem what looked to him like one of the slightest smiles he had ever come across.

"Its cool man everyone reacts the same way their first time through," he said.

Salem couldn't contain his emotions and looking over at Cherise. Having been through the same emotions her first visit she just smiled. There was another surprise coming up and Cherise couldn't bring herself to ruin the surprise. Cherise slipped her shoes off at the door and Salem proceeded to do the same. The mood from the outside to the inside quickly changed from handmade natural wonders to a place of enchantment. Salem's white socks touched down on pale blue tiles, which felt cool under his feet. Across the room sat a sectional couch, a love seat, and two long stretched single recliners. All pieces were beige and trimmed in darker beige. As he walked towards the seating area, he noticed in between the couch and the love seat, sat a waterfall. It was large enough to replace a huge bay window. The water ran down a brown marble slab, which was embedded into the wall, in such a way that guest could actually walk straight through it. Taking a closer look Salem noticed that the water flowed into a waterway that ran left and right of the fall itself into a filter. The filter was silver an ran around the boarder walls of the living room, and then back out into what Salem defined as the urban sanctuary. He guessed this is was what kept the grass and plants so green and healthy. Joint beckoned for them to take a seat while he ran into the kitchen. In the middle of the living room laid a huge beige and white rug, round in shape it was large enough so that all of the seating furniture rested on top of it. The two colors formed the Yin and Yang.

Cherise plopped on the plush rug and Salem followed her league. She grabbed a folded yellow plastic sheet that she spread across the rug, just in time for Joint to return with one hand balancing two extra large pizzas, and another holding on dearly two a large bag of hot chips. Sitting the food down and joining the others on the floor, Joint and Cherise looked at each other for what may not have even five seconds, and burst out laughing.

"Okay man, say what you have to say," Joint said relaxing the back of his head on the couch behind him.

Salem was at a loss for words.

"What, how the hell did you make this happen? I mean no disrespect, but you own a record shop, not Virgin records," he proclaimed looking around hoping that he hadn't missed anything.

The two now seeming more like a couple than ever to Salem couldn't seem to contain themselves.

"I told you he was a DJ right," Cherise said as she gave Joint a kiss on the cheek.

This didn't explain anything for Salem so he looked directly at Joint, who had finally decided to take off his shades. He was definitely black, and good-looking Salem thought.

"Okay man, when I was about ten my parents had an unlucky bout with an eighteen wheeler. My parents lost the battle with the truck, but my grandmother won battle with company's lawyers. She died a few years later leaving everything to me, along with the family's record shop. I missed my family and I needed something or somewhere to go to make me feel like I did when I was with them, so I thought up this. Now any time I want to feel that connection, I have the perfect place to go," he said smiling lying on the couch again.

Knowing that such tranquility came with a price, Salem's smile left his face.

"Hey, look, don't start that. I came to terms with my past a long time ago. Sooner or later you have to get rid of the grief and move forward," Joint said sitting up to open the bag of chips.

Cherise handed them both plates and began to serve the pizza.

"Joint here is not only good at designing flats, but he travels all over the world as a DJ, she said giving Joint a wink.

Joint almost blushed while punching Cherise in the

shoulder playfully. Salem didn't know whether he wanted to join in on their laughter or puke because of how close they seemed to be. The pizza was delicious, but he had a sour taste in his mouth.

"So why do they call you Joint anyway," he questioned.

Cherise almost choked on a slice of pizza trying to answer the question before Joint could even open his mouth.

"Well that's easy. Look at the fro, then the white jeans. Now imagine the shirt he has on being a white T-shirt. He only wore white as a kid and never got rid of the fro. He's like what we call a walking joint," she couldn't get the final words out with giggling.

It was really the first time he had seen Cherise's silly side full blown. He joined in on her laughter while Joint proceeded to explain himself.

"Hey to me Joint is an expression of who I am and what I do. I set joints jumping when I come on the scene. Forget that I become the joint when I enter a room," he almost shouted.

Cherise reached over grabbing Joints hand as she laughed, and at the same time Salem's laughter stopped. Joint notice the quick change and knew what was up.

"Hey, you know we're family right? Cherise here is my first cousin," he playfully said.

He wasn't sure if Joint had caught on to him, but either way he tried to shake any suggestions off.

"Oh, I was wondering why you knew so much about him. I thought," he said without being able to finish his sentence.

"You thought we were a duo, a thing, a couple right," Joint said asked.

"Well you seemed to be so close for just friends," he replied.

After stuffing his face with half of one of the pizza slices Joint pulled out two stacks of CDs and a stack of albums.

"Listen I have to go and check on the shop again and then I'm off to a show. Feel free to choose the music you want and make a list for me. Cherise stay the night or just lock up when you finished," he said winking as he jumped up from the floor.

Salem's heart felt as if it had suddenly dropped to

bottom of his guts. Joint grabbed a backpack and two more

slices of pizza. Saying goodbye to Cherise, and shoving

another piece of pizza into his mouth, he gave a sly look to

Salem as if to say big brother was watching and, slammed

the door behind him. From that point on it was just Salem

and Cherise. She seemed comfortable enough in her

surroundings, but Salem was a different story. He had no

idea where to begin. While he sat helpless chewing on a

piece of pizza, looking down at the rug, Cherise seemed

ready to get started. Laying down on her back and shoving

her face where his eyes met the rug, he was forced to notice

her.

"Well, are we going to get started, or are we going to try

and eat more than both of our stomachs can handle," she

asked.

She had broken the ice and Salem was grateful that she

had.

"Hey, I could do both, but I don't think you wanna witness me gorging myself, so I guess we just better focus on the music," he said laughing.

For about an hour they contemplated over the music they would use and after another two hours, they had confirmed their choices. Without realizing it the pizza was gone and their stomachs were empty again.

"So Cherise, what bought you to Columbia," he asked wanting to get a real conversation flowing.

Cleaning up the mess she seemed surprised that he had asked anything.

"A lot of things I suppose, but if you want to hear the long version, it make take all evening," she replied.

Salem looked at his phone and gave a quick smile to Cherise.

"Well, I'm waiting," he said.

"Okay, I guess it's better than hanging at home trying to avoid my roommates," she said.

"In that case I'll show mine as long as you show yours," he replied laughing.

"Well, I guess that means cappuccino is up for que. Would you like some," she asked.

She could have ordered him poison and he would have said yes. He decided to follow her in to the kitchen, which was painted a pale blue to match the white tile floors. The colors gave the apartment a continuous flow and all that

Salem could think of was what a genius Joint was. After getting over the kitchen he watched Cherise. She seemed to know where everything was and the way she moved across the kitchen reminded him of his sister. They both seemed a bit uncomfortable, but unlike Lamya, Cherise seemed somehow free, independent of who or whatever was around her. He liked watching her so much that he had completely forgotten to at least speak.

"Are you okay," she asked pouring some water into the cappuccino maker.

"Yeah, sorry, I was just thinking of how much I love this place. So do you stay here a lot," he asked.

Tinkering with the machine she didn't bother to look his way.

"Yeah, this is like my home away from home," she

replied.

"What do you mean," he asked.

"Well, it's like this. When I first moved here I was going to stay with Joint, he's the only real family that I had here. The only problem was that Joint was in the middle of designing this place and lived a straight up college bachelor's life style. You know I like to party as much as the next person, but for me there's got to be a limit. I couldn't hang so I moved into the dorms for a while and then found some roommates, but he gave me a key anyway, and whenever I feel like it I come over here. He's gone most of the time anyway,"

"So where are you from originally," he asked.

Carrying a tray with two cups of coffee into the main

room, she placed it on the rug, put her hands on her hips and proclaimed her status with a southern accent.

"I'm from Alabama baby," she taunted with an incredible smile that made Salem want to be from Alabama too.

"Sweet Home Alabama," he replied.

Rolling her eyes she gestured for him to sit down.

"Even though I hate that song, yes Sweet Home Alabama, she sighed.
"Why, it's celebrating you came from," he asked.

"I don't know I guess it's the country I don't like and I've always wondered when they sing that song is everything to them sweet in Alabama, or just some things to certain people. I f you know what I mean," she replied.

"So I figure that was one of the reasons you left home," he asked.

Reminiscing she put her arms behind her back and rest her elbows on the floor, as she looked up towards to the ceiling.

"Ahh, let's see. What brings anyone to Columbia? First and most important are those great scholarships, second my pride in an excellent school, and finally ambition," she answered.

Salem shook his head in agreement.

"Hey, I can't argue with you there. If it's what you want, it's what you want," he replied.

Still looking at the ceiling she had another thought.

"Other than school, I'm not that traditional southerner that goes and makes good only to return home. After school if I don't get a job soon I don't know where I might find myself," she said.

Sitting up she passed Salem a cup while taking a sip of her own. The cup hid everything but her eyes as she looked across at Salem.

"So that's it, what's the rest of the story," he asked anxiously.

Giggling she put down the cup and stared at him for a moment.

"Hope you're not saying that what I told you earlier was boring, because if so we may just have to get in to it," she said laughing.

"Hey, hey, I just like a good story and I feel that there is more going on than what you're telling me, he said.

"Okay, but there's really nothing else to tell, but here's the Cherise run down. Back home I left behind my parents, a sister and a brother, both younger than me. In four years I received double bachelors in journalism and psychology. Wanted a masters and I decided to get it in education. It has been eight years coming and within those eight years my then unwed sister has given me two nephews, my father died, and my mom struggles to understand how she conceived insane kids, excluding me of course. Now that I've expresses myself a little too much, how about you," she asked.

Salem was ready. At that moment he felt that he could tell Cherise anything. It wasn't at all like when he first met Mitch.

"Hey man, where are you from, because I thought you

were black, but I'm not so sure," Mitch asked as he sat behind Salem in a biology class.

"I'm from Morocco, so I would think I'm more African than you," Salem remembered saying with a smart-ass grin on his face.

"Morocco huh, you know my aunt is actually taking a little vacation over their right now. Sometimes we should sit down and you can tell me how wild it can get there for westerners. My aunts a little wild and I'd love to be able call her out on some things. Mitch replied grinning.

That's how they became friends, learning from each other one hangout night at a time. No long conversations just small snippets of information during surface talk, but as he hung with Cherise, he felt that he could tell her the world and still search for more to share with her.

"What are you smiling at," Cherise asked.

Startled Salem left the past behind and focused on who was sitting right in front of him.

"Nothing, I was just thinking. So Cherise wants to know about me," he asked.

He was kneeling, sitting on top of his toes. His hands were relaxed on his thighs, and playfully Cherise put her hands on top of his. Any thought of holding back evaded him. Until Cherise slid her hand away from his he watched her eyes, and could feel that they were reading him just like his mother. Not wanting to seem anxious, but not doing a very good job of it, he jumped up from his spot and walked back and forth as if he were a lawyer ready to make his case.

"Okay, I was born in 1983 in Fez Boulemane Morocco, and just after my sister was born my father thought it would be better if he moved the family back to the U.A.E. I spent most of my youth in Dubai and then we moved to Abu Dhabi where I felt as if my family was taking my freedom away. I found out early I loved drawing buildings or concepts of buildings and later felt that Abu Dhabi was not the greatest place for me to further my talents. So, I decided to move here, he said as he wrong his hands after every sentence.

Cherise gestured for him to sit down.

"So, that's all you've got after I spilled my guts for you here," she said folding her arms in protest.

"Well, if you put it that way, I can…" he started before he was interrupted.

"Hey, I'm just kidding," she began to laugh.

Cherise stretched out on her stomach with her hands

supporting her chin. She looked him square in the eyes, making him feel uncomfortable for the second time.

"So do you think that we have enough stuff," he asked afraid of what would come after her stare.

Having enough stuff meant that it was time to leave, and that was something he didn't want to see himself doing right away He played with his thoughts, because it looked as if Cherise was preparing to get up, and then it came to him.

"Oh, you know what? How can we have a dance party without any Michael Jackson," he asked, smiling ear to ear.

Picking up the last cup from the rug she rushes to take it to the kitchen, and quickly plopped down once more.

She sat with her legs crossed like a child in

kindergarten. Grabbing hold of her ankles she looked up towards the ceiling.

"Yea, I didn't think I was ready for that yet. I kind of browsed over some stuff downs stairs earlier. You like Michael," she asked.

"Are you crazy? I'm coming from the U.A.E. If you were to ask every other person you passed in the streets, most would say yes. We're crazy about him.

A shy smile came to her face.

"I don't know after his death it was really hard for me to listen to his music, but I do have a collection of his songs that I may want to feed through Joint's speakers. What we can do is, I'll put the music together and hold on to it. If I'm feeling okay, then I'll let it play. How does that sound," she asked.

He was glad that they at least had one thing in common and it made Salem feel good.

"Hey, do you like ice cream, because if so we could go grab some," he asked.

Agreeing with the idea they took the front door, which was actually an elevator placed between the kitchen and the guest bedroom. As the elevator doors closed Salem took one last look at Joint's place. He felt as if he was leaving the only oasis in the NYC.

7~

SELFISH DEEDS ARE SIMPLY HUMAN

The night before seemed like a dream for him, no, they didn't get to kiss, but he knew that Cherise was more than interested in him and only him. Still marinating in his own thoughts, he banged his knee as his cell began to ring.

"Yea," he shouted hoping that he didn't wake up any one in the apartment.

"What's up, you could have told me that you had the music straight and that Joint was in the house," he yelled in a high-pitched voice, which he always had when he was excited about something.

"Hey, I'm sorry I was too busy hanging with the DJ's sexy cousin," he almost yelled remembering his parents were probably up lurking around.

"Ohhh, I see. So you finally got her to notice you huh," he asked.

"That's right. I got the music, the DJ and the girl," he said trying his best not to sound too excited.

Mitch belted out a laugh and then stopped abruptly.

"Hey I hope you play it cool with miss shorty. I need my boy for the party. Hold it off Salem! Hold it off. Remember the party is what is important right now. Trying to get us hooked up with a place at this very moment," he whispered excited at the opportunity.

While Mitch hunted around for a place, Salem felt that he needed some alone time. Peeking out of his bedroom door he listened for any sounds, but couldn't hear a thing. Tip toeing down the hall to the kitchen he made himself a huge bowl of cereal. His mind went back to Cherise. He was amazed at how much he was attracted to not just her ways, but also her style, which made him remember his father and the bra the day before. Was his father sneaking around? Becoming a little nervous he stood up to go and check his room, only to be stopped by the happy good mornings of his sister.

"I hope you're not in a hurry after staying out for what seemed to be the whole night? Because guess what, I have some news for you," she whispered.

He always had time for his sister, and as she whispered in his ear and took a spoonful of his cereal, he knew the room check would have to wait.

"Spill it," he whispered back.

He felt that he sounded rushed, and it may have been for the fact that no matter how he tried for the first few minutes he couldn't keep his mind off of his room.

"Remember I told you that I'd be looking for a job? Well last night I received an email from BioNeuutral Laboratories Corporation. They want to see me NOW! I'm going today, but I told mom that I was going to the movies with Taif," she said, as the last of her words almost escaped Salem's ears.

The thought of the room left him, but it was only exchanged for fear of what Lamya was planning on doing.

He knew that she was serious about the idea, but he didn't believe that things would move so quickly.

"So are you going with me," she asked.

He knew that even though she formed it as a question, it was a command.

"How come you didn't at least call and tell me this yesterday," he whispered back.

"I wanted to, but with you and Abu gone, mom wouldn't let me have any time to myself," she said looking around the room as she whispered again.

"So what time is the interview," he asked.

Though her move scared him to death and he didn't wholly agree with it, he liked all of the excitement that came with it. He had to ask himself, what if she worked in the states. She wouldn't have any problem affording her own place, and they would be close to each other. No matter how much he hated going home; sometimes the absence of family did bother him.

"I guess you better get ready before they wake up then, he whispered once more before getting up from his seat.

Kissing him on the cheek she headed for the bathroom. He noticed as she turned the corner that she had on Betty Boop pajamas. Her sassy face with the big head full of black curls and the pouty red lips made him wonder. Did Lamya have a little of Betty within her?

It was 9 am by the time Salem was dressed and ready to go. Lamya sat quietly in the living room planning to meet up with Taif and praying that their parents wouldn't wake up. On eye contact they both tip toed quietly out the door.

Closing the door behind them they both took their ritual breaths of freedom as they headed for the elevator. Lamya's interview was in Manhattan. Catching the N line the both of them sat quietly watching others get off and on the train. A couple about their age hopped on the train halfway through their trip. The guy wore skin tight, black skinny jeans, a black t-shirt with a screen print of Victor Fort and the Corpse's Bride. A silver plated belt decorated his waist, while blue nail polish and black lipstick decorated his skin. Salem was sure he had on eyeliner too, but couldn't be positive because of the black and blue hair that fell just past his nose. Lamya couldn't help but to whisper into her brother's ears.

"That is a boy right," she asked not taking an eye off of the couple.

His people were so analytical about everything. Even Lamya was a little bit more eastern than she wanted to admit.

"You see he has a girlfriend. What does it matter anyway," he asked.

For a moment he had lost his manners snapping at his sister even though she was the oldest.

"Sometimes you just have to look past what you see. You may be living here if you get this job, there are going to be a lot of different things that you see," he said shrugging his shoulders as he spoke.

Lamya understood where he was coming from and felt guilty for her actions, but old habits die-hard. She decided to focus on a little girl that stood further away from them, holding her mother's hand. Ironically she was dressed like Britney Spears during her Baby One More Time phase. Imagine she thought, that little girl was dressed in black loafers, with black knee high socks which came up just a little past her knees. They left her thighs exposed except for the little black mini skirt wore. She even had the nerve to have on a white girlish T-shirt that purposely exposed her belly button. If it wasn't for the pigtails, a lot of people could have seen her as just a short woman still hanging on to her mother's coattail. Lamya turned her head in discuss and refused to believe that she was wrong about judging that scene.

Her brother on the other hand was focused on the couple still standing in front of them. Looking at the girl he noticed that she was dressed in black too. She was the larger version of Lamya's pigtail enemy, with an added bit of sexy. In black loafers, knee high black socks, and a red and black pleated mini skirt, the little girl in pigtails looked back continuously, obviously ready for new inspiration. The girl was probably focusing on the black leather jacket that hid her white T-shirt, and a black-feathered fedora that made her look complete. The girl could see the youngster looking at her, but she also felt that someone else watched her too. Out of the corner of her eye she gave Salem a sly wink and a sneaky grin.

"Hey, where did you get those Betty Boop pajamas from," he asked.

"Why," she replied still annoyed about the whole little girl situation.

"I just didn't think she was your style," he replied.

"What are you saying; I can't be a Betty Boop? Not that I want to," she said looking first at the little girl and then the sexier older one.

Salem didn't want to say another word. He thought after his earlier remark that it was better to keep his mouth shut.

Turning back to the couple he watched as they hopped off of the train, and wished that he were doing the same.

By 11:15 they were in Manhattan. Deciding to get lunch Lamya made the restroom her make shift changing area, while Salem ordered them two omelets served with a slice of turkey, hush puppies and fruit cups. After she dressed Salem decided that it would be best if they went over some interview questions, and just as they were making head way Lamya's cell phone rang.

"Salam Alaikum," she said with a stiff smile.

Salem knew exactly who it was.

"Okay, Ahma okay, hudahafez," Lamya confidently said.

"Well what did she want,'" he asked.

"She just wanted us to pick up some things from the market if we don't stay out too late.

He disliked the fact that parents kept tabs on their children tighter than a leech on an unsuspected body. Wanting to wash down the breakfast, they decided to take a pit stop to the New York Milk Shake Company on Vandervelt Avenue. Lamya wore casual black boot cut pants, with an elegant white tank under a matching black jacket. He didn't say anything, but he was impressed with his sister's determination. Talking as close siblings do, by 2 p.m. the two decided to head over to the interview. She was due to appear at two forty-five and she seemed as ready as ever. At two thirty they took the elevator to the twenty-fourth floor. Salem sat in the lobby while Lamya talked with the receptionist. There were a lot of white lab coats walking to and fro. Meshed with the white hallway in which he sat, he felt as if he were in a hospital waiting room. He wondered was the hallway the same as Jackson's family stood waiting for the news. Did he know that they were outside? Did he know that he was gone? Who knows he thought, but what he did know is that he wanted to impact the world just as Jackson did. It was around four o'clock when he forced himself to leave his thoughts behind. He could also see Lamya walking down the hall towards him. He imagined her in one of those white coats, but when he did the feeling seemed to make him shiver. He could see her smile as she drew closer to him and with that he exhaled, jumped up from his seat, and headed towards the closest elevator he could find.

Heading out the door a phone call from Mitch would keep Lamya from sharing her experience with Salem.

"Guess what? I've got a place on lock down that's goanna make you piss in your pants boy!" Mitch yelled through the phone.

Salem had heard this excitement in Mitch before, and most of the time he would come through on his promises, but once and a while promises that seemed drenched in gold would sometimes fall short of even the silver mark.

"So where is it," Salem asked.

"Alright, listen. We had to compromise a little because the place was given to us free of charge," Mitch said.

Already it was sounding more like silver than the expected gold.

"Man come on with it, because I know something is up," Salem replied.

"We were too last minute for any outside venue, so I talked professor Chow into giving us Alfred Lerner Hall.

Shit my family kind of liked that idea better anyway and my dad is paying for security.

Clinching his teeth, he wanted to reach out and smack Mitch, but instead had to revel in smacking himself in the forehead for not being more aggressive in helping him find a place. Now Salem wasn't what one would call a party animal, but when he did party he made sure he was well satisfied. After his first year of campus parties, the remaining years he rarely went to parties on campus. It was something about the being around the same crowd that troubled him. People always got the idea that they knew him, and what he was all about. He didn't like it. No, he was really looking forward to something more distant. It was suppose to be a party where he let it all hang out, where he could put the college boy to rest, and let the new found man loose.

"Look, I don't know what you want to do, but we're grown men. You can do what you want, and you have to be honest, the place is goanna make some haters envious," he said laughing.

Mitch was right the place was perfect. Nicked named the domain by students, it was one of the more modern structures on the campus. The Domain was the place where most of the professors held their social gatherings. Set on the corner of 2920 Broadway, it was surrounded by city life. Outsiders always wanted to take a peak to see what was going on within those campus walls, while lights, music and other various sounds of entertainment tempted them. The school planned on putting in a pool over the summer, and with so much construction most of the professors had decided that it was best to hang elsewhere.

"I guess we just gotta work with it then," Salem replied.

"Hey, look. It's gonna be great. No one said the party had to stop at the Domain, it's just where we have to start it," Salem said laughing like he knew something Salem didn't.

Lamya was beginning to look cross.

"Hey, I'm still on family time, so can we catch up a little later," Salem asked.

Mitch said his goodbyes and that was it, the party was set. Catching up with Lamya who had just stormed out the lobby doors to meet Taif, Salem felt good. It was as if he were on cloud nine. He was going to end his college career with a bang after all. Making his way through the lobby doors as his sister did, he could see Taif wobbling down the sidewalk. She wore faded blue boot cut jeans, a long sleeve loose fitting red and white tiny flowered blouse, and light blue colored scarf. She tied it to the left of her head letting the remaining cloth hang across the front of her shoulder.

Exposing the bottom half of her hair, she resembled a

fortune telling gypsy. Though any type of fashion sense

seemed to have evaded Taif, it was something about her

presence that seemed to always bring about a different side

of Lamya. She decided not to change her clothes,

expressing instead that she felt more like a woman without

the covering garments.

"Hey, so what happened with the interview? I almost

forgot about it," he asked excitedly.

The girls were more interested in what film they wanted

to watch more than anything else.

"When I wanted to talk to you about the interview you

were too busy to care. Your Mitch was more important."

Rolling her large eyes, Salem couldn't help but think of Betty Boop again.

"I'm sorry about putting my thoughts above my big sister's even though I spent the day on her behalf, stuck in what felt like the hallway of a morgue," he replied.

As they fussed Taif decided to stand between them. She had forgotten how futile she thought their fights were. There she was sneaking out of her parents house to meet them, and neither of them had the courtesy to say hello. Instead they turned to her with frowns on their faces, there was no need for her to even try and intervene, instead, deciding to just follow behind them. Sometimes she felt as if they treated her like their little rag doll, along for the ride just when they needed her.

"As you know I went to talk to the receptionist, and even though we were fifteen minutes early the first interview was over and she said I could just walk on in. I was trying to signal to you from the window, but you were in your on world or something," she said looking at Taif for support.

Taif may have gotten her drift, but decided to ignore her as they jumped on the train heading away from the Bronx into Manhattan.

"Instead of trying to stab me with your sarcasm, can't you just go on with the story," he said following the girls on the train.

She was getting on his nerves and she knew it. It was moments like this that would get him pretty testy and she knew it was coming, but just like he could get testy, so could she. Rolling her eyes towards the back of her head she thought that it was best to finish the story when they reached the theater. With the two siblings quiet Taif could finally hear herself think, and what she thought was that she loved what Lamya was doing, she was taking a stand for herself. No, she wasn't sneaking out of the house to do what she wanted. She wasn't throwing a fit to her parents because they were trying their best to keep her in. What since would throwing a fit really make? She was making smart moves as an adult. Taif thought long and hard as Lamya grabbed money from her hand to buy popcorn and nachos.

"You know I wasn't blaming you for anything. I was just trying to tell you the story point by point, she whined, handing the attendant money and stuffing a handful of popcorn in her mouth.

Getting tired of their on and off again relationship Taif grabbed the food and decided to take a seat. They had about ten minutes before the movie started. Munching on some nachos as she watched the brother and sister duo, she felt jealous of their connection. At least they had each other; she only had sisters, which left her pretty much stagnant in moving around freely.

She recalled one day when she was around six years old. Her and the family were on a beach outing. She was maybe nine, and at that age whatever her mother felt comfortable with her wearing was okay. On that particular day she was sporting a bright pink swimsuit. She also wore wide rimmed sunglasses that drooped on the end of her nose. A white girl around the same age asked her if she wanted to build a sand castle with her. Her swimsuit just happened to be pink too, but unlike Taif's; this girl's suit had an opening in the front that revealed her belly button. Taif's mother sat further back off the beach dressed in a long sleeve white T-shirt and light grey sweat pants. To cover her eyes she wore larger rimmed glasses than her daughter and a large straw sun hat. Taif never had a clue as to how her mother noticed the two of them, but before she could say yes or no to the girl, her mother had run down the hill, through a couple sunbathing, tripping in a small sink hole as she grabbed her daughter. Kicking and screaming not knowing what she had done wrong; Taif was covered with a towel, thrown in the back of their Sudan and taken home immediately. The next time they went to the beach and each time after wards she was made to wear what looked like a black diver's suit. No one ever approached her on the beach again, unless they thought they could share a shady area with her. Taking her mind off the awful memory she studied Lamya's dress as the two continued to talk. Taif hardly ever wore pants. She didn't want to have to bother with hearing her mother's mouth. No, she thought, her style was short sleeve shirts over long sleeve shirts of different colors. Her skirts were usually jean material and if it were hot then a cotton material of different colors would suffice.

In comparison she began to stuff nacho after nacho into that plump face of hers while pushing those wide rimmed glasses back up on to her nose. It was then that she decided that it was time for a change. Pushing her bangs back into her scarf she looked down at her beaded flip flops bought from Aldos. They were the only items that showed she knew what era it was. She felt like choking herself.

There were only two nachos when the sibling duo walked up to Taif. Lamya looked in discuss and dared not to ask why.

"So, like I said. They liked my resume and want to have another interview with me. The secretary said she will call me later on this week," Lamya continued.

Taif jumped up ready to drown her thoughts in a good movie.

"You see, just great. More good news for the Tamimis," she fussed.

Like Lamya had grabbed the money from Taif's hands earlier, so did Taif grab a drink from Lamya's hand, while simultaneously grabbing Salem by the shoulder and leading them both into the theater.

If her cousin could make a change by staying in the states on her own, then so could she, she thought, right after the movie was finished and the popcorn was done.

8~

LOSING SELF TO FIND SELF

Almost two weeks had passed and in that time Salem

had stopped a forced engagement, and had his dirty hands

involved with keeping his sister safe in the states. He

wondered what his families visit would conjure up next, but

until then he knew he didn't have long before graduation,

and he needed to find a way to get closer to Cherise. Lying

on his bed, he put his arms behind his head, and before he

knew it he was off to dream land. The deeper his sleep the

younger he seemed to become and before he knew it he

found himself back in the U.A.E. He was ten, back in the

villa above a local market where they once lived in Al

Aine. They stayed on the top floor. Each villa was right off a main hallway, which had three triangular glass domes where residents could look down and watch other local residents shop for their weekly groceries. Many evenings Salem would sit next to one of the domes closest to his villa making sketches of things going on below him. His favorite subjects were women, mostly those who wore abbyas. It was fun for him to imagine what they were wearing underneath those shapeless clothes, and he spent many hours dressing and undressing them with his pencils. In his deep sleep he sketched at an amazingly rapid pace, but then suddenly stopped. One particular lady walked beneath him, and he couldn't help but focus on a single strand of hair that fell from her abaya, dangling down the right cheek of her face. He had this sudden urge to touch it, and in response placed both of his hands on the glass as if he were preparing to crawl across it. As he looked below him the market and its people began to spin round and round out of control. The faster it went the dizzier he became, until he could see nothing more but a blur beneath him. He collapsed on the glass being absorbed within it, held like a prisoner with no room for escape. The piece that imprisoned him broke from the dome and began falling within the market. Screaming Salem tried repeatedly to break free of its hold. He was afraid he'd hit the ground and starred intensely below him, but the closer the glass came to hitting the floor the darker the market began to grow. It grew so dark that soon there was no market at all only darkness. He began to fall faster and the faster he fell the more he began to see. The dark revealed the lives of others those he did know and others he didn't. Each life passed seemed to slow his fall, but as soon as it was out of sight he fell even faster, that is until finally the darkness thickened and the fall slowed to almost a halt. It was then that he saw one after the other lives of those he knew at present. Slowly the darkness around him turned a bright white he found himself in the living room of Joint's home. Cherise and Joint were sitting on the couch, where Cherise was crying and Joint was trying his best to console her. Passing over them the space grew dark and as he turned to face another direction the space brightened again. He could see himself standing in front of Joint's shop, walking away with his head held low. Had he hurt her some way, he thought, but before he could find out the space drew dark again, only to lead him into the lives of his parents. They stood in a beautiful condo made up of windows instead of walls. The purpose was the beautiful structure that over looked the whole of Manhattan. He seemed to be hovering right above them, but couldn't hear a word that they were saying. Mrs. Tamimi pointed her right hand at her husband angrily, while Mr. Tamimi looked down at the floor shaking his head in despair. Salem wanted to reach out to them to ask what was the matter, but he couldn't move from his incased prison. While screaming in defiance he was pulled away from his parents on to a huge balcony just outside of where

they stood. It was huge and so white that when the light

reflected off it the shine constricted his sight. He hovered at

one end of the balcony, and could see Mitch at the other

end. His back was facing him, but he could see that Mitch

had his arms around his girlfriend. He put his hands under

her chin to lift her head, and at that point the triangular

prison moved in closer. Mitch moved into to kiss her and as

his head tilted slightly to the left, Salem caught a glimpse

of the girl's eyes. They were not the eyes of Mitch's

girlfriend, but instead the eyes of his sister. Mitch was his

closest friend, but the sight of seeing his sister with him

filled Salem with anger. He struggled to reach through the

glass and grab Mitch by the neck, but he was dragged to the

edge of the balcony and as he screamed Mitch's name the

glass began to drop at a rapid speed away from Mitch,

away from his sister and away from his parents. Unlike

before he could feel the strong wind as he fell which moved

like an invisible current pulling him towards a concrete floor. His arms and legs dangled in the wind like those of a puppet being directed to its death with the pull of its strings. And then in the flash of a moment his back hit something hard. His head flung forward and then back hitting the concrete with such force that a stinging sensation prickled through every inch of his body so much so that he couldn't move. His muscles began to constrict, and as quick as they tightened they relaxed to the point that Salem felt he would melt from the sensation. Then just as that feeling took over him, his body would constrict again, becoming so unbearable that he had no intention of taking another breath of air. The lack of air constricted the body sucking in his skin, and crushing his bones. He began to crumble, disintegrating under the pressure breaking apart into tiny little pieces. He had become one with the glass shattered on the concrete ground. The only thing that remained was a small shard, which contained half of his right eye. It looked up, then left, and right as if pleading for those looking down at it to put its remains back together.

"Hey, get up and stop whining in your sleep. Your mom has breakfast ready," Taif yelled into his room.

Glad that it was a dream Salem jumped up touching his eyes to make sure they were still intact. Annoyed with who awoke him, he threw his pillow at Taif who went giggling down the hall behind what sounded like the louder laughs of his sister. It was a Tuesday morning, and from the looks of it, it didn't seem as if the day would be anything else but another nightmare. After breakfast and quick plans for a graduation dinner hosted by his mother, he decided that he had enough of the family for one day. His mind was on Mitch, and he decided that he would go and pay him a surprise visit. By the time he reached the number six line, taking him from Astoria to Harlem, he could feel that New

York vibe generating through him. Reaching Mitch's door he could smell flavors of the south coming through the kitchen window, reminding him of his summer visits down south to see cousins. Walking up to Mitch's place Salem would usually get an ear full of house or at least some hip-hop, but this time the sounds of rhythm and blues filled the air. Usually he would just walk right in, but he felt that it was smarter to knock. Knocking three times, his last rap on the door bought about the sassy sounds of a female's voice.

"Mitch baby, I just don't want to answer your door and we're all the way out here in Harlem," she shouted.

She had a southern accent so captivating that his ears clinched onto every word that came from her mouth.

"You can answer the door. No one's going to bother you," Mitch shouted.

Hearing footsteps he straightened his posture, hoping who ever came to the door didn't think of him badly.

"Well, look at here. May I help you," the woman asked as she eyed him up and down with a charming smile.

Averaging around five foot six, she was what Mitch would call high yellow. She had short-cropped hair, and big round eyes attached to lushes eye lashes that made her resemble an adult version of Strawberry Short Cake. Her lips were short in length, red in color, and came to a sharp point at the top, which made it look as if she was always puckered read for a kiss.

"Well, can I help you," she asked getting agitated.

She seemed to Salem to be bossy in tone, but her looks allowed it. As she looked him up and down he couldn't help but notice her too, especially her full chest which was accompanied by an even nicer, waistline.

"Oh, I'm sorry. My name is Salem. I'm a friend of Mitch's," he replied nervously.

Putting one hand on her hip and the other just slightly above her top lip, she gave him a grin.

"Okay Salem, any friend that looks like you, and is a friend of Mitch's, can always be a friend of mine," she said.

Still holding her hip she turned around gesturing for Salem to follow. Walking with more than just a noticeable twist, Salem was entranced with how firm and round her backside seemed to be. He had never considered himself an ass man, but the way she looked made him believe otherwise. The unfortunate part of the situation was that his first self-realization was also the way he met the rest of the people visiting Mitch that day.

"You okay baby," Mrs. Pettiway asked seeing him eyeing his leader.

It was like he had been caught with his hands in the cookie jar. Snapped out of his trance he looked up just to see a large group of people starring right back at him.

"Hi," he said with a quivering voice.

The response was laughter, which grew the longer he stood quiet.

"Its okay baby, Gwen just loves to make men drool over

her. Even if they are a little too young for her," she said cutting her eyes at Gwen.

Ignoring the older woman Gwen turned around, gave Salem another flirtatious grin, and disappeared within the group.

"Hey man, it's cool. Cousin Gwen has a habit of flirting with everybody," he said running over out of the crowd to give me him a slap on the back.

Along with the slap on the back Mitch gave him a manly hug. Salem wasn't sure whether to hug him back or punch him. As soon as he saw Mitch's face all he could think about was the dream and his best friend attempting to kiss his sister.

"Hey, everybody this is my good friend Salem. Mom I told you about him," he said proudly.

"Oh, nice to finally meet you baby. Come on in and let me fix you a plate of food," she said scurrying from her seat to the kitchen.

Salem followed Mitch and his mother into the kitchen and as he walked he felt a strong tug on the back of his shirt. In fear that it was Gwen he ignored it moving closer behind Mitch.

"Hey you, I didn't know that you were going to be here," Someone said behind him.

It was Mitch's girl friend, and ecstatic that it wasn't Gwen, Salem turned around and gave her a heartwarming hug. Michelle was cheerful and as happy as ever, which meant that her and Mitch were happy together. She was bringing in meat from the back yard and motioned for help. The memory Mitch and his sister connected in a loving embrace melted away.

"I'm sorry; let me help you with that. I thought you were Gwen," he whispered.

"Oh my god, she gets around doesn't she," Michelle whispered back.

It seemed like every time Salem met up with Michelle she would sound whiter and whiter. Now it wasn't that anything was wrong with this, there were many in fact too many that had the white dialect going on. Infact he had so many cousins using this dialect that it literally made him angry. He knew many of his cousins were just faking it, which made him also questions why Michelle spoke as she did. Then he figured there were only two ways this was possible, growing up around and in an area where the majority of people were white, or just wanting to be white which meant changing the personal dialect. To him Michelle's look contradicted her speech. A petite girl like Cherise, Michelle had short jet-black hair that was tailored to her face like Halle Berry. Her features were keen with a sharp nose and thin lips, while her skin was as dark as coal. She was flawless in looks and the smoothness of her skin gave Salem every excuse to pinch her cheeks each time he saw her. Too bad his hands were full. He liked Michelle a great deal, and what he hoped is that she was being true to herself in every way possible, because if not, how could she be true to Mitch or anything else in life.

"Salem just sit it on the table and go and grab a plate," she said bustling around the room.

Mrs. Pettiway directed Salem to the table before he could even grab for a plate. As he sat he wondered if Mitch had anything to eat at all. As Mrs. Pettiway handed Salem a plate of food, Mitch sat across from him with a plate of his own.

"Hey, have you eaten any of our food before," he asked as if he had just discovered a deep revelation.

Having to think back in the four years that he had been in the states, not once had he tried any of Mitch's food. He felt guilt building within him, because every time he would find a new Arab restaurant, Mitch was always willing to go.

"Mitch, you know I haven't ever tried your food, not once man,"

Mitch's mother couldn't help but laugh.

"Well baby that's okay. You don't need to try this type of food in no old restaurant anyway. You got the real deal right in front of you," she said passing him a plate.

She giggled again and in the process grabbed Salem by his face and planted a big one on his cheek. Still laughing she walked away without another word. The two found themselves alone.

"Wow, when you said family I figured you meant just your mom and dad, but you have every generation starting from the 1920s out there," he laughed.

"That's how we do! I may be partying with you on the twenty-ninth, but before that my family is the party before the party. Hey, I would have invited your family over, but I wasn't sure how well they would mesh," he said laughing.

The word family bought back the images from his dream earlier that morning, and it didn't sit well with him.

"Yeah, I don't know how that would have worked out either. You haven't met any of my family by the way have you," he asked suspiciously.

Asking the question, he held his breath as he waited for an answer. Mitch on the other hand had taken a bite of food from one of the dishes sitting next to him and his mouth was full. He was much more interested in savoring the taste of the food rather than answering his friend's question. Salem needed an answer and as he watched Mitch's jaws chew slowly on the food, the silence annoyed him.

"Mitch, have you met any of my family or not," he asked again.

The question sounded too suspect the same as the expression that Mitch had on his face as he starred at his friend.

"Why," he asked.

He sounded uneasy which made Salem antsy.

"So you have met them," he asked with a pushy force.

Mitch quickly swallowed a big gulp of his food while intensely starring at Salem.

"Man what's wrong with you? I feel like you're trying to interrogate me or something," he asked.

Salem could feel that the answer was yes and he just wanted to hear it from Mitch's mouth.

"You didn't answer the question," he said.

"Man you been smoking something," Mitch asked.

Though the apartment was cool, the heat from the stove made Salem perspire. His eyes grew wider, and Mitch couldn't help but believe he had smoked a huge bud before coming over.

"Just answer the question Mitch," he said.

"No, Salem, I haven't met your family. But then you should know this because you haven't introduced them to me yet," he rebutted.

They both looked at each other for a few more moments one making sure the other was okay in truth and attitude.

"Man, I think you should eat something, because either you've got the munchies real bad, or your ass is going crazy," Mitch expressed.

He was telling the truth, he hadn't met any of his family, and Salem could breathe for a little bit longer. Taking a swallow of a cold glass of coke, which Mitch's mother provided for him, he took the first bite of his food. It was good, more than good and he closed his eyes savoring the food as if he was eight years old again.

"Man, what is this," he asked.

A smile returned to his friends face. It made him feel good that Salem could appreciate the food.

"Shit, that's your first taste of collard greens covered in ham hocks with a side of smothered chicken to make the meal complete," he said smiling.

"It was then that he remembered why he never ate any of Mitch's food, it was filled with pork. After enjoying a big mouthful he sat almost shocked with his mouth open, mugging Mitch in disbelief. Not wanting to seem rude he swallowed what was in his mouth.

"What," Mitch asked.

Salem shook his head and as Mrs. Pettiway passed through the kitchen she noticed that something was not right with her guest.

"Baby what's wrong? You don't like the food," she asked.

Hesitant he didn't say a word. It was one thing to spit someone's food out, but just wrong to have to say it was no good for him. Mrs. Pettiway looked at her son and then at Salem. Simultaneously both Pettiways burst out into laughter. Walking over to Salem she put her hands on his shoulder, while leaning over so she could see his face.

"Baby I think Mitchie is just pulling your leg. With all the diabetes going on in families these days, this family doesn't eat pork, just things that give us the flavor of pork," she said.

Salem began to smile and as soon as Mrs. Pettiway left the room Salem threw a wet hand towel at Mitch.

"Oh come on man. I was just trying put you in a good mood after you came in here acting so strange," he said raising his right eye brow.

"I'm sorry. It's gotten a little stressful with the family in toe," he said shamefully hoping

Mitch wouldn't enquire any further.

"Stressful, shoot look at this, you've never been like this before, so you gotta shake it off and get to having some fun. My family has booked two big suites in Manhattan for the rest of their time here. Their leaving tonight so I thought Michelle and me would throw a little party. I was going to call you later this afternoon, but since you're here just stay. Picture drinks, two free movies, and an excuse to call Cherise," he said with a witty smile.

Salem was sold on the party and decided that while Mitch continued to mingle with the family he would give his sister a call.

"Yes Salem," she said playfully.

He could hear two or more of his cousins in the

background.

"Staying away from the girlie sleep over, tell mom that I'm goanna stay over to Mitch's tonight. His family is here and they've asked me to stay for dinner and movies," he lied.

"Really, what are you talking about? You have enjoyed these sleep overs more than ever have, but the afternoon with your friend sounds like fun,"

Salem always felt guilty leaving the family and doing his own thing even though most of the time he was doing his thing with them.

"Listen tell them that I asked you to help me find a graduation gift for Mitch, and that you need to meet me in Manhattan around 11 am tomorrow," he said.

"It sounds like sneaky fun to me. What are we up to," she asked.

"What are we up to? I think it's best if we go ahead and pick out that outfit for the party, unless you want to wear whatever you have packed away in your suitcase," he said.

"Oh shut, I almost forgot about it. Yea I have to get something, of course I help pick out that gift for your friend," she said giggling.

He could hear his cousin whispering in the background.

"Taif thinks she wants to tag alone," she whispered.

"The more the merrier, so see you tomorrow," Salem expressed.

Feeling better he slips his phone into his pocket and joins Mitch and his family for cards and conversation.

It was later after the three had taken some rest that the party began. While Mitch set the music for the evening, Michelle fixed plates of the leftover food in the kitchen, and Salem was assigned to greet people at the door.

"Oh my gosh is Salem, is that you? I thought you had gone home a while ago," Israa asked with surprise.

Israa was the first girl he ever dated in the states. He didn't actually have a thing for her, but at the time she kept him from being home sick that first year. She was a beautiful Moroccan girl with what Salem defined as a good body, not great, but very good. He almost didn't notice who she was. In fact it looked like she had gained double the body weight of what was once a hundred pound girl. The sight made him feel good about the fact that their relationship stayed plutonic, and then it made him think about Gwen. Intimidated by her to the point of pure embarrassment, he couldn't help but admit her beautiful assets would have done him a world of good at that moment.

"Israa, you... You look so great," he said trying to hold a fake smile on his face.

He didn't want to lie, but what else was he suppose to do? Walking in behind her was a talk robust white guy. He put his hands around her waist as she smiled at Salem.

"This is Greg, and Greg this is Salem," she said.

He never figured someone like Greg to be her type, but he also never figured that she would be so big. Shaking her boyfriends hand to get rid of the awkwardness he directed them toward the food. He thought it was best that he moved away from the door at that point and decided to go and listen to some music. Sitting on the couch he discovered that Mitch had all house music lined up for the night. Bobbing his head to the beat and realizing that everyone else was in the kitchen, he began to stand up and dance. This house had no words and it made him imagine how he would call Cherise and ask her to come out. He hadn't called yet because as usual he was nervous about the whole situation, and he knew that if he didn't call right away there soon be no use no to call. Not knowing what to do he started playing around with his dance moves and being silly Beyounce's scissor legs move was his choice of dance. With his back to the living room entrance, he didn't notice that more people had walked in and he had become their entertainment.

"Whoa, Moroccan lover boy is giving us some of that

dessert flavor," a voice said loudly.

Of all people Jim Themes decided to join the party. A wrestler from Nebraska, Jim was your typical American red neck. The blond headed grey-eyed devil had paid his way through college on a wrestling scholarship. What was unbelievable was that Jim had made it through four years of college, let alone an extra two. A sixteen year old in a buff wide neck, twenty-four year old body, he was popular high school football player, and Salem the geeky nerd.

"Long time no see dessert boy," Jim said.

Salem hadn't turned around yet and really regretted doing so.

"Yea, I see your neck is still red," Salem said with an annoyed smile.

Jim had been waiting for his response. It was the way they always greeted each other, whether Salem wanted to or not. Raising an eyebrow with a grin he used his shoulder to nudge Salem away from him and then headed straight for the kitchen. Behind him followed an entourage of protégés and what looked like a sixteen year old who claimed all night that she was Jim's girlfriend. Usually Jim's bullying tactics didn't bother him, but that incident took him away for a moment, back to Khalifa city. Their parents had just rented out a villa in City "A" and they celebrated by joining other family members for dinner. Salem was in traditional Moroccan dress and was allowed to go and explore the rest of the market area. Deciding to buy some candy for himself and his sister, walking out of one of the markets he was confronted by two locals around the age of twelve, the same age as him. Knowing what was to come he quickly walked passed them to catch up with his father.

"Salam Morocco, who are you taking the candy to," the first boy asked.

They were walking fast to catch up to him and before he could reach his father they had pushed him to the ground and began pulling him into one of the market alleys. One boy grabbed his arms, while the other his legs. Swinging him back and forth they promised to take him higher if he didn't give them his candy. Dropping him on the ground the taller of the two picked him up and pushed him against a wall.

"Oh look and he's a pretty Moroccan boy too," the second of the boys teased.

Salem was determined that he wouldn't let them get away with his candy, and so he kicked the second boy in groin while the first boy punched him in the stomach. He felt no pain just revenge. Angry at his attack the second boy stood, and gave him a punch to the face. Salem fell immediately to the floor and as he lay there the first boy thought it would be funny to pull his clothes up over his head. Both boys stood up starring down at him as if they had just seen some sort of alien. Neither of them said a word. Struggling to pull his clothes down Salem jumped up, it was his chance to get them back.

"What's wrong? Are you scared now," he shouted to the top of his lounges.

Pushing both boys to the ground he quickly punches one twice in the face and then the other. Jumping up he kicked them both in their sides and found his way out of the alley and safe back with his family. He remembered his father being so proud of him, so he never mentioned what caught them off guard and led to his victory. It was better that he didn't. Maybe he hadn't turned out to be the Hulk or the Rock, but he won that day and promised himself he would never let anyone bully him again. Emirates were tuff, and they made him tuff too.

Stuck with a stupid grin on his face he was knocked back to his real predicament when Jim yelled at him from the kitchen.

"Hey dessert boy continue dancing for us," he said.

Salem thought of himself as more mature than Jim, so he gave him a smile and continued with his dance.

By eight o'clock Mitch's apartment was full. People were eating, listening to music, or just sitting back and enjoying a drink. Salem got caught up in an in-depth conversation about westernizing the Muslim world with Israa, and had completely forgotten about calling Cherise.

"Hey I'll talk to you later, I'm gonna go and dance with

Greg, she said giving him a kiss on the cheek.

Salem grabbed his third drink from the kitchen counter. He thought it was too late to call Cherise. Going to the living room he plopped down on to the couch. Smiling he felt alone as he looked out at everyone else. It was as if he was in a theater and his friends were his personal film. He watched Michelle tease Mitch, Israa dance with Greg, and he imagined himself dancing with Gwen. By eight thirty his eyes were half closed and the room began to spin. His head felt heavy and so he rested his chin on his chest. He looked down at the floor and what he discovered were two pair of feet dressed in black Japanese influenced heels. The shoes were fascinating to him. He couldn't take his eyes off of them, that is, until the heels were lost behind the bent knees of their owner.

"I think you may need to take a little break from

drinking," she said.

He watched as the knees dropped to the floor and what took their place was the face of Cherise looking up at him. Not alone any more he sat up and smiled. She was a welcoming surprise, but he knew that it was no coincidence. Mitch sat on the other end of the couch kissing his girlfriend. Taking a break from Michelle's lips Mitch rested his chin on her shoulder giving Salem a wink accompanied with a thumb up.

"You know you're not just goanna sit there. Come on, get up and let's get some fresh air," she said smiling and dragging him from the couch.

The drink had really gotten to him. After standing he nearly left Cherise behind just to reach Mitch's back yard. It was nothing like Joint's paradise in the city, but at that moment, opening that door to Mitch's square inch of New York yard felt good. The fresh air nipped at his senses, which made him realize that he was leaving Cherise behind. As he turned she was standing just within the door with her arms folded leaning against the frame.

"I'm sorry. I didn't realize how much I needed this," he said sheepishly.

Stretching his arms above his shoulders he looked up into the night sky.

"Hey, I can see just a few minutes has done you some real good. Now how about some food," she asked smiling.

"I don't know if you noticed or not, but there are a lot of people in their trying to grab food. What if I text Mitch and tell him to hold us too plates back, and mean while we can talk about party plans" he asked.

"You know, I'll tell you honestly I'd rather talk about things on Mitch's dance floor a bottle Heineken in my hand while we wait for the food," she said smiling uncontrollably.

A little too excited Salem grabs too bottles of beer from the cooler and leads Cherise back into the house. The music seemed louder than before and everyone in the apartment moved to his or her own personal beat. The mood swept them up in the moment. One song turned into two and two turned into ten. By that time Cherise was on her fourth beer and Salem on his fifth. Hunger had finally conquered them and so the two headed towards the kitchen. Salem leads and Cherise follows by grabbing hold of his arm and locking hers within his.

"Hey wait up. Are you so hungry that you've already forgotten your new friend," she asked.

He didn't dare to turn back, he was smiling too broad to ever let her see. As he entered the kitchen he found two plates wrapped in foil waiting for them. It seemed that as soon as he grabbed the plates, everyone else got the same idea. Grabbing a fork he grabs two seats where he and Mitch had sat eating earlier that day. Taking his fork he scoops up a bit a food from his own place and offers to give Cherise a bite. She looked as if she was going to refuse so he moved the fork closer to her lips. Barely opening her mouth he moves the fork a little closer and gives her a gentle smile, so gentle that she slowly took in what he offered.

"You know we could share. There is more than enough for us," he said.

Taking a bite himself they both burst into laughter as some of the food he was trying to eat dribbled down the side of his mouth. Cherise then grabbed her own fork and they dug into the plate together. He wouldn't have believed it if anyone else had told him, but the food that he put in his mouth that night was five times better than the same food he had eatten earlier that day. Mrs. Pettiway really had gift he thought, and then he looked across at Cherise, maybe she was the pop in his midnight delight.

With everyone full from the food the mood and the music seemed to shift gears. Blame it on the alcohol was the next up and everyone, including Salem and Cherise made their way to the dance floor. From that point on Salem couldn't help but to think that Jamie Fox was actually an undercover pimp, because the song gave almost anyone the reason to things they normally wouldn't put themselves out there for. Feeling confident he put his right arm around Cherise's waist pulling her closer to his body. His heart beating fast, he moved to in time to the rhythm of her hips. She was relaxed, and in her relaxation her hands fell to her side. Leaning back she smiled as she looked up at the ceiling. To keep her from falling he pulls her closer and their bodies touch. The food did little t the time to sober ether of them, and he could tell. The top of her body seemed suspended in air and Salem believed that she looked like an angel as she twirled her around. She liked the way he held her and wanting to be even closer, so she took her right hand and caressed his neck, while pulling herself up and resting her forehead on his shoulder. It was as if no one else was in the room, and then the lights went dim except for a small lamp with a red bulb that gave the room a sassy nuance. The music was louder, not as loud as the beat of his heart. His face was flushed red and he knew that dripping sweat was next to come. Taking a swallow of guts he took a deep breath. Removing one hand from Cherise's waist he gently put it under her chin pulling her closer, so close that their lips nearly touched. He opened his eyes wider just to look into hers. She was aware, but was she willing? Moving his eyes from hers he looked down at her lips. At that time it wasn't the color that enthused him, but instead how plump and lush they looked as if they knew what was about to happen.

"Well, are you goanna kiss me," she whispered.

He was going to, but he couldn't completely let go. Instead he moved away leaving only his hands on her lips. Slowly he let his hands slip away from her. A reply to her question was interrupted by a familiar voice.

"Hold on. You're not hitting on my cousin? Are you coz," he said with laugh that seemed exaggerated to Salem.

He had dropped the ball and felt as if everyone was watching him. He never answered Joint's question. How would he explain himself especially to Mitch? He couldn't even figure out what was going on with himself. He looked up at Cherise who had turned to give her cousin a hug. She still had a smile on her face as she looked back at her crush. Her smile just embarrassed Salem more. He needed to clear his head and decided to escape to the bathroom. Washing his face he looked in the mirror. The reflection was as good looking as ever, but that night he hated what he saw more than ever. Turning his back to the mirror he sat on the sink, with his head low and one final thought in his mind. What was Cherise really thinking? With that thought he slid to the floor falling asleep with his head against the bathtub.

9~

REALIZATION DROWNED IN DRINK

The night before was like a daze for him. The next thing he knew he was sitting on the train heading for home. The ride seemed longer than usual, or it may have been that churning of his stomach that made it so. He couldn't get Cherise out of his mind. There she was this beautiful specimen waiting for his kiss, and all he could do was hide his fear within the four walls of a bathroom. Resting his elbows on his thighs he held his head down in shame staining at the floor. Three people shared the car with him and they all looked as gloomy as he did except for one girl who sat at the opposite end of the car. Sitting just as Salem was she turned his way. Her face was familiar and Salem tried to remember where he had seen her before. His eyes began to wonder. Sitting just across from him was young man around his age. In black jeans, and a dark grey sweat shirt the man covered his head with his hoodie. Slouched in his seat, with his hands folded resting on his lap, he only faced down unless the train made a sudden stop. When he did lift his face, the white of his skin and the blackness around the eyes told of a man who'd rather live life through a mist of drugs rather than a natural high. He was so high, that he looked depressed. Looking away Salem figured he had his own problems to worry about, and turning his head to avoid looking any further he noticed a woman around the age of fifty. She was the only one standing. In an off white knit sweater with beige khaki pants to match she starred intensely out of the window. She knew Salem was watching her, but she chose to look straight ahead. She looked as if she just wanted to reach somewhere desperately, even if she didn't know where. Salem seemed to understand this and had no difficulty in feeling empathetic towards her or anyone else in the car. He just hoped that he'd never have to ride the subways so early again. At the next stop the guy high on drugs and the woman down on missing home got off the train. Salem could only imagine what would happen if they were to start a conversation with each other.

Five minutes of heading into the next stop, the familiar looking girl stood up and looked directly in Salem's direction. Walking slowly with her head down and hair dangling in her face, she takes her right hand grabbing on to the safety pole sliding it along as she walked. The pole led straight to Salem. He was wary of the girl, and like the older woman he looked in the opposite direction, hoping that she would go the other way. But like almost everything else that week, there wasn't much luck in the cards for him. It took her only a few seconds to reach him. He didn't look up right away and the only thing he saw were black jeans with matching Beetle Juice, black shoes. It was then that he remembered the last time he and Lamya were on the subway. There was this girl with a guy who gave him a wink. This was the same girl who had decided that she could just invade his privacy.

"Hey, so what are you doing on the bus so late," she asked.

Early or late he thought it didn't matter. Reaching into his pocket and taking out his cell phone he discovered that it was five to six in the morning. He didn't care, but what he did care about was the fact that this stranger talked with him as if she knew him.

"Do I know you," he asked.

"Of course you do. You don't remember saying hello to me earlier this week, "she asked.

He pretended not to remember her and shook his head.

"I'm sorry, you must have me confused with someone else," he said.

He never did say hello to her, even though he did remember her. He felt kind of like he was telling at least a half-truth. As he contemplated the choice of his words, the girl kneeled down in front of him, and put her hands on his knees. Resting her chin on her hands, she looked straight up into his face.

"Come on, you were looking at my skirt with your wife the last time around. This time why don't you try starring into my face," she asked.

The redness in his face told the whole tale.

"You see, I knew it was you," she said as if she had been holding her breath.

Standing she quickly planted a wet one on his lips, taking the kiss that was meant for Cherise. Surprised Salem jumped back into his seat. She was amused by his reaction and decided once more to get as close to him as possible. Grabbing him by the chin she puts her lips as close to his as she can without touching.

"What are you doing," Salem almost yelled.

"What do you mean what am I doing. You don't like me being so close," she asked still with a pretentious smile on her face.

He was thinking the girl was eccentric, but after her actions he just thought the chic was insane. He wish then that the two travelers that were with him earlier had never got off the car.

"Look, I hope you don't do this to all of the guys that you think have a thing for you," he said.

Forcing herself closer on him she whispered in his ear.

"Funny, because I don't think that you had a thing for me that day. I just think that you had a thing for the skirt I was wearing. That outfit always gets people, and either way you were interested in something. So where are you going," she whispered sarcastically.

"Home," he said stubbornly.

"Oh so the pretty boy can party. You had a big night out didn't you, she asked?

That was something he definitely didn't want to answer, since his night out turned out to be a big disappointment.

"So are you really tired, or could you stand some more fun," she asked.

If he stayed out any later he would miss time with his family. He was supposed to meet up with Lamya, and the thought had completely escaped him then.

"Come with me there's an after party at one of my friend's place. You'll love it," she said.

An after party at 6 a.m. was what New York was all about. You could build your dreams or drown your dreams in the city, and for some reason Salem was in the mood to drown away any failures. One stop before Astoria the girl pulls the cord. Raising her left eyebrow she took one step out of the car, while using her left hand to keep the rest of her body inside. With her free hand she curled up her index finger beckoning for her new friend to follow her. Why not he thought and with a very indecent smile he used his pincky finger to lock hands with her. Pulling him from the car she led him down corridor of what Salem always called the subway underworld. The white walls plastered with New York's finest advertisements for restaurants and great shopping areas began to grow on the subway tracks where they followed the trail for a couple of minutes. After walking for what seemed to be half a mile she jumped onto the subway tracks and Salem followed. He was getting just a little worried about the decision that he had made. He feared that a train could appear at any second and so he pushed himself further away from the track and closer to the wall. About a minute later the girl stopped at what appeared to be a door leading into a tunnel. This didn't do much to relieve his anxiety and as the tunnel grew darker and darker, he was seconds to turning around and running for dear life.

"Hey, where are you going," he yelled.

The girl didn't answer, instead she kept moving ahead towards the light. Salem continued to follow and his nervousness quickly left him, because the closer they got the more voices he began to hear. With the voices came a consistent sound of base and after the base full-blown music. The light was blue and by the time they reached an open door it revealed what seemed to be all the alternative world of New York. Though the light was blue the theme was rocking black. The music was rocking as well, contradicting the eighteenth century paintings that hung on the walls. Strange enough it was the paintings that seemed to set the mood. What looked like white satin fabric draped the mocha colored walls. Falling just above the paintings, it became a make shift trim around the room, which made Salem think of icing on a cake. Still following the girl she led him to a round table that was cut in half. The table included a half moon cream colored couch one time larger than the table. The tables were a dark wood and half a foot in front of the table hung silver beads that created a curtain around the table. With this each table became its on private room. Dividing the curtain the girl jumps into the room and slides into the couch. Welcoming her were two other guys dressed in black. One was wearing an AC/DC T- shirt while the other sat in a plain black T-shirt joined with suspenders that probably connected to some tight black jeans. Salem slid into the booth with her the first guy gave

Salem a smile, and a wave of approval. Obviously he knew him, but Salem failed to recognize him. The girl gave him a shove in the shoulders.

"This is my boyfriend Levi, "she said.

Levi stood up to shake his hand. The AC/DC T-shirt was covering another T-shirt. It was white and fell a little further than the first. Like his neighbor he also wore suspenders though he let his fall to the floor. Salem guessed that he wore them that way to add color to his plain black jeans. The jeans, it was the jeans that jump-started his memories. The guy he was meeting was the same one who was on the train with the girl the first time he saw her. The memory almost ruined his mood. It wasn't as if he thought anything was going to happen, but he didn't think he was going to meet her boyfriend. The questionable situation pulled his attention to the guy sitting next to her boyfriend.

He was Asian, probably Japanese, with long black hair, with blue streaks that ran through it. The guy felt Salem starring at him so he looked up to acknowledge him as he combed his hair back away from his face with his hands. Giving the stranger a nod Salem turned his attention back to the girl and her boyfriend.

"So he's Levi. What's your name," he asked.

She had that Goth look, but not exactly that Goth attitude. Unlike a lot of Goth enthusiast her hair was as brunette as the day she was born. Cut lightly above her chin, her hair was tucked neatly behind her ears.

"Serene. I guess I should ask your name too," she said.

He wasn't impressed by her response; he had met her type before. Laughing at himself he sat back in his chair looking at the three of them.

"I see that you're really trying hard to contain your excitement yourself, so I'll just tell you my name is Salem," he said.

Completely wishing he were somewhere else, he turned his attention back to the Asian guy who sat idol watching the three of them. He wanted to know the guys name, and it looked like that was going to take some work. Fiddling with a matchbox the guy looked directly at Salem. Hesitant he opened his mouth to speak, but paused.

"My name is Jin Jin, but just call me Jin for short, he said barely smiling.

After revealing his name he seemed more at ease, reaching across the table to shake Salem's hand. Being a gentleman Salem met his hand with a strong grip releasing right away, but Jin did just the opposite. His hold was gentle and as Salem was letting go he tightened his grip as if he wanted to hold on just a little while longer. Feeling uncomfortable Salem snatched his hand away while Jin Jin just smiled. In midst of the awkwardness a server came by balancing four shots of a pink liquid. He shook each and every persons hand, including Salem's. He knew the group well and reaching into his camouflage pant pocket he pulled out a Zippo that he had borrowed from Jin Jin, flicking it across the table. Serene and Levi grabbed their own glass while Jin Jin grabbed two handing one to Salem.

"I have a feeling that you haven't had this before. Chug it. It's called the Pink Fuck," Jin said chugging his shot down.

Salem took hold of the shot and proceeded to gulp it

down when his cell phone rang.

"Where are you Salem? His sister whispered. You were supposed to call me," she whined.

Just that fast he had forgotten about the plan with his sister and there was no excuse for it.

"Lamya, I forgot. I'm stuck here at some underground party, literally. I don't want to be rude and it's kind of interesting so go on with your regular plans and we'll come up with something when I get home later," later he said.

Lamya knew her brother well enough that he would keep his word. She could hear the music and wished that she were where he was. Salem knew she could hear the music and knew even though she might have wished she could be there, she wouldn't like the type of crowd.

"Okay brother. I'll see you later, just don't have too much more fun please," she said gently closing her cell phone.

He gulped down the drink, and as it went down it coated his throat, but not in a good way and he struggled not to cough. Another round was passed and he didn't hesitate to take the second gulp and as he did his cell rung again.

"Sali, where are you? I've been over to Mitch's all night," he said.

"I know, Mitch just came by here," he said.

"The second gulp had become stuck in his throat. He thought that it was good he didn't say another word.

"Well, I left about an hour ago and everyone was sleep,"

he said.

Swallowing the solution he stood up turning his back on his host, as if to hide what was certainly being read on his face.

At the other end of the phone his father stood in the doorway of his room. Peaking down the hall he watched to make sure neither his wife nor daughter was near. Whispering into the phone he covered his mouth.

"Sali we are father and son. You can tell me anything. Your not home, could it be that you're out with a girl," he asked.

Salem turned around to look at the new group of friends he had recently acquired. Serene snuggled up to Levi, but as Salem looked her way she gave him a wink. Turning around he thought how much he hated his father's questioning and how much more he hated answering them.

"I'm with friends dad, is that okay," he asked.

He knew his father wanted to hear something better than what he had told him, but that was all he would get. Somehow his father's voice took him back home again. It was if tar and the family were breaking their fast. A moderate family, on this day the men and women mingled together, and so did the children. Mr. Tamimi helped their maid bring in cushions for the growing guest. Walking in and out of the living room he noticed that while the other boys sat amongst each other, his son sat amongst the girls. Whispering in his son's ear he expressed his concerns.

"Try and get along with them. What's wrong," he asked sincerely.

Another thing about his family that he disliked was the continuous family gatherings. It was during those gatherings that he always felt under pressure to confirm to Arab tradition. Amongst the gathering were two other boys Mohammed and Khalifa, who sat with the boys. Looking back at Salem and his father, they snickered to each other knowing what the whispering was about.

"They only talk about stupid stuff. It's like they have nothing else to say. Talking with them makes me crazy sometime," he said hold his as if he had a headache.

Mr. Tamimi puts his left hand on his son's left shoulder. Taking a tight grip he whispered again.

"Go and try. Playing football with them every now and then doesn't mean that they will automatically accept you," he said pushing his son to make a move.

The last thing he heard his father say before hanging up gave him a defensive demeanor.

"Listen has fun, I think it's good for you, but just keep it to yourself," he said with a jolly voice.

Putting the phone back into his pocket and looking back at Serene, he decided he was going to have fun, but not because of his father's words, because he thought maybe he needed to loosen up a little more. Nodding to his host he gave them what had to be the hugest smile of the night. The pink solution began to take affect making him feel as light as a feather. He began to talk uncontrollably and suddenly wanted to know more about his new friends. His took his seat next to Serene closing the beaded curtains behind him, but not before friendly waiter passed them another shot.

10~

CHAINS OF THE PAST INFLUENCE THE

PRESENT

Opening the doors the sun seeped in through the existing

tunnel revealing a dirty white cigarette budded floor. The

glamorous tables with their beaded curtains looked as if

they had been abandoned for years, except for one lonely

guy who laid flat on his stomach, hung over, and spread out

across one of the couches. A bar tender dried the remaining

glass making the rack complete for the next time around.

Above him was a large round hole in the ceiling, covered

by what looked to be glass. It must have reached the streets, because a beam of light began to heat up the back of his neck. Shielding himself with his arms he resembled a vampire who had forgotten the rules. It was time to go home, and dealing with the family meant he had to muster up all the strength he had. Closing the door behind him he didn't have far to go. In-front of him he could hear the train and above him the sound of the world awaited.

It was four in the afternoon when he reached home. Walking up to the door he heard what sounded like silence on the other side. He thought maybe they weren't home, but to make sure he slowly put the key into the lock. Turning the knob and pushing the door slightly, he had just enough room to squeeze his body inside. The place was dead and Salem felt that he could breathe little easier. Entering his room he plopped into his desk chair and closed his eyes for a moment.

"Well someone had a big night last night. I'm glad your mother and Lamya are already gone to your cousins or else they would be asking all types of questions, Mr. Tamimi said.

Salem opened his eyes to his father who stood straight over him with this goofy smile on his face.

"It was this underground party next to the subways. I had to check it out," he said believing he was sounding exactly as he father would want him to sound.

"You don't have to explain, but since you're here your mother would stop speaking to us both if she found out that you came home and I didn't bring you to the house. You better go take a quick shower," Mr. Tamimi said while pointing at his sons face. Salem ran to the bathroom taking a look in the mirror. A black lipstick smudged his lips and the imprint of red lips was on his right cheek. He didn't remember any kiss the night before. In fact he couldn't remember anything. Thinking that it would jump start some memories he drew his face closer to the mirror the only thing it revealed is that his father was standing right behind him.

"I don't know what happen, but you don't have time to explain either. Get ready so we can go," he said shutting the door as he spoke.

At that point a shower sounded like a good idea. He didn't remember what was up about the night before, but he knew he wanted to wash away whatever proof there was of a night at all. After his shower his father wanted him to wear something traditional, but he decided on a pair of casual pants and a T-shirt. Family gatherings for some reason or another dulled his since of adventure in dressing up. They walked the six blocks to his cousin's place on the request of his father. A block into the walk Salem slowly took in the fresh breeze, which seemed to be a complete cleansing to begin the evening.

"Why are you drinking," Mr. Tamimi asked.

He was surprised that his father didn't ask earlier.

"I don't drink all the time. I don't know if you realize it or not, but there are some students coming from the same background as me that do, and they never look back.

"Sali, we are Muslim, We don't drink at all," he said almost pleading as he spoke.

Stopping in his tracks, Salem remembered his lipstick, smudged face in the bathroom mirror.

"It's not okay for us to drink, but its okay for me to do whatever with girls," he asked.

Mr. Tamimi didn't say a word. Instead he looked down towards the pavement.

I know there is a difference in the level of things that are harom, but let's be honest.

"I don't mean to push anything on you, but I'm just thinking about your future," Mr. Tamimi said.

He didn't understand what his father was talking about exactly, and he refused to ask into it anymore.

"I think the most important thing in my future is to do my best at this new job so I can have an even brighter future later. Don't you think that's most important right now," he asked his father.

His father didn't say anything at first, but instead continued to walk. Salem's question made him think of the day when he convinced Salem to go fishing with him. His son was eight at the time, and had talked his father into wearing matching Addidas tracksuits. Both dressed in white and blue it was the only way that he could talk him into going with him. After leaving the dock he watched as the other boys intensely watched what their father's did. Mr. Tamimi had tried everything possible to keep Salem focused on the reel instead of the partially built model boat that he had bought with him.

"Well, what do you think," Salem said again.

He never seemed to be able to stay angry with his father. So slowly he put his hand on his father's shoulder getting him to slow down. Mr. Tamimi looked up but didn't know exactly what to say. Sometimes he believed there was a lot he didn't understand.

"I just want you to be happy. I don't care if you're doing it for yourself or for us. Just that whatever comes about in life that you're happy with yourself," he said.

"I'm doing everything for the family dad. Don't worry because along with that I plan on keeping myself happy as well," he said smiling.

"I partied before. I mean not like you do here, but I have had my fun. Then I got married. Well I chose to get married and then I had to stay in my boundaries," he said as if he hated saying anything.

Not another word was said. They had reached the fifth block and it was time to get back to family.

It had been almost two days since he had seen or heard from Lamya. When he walked into his cousin's apartment it was obvious. While his mother acted as if nothing was wrong Lamya gave him the cold shoulder and forced her cousin to do the same. Walking into Taif's place was like flying home for a visit. Salem believed that they had to be the most traditional Arabs in the area. Irani rugs covered the floors and walls. Long round pillows placed on top of wide rectangular cushions of gold, red and royal blue colors trailed the living room walls from end to end. The home wasn't the only thing traditional, so were the young men in the family. Giving his mother and aunt a kiss and hug, he walked over to his cousin and sister giving them both a playful rub on the on the top of their heads. Lamya rolled her eyes, and that all she had time for. There was no time for anything else. He had to join the other guys in the next room. First saying hello to the uncles, he shook hands and held short conversations so that he could get around to everyone. He wanted to make his father happy, and it seemed to work. With his job done he walked in to the next room. While the tweens sat playing videos games, the guys his age sat whispering about the girls they had fooled within the past. Mohammed, Ahmed, Khaled, and Sultan sat huddled in a group looking like men, but talking like boys.

"Uh hum, Marhaba. Semi how have you been? I heard you were a little too busy to come before dinner," Sultan said laughing.

Rolling his eyes while taking a seat he still managed to give them a smile. In a way the smile was real. It was the first time in one of these gatherings that he was the object of such conversations.

"So I'm late. Does that actually mean I was out doing

what you're hinting at? It could actually mean anything you know," he said raising an eyebrow.

Giving him a sneaky grin Sultan slightly shook his head.

"Okay so your saying you're saying you've just been hanging out with other guys alone all of this time," Sultan asked.

"No Sultan your right. It's just sad that you don't want to tell the guys that the one I was hanging out with was you, and we set this whole plan up where I had to come late make sure it didn't look like there was a connection. Hey, its okay though isn't it? We had fun last night," Salem said with a smile.

Like almost all of this cousins, whether visiting or living permanently, they mostly stayed in their Arab communities. This had their conversation skills stalled at certain subjects and to cross the line was sometimes too much for the guys to take. Sultan of course let the smile go and took on another action. Even in the American world for an Arab to jokingly be called gay could raise some unwanted reactions. Sitting across from Salem he reached across the table, and pulled at the neck of his shirt, and then gave him a solid slap in the face. Just as quick Salem returned the forced offer by grabbing the hand Sultan slapped him with and twist his wrist just enough to have his cousin sprawled across the table turning red as he begged to be let go. If he had held the grip any longer Sultan could have found himself a lifeless piece of fresh meat for the rest of the guys. Lucky for him Lamya's father walked into the room to break it up. He caught the two young men with Salem on his knees and Sultan on his back. They were both embarrassed. Sultan gave Salem an upside down smile before proceeding to cushion the moment.

"Chalous, Chalous. Sorry, it won't happen again. Our

play got out of control," Sultan insisted.

"Playing is the game of football or parchezzee, not back breaking each other over tables," Mr. Zaidi fussed going back to the room to enjoy his shisha.

And that was it. It wasn't like furniture was such a big deal for the Zaidis anyway. Historically like the rest of the family they were bedouins. If it were possible they would be their happiest spending the rest of their lives in the Arabian dessert, even after being spoiled with their air-conditioned apartment. Mr. Zaidi's real concern was thought of paying for eight years of college if after graduation the only thing his hard earned money turned out was a bunch of conservative animals.

Though they were Moroccan, living in the U.A.E. made them slaves to the kernel, and anytime they could get their hands on some KFC, it was always the meal of choice.

After Sultan pulled himself off the table, he and Salem joined the rest of the guys who were already seated on cushions surrounding themselves around buckets of chicken and two large dishes of Byrianni. Salem listened for his mother's voice in the other room, while over hearing his father's laughter in the room right next to him. The Byrianni looked great and as he took his right hand scooping up a bit of rice and lamb he took the privilege of admiring the moist silky substance that has filled his hands since he was a small child. It was the simplest of pleasures for him and at that moment the sound of familiar voices, the rich colors that covered the oblong cushions, which in turn cover the rich Persian rugs reminded him that he belonged. This feeling gave him a rush and then it was dropped like a brick into deep waters. An empty heart like any other needed to be fed and so he took a mouthful of byrianni, and another, and then another until he felt as if he would explode. He was full, but something in his heart was still empty. He seemed to always feel that way among family gatherings.

Looking across the table Mohammed starred back at him. It was normal for him and Salem to act this way, since around the age of seven their relationship had been the same. As first cousins and both boys they were as close as family could be. They grew up together and though there was never much conversation between the two of them after the age of seven, they both found themselves in the U.S. around the same time. Unlike Salem, Mohammed wasn't as charismatic as his cousin. He was fair skinned with reddish hair and freckles that surrounded the outer lines of his nose and the silver round frames he had worn since he was in high school. Though the same height as Salem, he had an extremely slim build, and when he walked his back hunched over making him look gawky and out of place. Of course where he failed in looks he more than compensated for in brains. In one year Mohammed would be a surgeon and no one who knew him was surprised. Salem was always uncomfortable in the way that Mohammed starred at him. On that day Mohammed couldn't be more obvious as he held his chin down near his chest so he could see Salem over his frames.

"Man your hungry today aren't you? Whatever you did last night it was rough one," he said with a soft smile.

Just as he didn't like the look Mohammed was giving him, he also hated his comment.

"Yeah, a long night, don't know if it was any fun though," he replied.

Mohammed held his head down lower. Salem could feel that he was trying to analyze what he was really saying. He had Salem think back to one of the last times they acted more like friends than cousins. Salem was entranced with the red cummerbund Mohammed wore to match his black tuxedo. It was the celebration of national day and the whole family decided that it would be fun to throw on some western cloths for the celebration. It had been a long day and eight in the evening Mohammed and Salem were the last allowed to take a cool bath to wash the sweat away. Instead of a tuxedo Salem wore a suit with a black bow tie, and the shoes to match. Mrs. Tamimi was busy with the rest of the women serving food for guest, because the maid was given the night off for family. The two boys were put in the care of their uncle Bakir. He was a big guy for his age of twelve, but suited just right for taking care of two seven year old boys. Bakir was always that family member that made them laugh, and it seemed that night that it would be the same.

"Oh look its tweedle dee and tweedle dumb. Two little penguins, one in red and the other in traditional black and white," he said laughing.

While running bath water for the two he danced around them as if he were a penguin himself. Wanting retaliation the boys scooped up some bath water in their hands and threw it at him. All seemed fine at first, even though they left Bakir's hair drenched in water.

"Well take of your stuff, and I'll be right back," he laughed wiping his face dry.

Running out of the room he ran to the next room to catch a bit of the football game. Taking off their jackets Salem couldn't help but to touch the red belt. Peeping in to see if they had undressed yet Bakir watched casually as Salem put his arms around Mohammed's waist to undo the belt. Too interested in the game to even tell the boys to hurry, he rushed back to the other room to join the other boys. Bakir didn't realize that his cousin Khalifa stood right behind him hiding in the corner of a wall. Though most of the time Bakir was okay with his weight, the other boys loved to tease him, so much so that it had become a regular to put him down by using words, especially Khalifa. Seeing Bakir watching after the boys in the bathroom gave Khalifa newfound ammunition. The problem was on that night not only was there family, but strangers too. Bakir ran into the room where they were watching the football.

"Pudgy, pudgy. Hey doughboy. Are you all sweaty and wet because you were starring at the boys in the bathroom.

A crowd of laughter burst from the room. At first Mohammed had no idea what was going on, until those laughing pointed their fingers at him.

"What? Mrs. Tamimi told me to watch them and make sure they took a bath. I wasn't starring at them," he shouted back.

"Yes you were and while you were starring you were also licking your lips and rubbing that fat stomach of yours," Bakir laughed back.

He was pointed at Mohammed as he accused and the hate on his face made Mohammed hate him right back. Though Mohammed was a big boy, he was as soft personality wise as a puppy. Khalifa was about the same size, but all his weight was turning to pure muscle. Mohammed had never been in a fight and didn't want to get in one at that point. He was a shamed and though he had been made fun of many times before the strangers that laughed with his family put a pain in his stomach and heart that he just couldn't seem to shake off. Salem had just removed the commburbond as Bakir ran into the bathroom to escape the laughter. As he entered Salem held the belt in both hands as if it were a block of gold. For a while Bakir just stood there starring at them without a word. He just sat on the side of the tub as the boys undressed. Turning off the water he helped the two climb in. Without getting it wet Salem wrapped the belt around his head making both boys laugh. As they giggled the boys in the next room continued shouting taunts Mohammed. Not wanting to him them any longer Bakir slammed the door. In a low voice he tells the two to be quiet, but they didn't hear him. Repeating himself he said it louder, but they just ignored him. Finally fed up Bakir put his hands over his ears and shouted for them to shut up. They stopped their giggling and then there was silence except for the sound of the game on television that had been turned to its highest level. Mrs. Tamimi knocked on the door without opening it. Wanting to get back to the other women she quickly pops her head in and out.

"Is everything okay," she asked.

"Yes, I just had to get them quiet. They were making too much noise. How much longer will you be busy," he asked.

"If you can just watch them for ten more minutes Bakir I will have the perfect surprise for you. You just have to be patient, fifteen more minutes," she said.

He shook his head in agreement and with that she ran back to the kitchen leaving the door cracked. Bakir kneels down near the tub and grabs the soap. Unexpectedly Bakir ran into the bathroom, grabbed Bakir by his large curls and dunks his head in the water while others looked on from outside the room. After having dominated Mohammed, Bakir ran out of the room slamming the behind him. The younger boys following in lead with the older boys began to laugh splashing water on each other. Bakir turned red and not having the guts to take his anger out on the bigger boys, he instead took it out on Mohammed and Salem.

"Stand up Mohammed. Stand up he shouted," Bakir shouted at him.

Nervous Mohammed jumps up almost slipping in the tub. Bakir grabs him by his arm and then tells Salem to kneel down in front of Mohammed.

"Hold his stuff with your hands you little fagot," he said angrily under his breath.

Salem unwillingly takes hold of Mohammed's private in his left hand. Bakir held Salem's head down and forced him to open his mouth, making him orally massage Mohammed to the point of ejaculation. Bakir's eyes were cold and distant as if he weren't even there. He barely looked at the boys, instead just starred at the wall. Next he made Salem stand and had Mohammed perform the same action on his cousin. Mrs. Tamimi's voice could be heard through the door and it was at that instant that Bakir jumped as if knocked out of a trance. Forcing both of the boys to sit in the tub he splashed them vigorously with water nervously answering Salem's mother, whom this time decided not to stick her head inside. Confused all boys sat in silence for what seemed like eternity to them. Finally Bakir stood up, grabbed a towel and wiped his face off. Picking them up out of the tub he puts a towel around the each of them, watches them dry off, and says the only words he would ever say to them again.

"If you say anything to anyone about this I will wait until your whole family is sleep one night and I'll take them away and store them in a hidden spot where you will never find or see them again," he said with his back turned and head held low, walking out without closing the door.

That night Bakir's reward for getting the boys clean were two American cupcakes. The boys acted as if nothing had happened, but as they both watched a slight smile curl up on Bakir's face, neither he nor they knew what would come next. A month later Bakir would be found dead, face up in a bathtub due to a low blood sugar induced seizure.

The final events of that night snapped Salem back into reality. There had been other bad nights since then, but nothing that clung to him as long. He figured that it was the same for Mohammed, and the reason neither of them could say more than a few words to each other whenever they met.

"Hey are you gonna eat that or not? Watch out or the dumb dumbs, will take it from you, Mohammed said leaving the room.

An Arab gathering was one that guest had to take seriously. Starting around five in the afternoon a party could keep going late into the wee hours of the night. There was always a lot to talk about and many things to do. For Salem he wanted to take himself away and the best way for him to do that was by thinking of Cherise. He knew he still had a chance and it changed his mood. It was usually looked down on, but since he was child Salem had a habit of running to the kitchen and watching his mom cook. Dinner was over that night and he knew that the women would be cleaning up. He didn't care what anyone thought and walked into the kitchen where Lamya and his cousins were putting dishes in the sink. The sight of Salem seemed to make them delve into their work even more. Salem loved to see women in the kitchen, for some reason it always made him feel safe, even though it was just his sister and annoying cousin.

"Sorry I didn't get here this morning, but I'm here now," he said half smiling.

They didn't seem too impressed with his words so he decided to change the environment. Grabbing both of their hands he pulls them out of the front door. The rest of the family looked in awe, but Salem didn't care and he hoped the girls felt the same way.

"What are we doing," both girls whispered tripping out the door.

"Were just going out for some fresh air, I think we could all use it," he said

Dropping down and sitting on one of the stoops the girls follow behind him.

"So what's was so important that you had to drag us out here. You know right now their talking about us in there. Even though I'm your sister and Taif is definitely not a love interest," she said nodding her head at Taif.

Taif didn't respond instead she focused on Salem.

"I had my fun yesterday, some unexpected fun earlier this morning. So I thought it would be good if Monday we focused on you guys and shopping for the party, Salem expressed.

He didn't want to mention the negatives parts of his fun time out, and since Lamya didn't ask it made it easy to move on for the moment.

"That would be the best, but it just happens that your mother wants us to spend some family time together tomorrow. Probably because you weren't around today,"

Lamya said.

Okay, so if we can't go on Monday let's do it on a Tuesday. Taif, if you can spend the night tonight it would make things much easier," he said.

As usual the Tamimis think of everything, but I'm in. I certainly have nothing in my house hold to loose from it," she expressed.

Though she was curious as to why Taif seemed too be agitated each and every time her and her brother got together, she was being her usual self, which meant carrying only for Lamya at that moment. She completely blew off her comment and focused on the plan at hand.

"Okay if you want to go, go ahead and ask your parents while they're in a good mood. You know our parents will say yes because they think of you as their second daughter," Lamya said pushing back towards the door.

With Taif out of the picture for a moment Salem decided to catch up with Lamya, if she would allow him.

"So what else is going on with you that I don't know about," he asked.

She looked down the sidewalk as he talked and noticed Asian women she figured Japanese around the same age as her. She walked with a briefcase in one hand and a cell phone in the other. As she passed it was obvious that she was still talking about work, even at such a let hour. Lamya turned with her arms crossed grinning at her brother.

"What's going on? I'll tell you this it's good that we're going out Tuesday, because that morning I have my second interview," she said standing on her tip toes holding her arms high in the air and twirling in place like some little at an amusement park.

"Wow, whoa. So you could really get this," he asked.

Lamya was agitated at the fact the he could even think otherwise.

"What's wrong with you? You know that I'm serious about this whole thing, and if I'm serious then I do my best to get what I want.

Salem couldn't help but agree with her. What Lamya wanted she usually got. He was happy for her, but not what the situation could bring about. Lamya could read this in his face and wanted to get to the point.

"Okay Salem, it might be a lot for you to swallow, but we can adjust. I can take care of myself as long as I have the tools, so don't worry," she said in an assured voice.

There were very few times when the two would get angry at one another, and that moment would prove the point. Looking at each other without saying a word they both broke out into laughter.

"Okay, so if you got this job, where would you live, he asked.

I don't know, but what I do know is that I want the whole American experience this time around. A Volks Wagon bug, a blond boyfriend and an awesome flat to match. Salem cracked half a smile at her comment. He wasn't sure if she was serious or just fooling around, any way he thought he would find out soon enough. By this time Taif had rushed back out of the house.

Raising her hands like Lamya she ran down the stoop where they sat giving both of them a hug.

"It's on, I can't wait. And you know, I've been thinking. What if we were roommates? You wouldn't have to bother with your brother at all and we can keep each other company," she smiled.

Lamya looked at her brother, her brother looked at her, and they both looked at their cousin.

"Well, what do you think," she asked.

Taif was not the most attractive in the family, and whenever she was frustrated, it didn't make things better. She looked at the both of them with intense eyes and clutched her teeth together. It left the two no choice but to shake their heads in agreement.

"Yeah, is that okay with you Lamya," he asked questionably.

Lamya in secret was a bit relieved. She loved her brother, but sometimes he had his ways. It would be good to have some other family support. Taif already had the job, so she could definitely pull her on weight.

"Yeah, we'll make great roommates,' she said hugging Taif.

The Tamimi's were walking out the door. Seeing it as her queue to leave, saying good night Taif headed back into the house to see the other guest out.

11~

DECISIONS MUST BE MADE

It was Sunday and Salem believed that it was a day for him to get back to business. Besides he thought if he kept his mind busy, he wouldn't think much about the past two days. In a rush to find a job after graduation, he failed to delve more seriously into the company he would soon be calling his second home. Headed to the campus library he was unexpectedly greeted at the front door. It was barely nine in the morning and obviously Taif needed some freedom sooner than later.

"So where are you off to," she asked. She was close and he always hated when she inquired about his where about. It was the look he always got from her intense eyes. It made the hair on the back of his neck stand up straight for days. Invading his space he caught a whiff of her Arab perfume. It was good he had to admit, but when he looked down cautiously he caught a glimpse of the sweat, which had begun to bubble up on her top lip. Any attraction she held with the perfume just disappeared. Stepping back he opens the apartment door and with his left arm out he directs her to enter. Stepping in she opens her mouth to say something else, but Salem puts a finger over his lips signaling for her not to wake the others. She gave him a smile and a wave as he backed away and closed the door. Closing his eyes he opened them again to find himself at the age of twelve again. Taif was spending the summer with her grandmother since May she was allowed to join the same school that Salem attended. They also happened to have the same classes, but while Salem sat in the front to the far left, she sat in the back just opposite of him. Every morning would start off the same. She would make sure Salem was already in the room. She would then take out a piece gun shoving it into her mouth and chewing ferociously until she had made it soft. She had the habit of wearing half of her thick black curly hair in a single ponytail, while allowing the rest to fall down her back. Salem always figured that she wanted to make sure everyone saw the round large light blue glasses that adorned her face each day. Whether or not this was true he never found out, but what he was sure about was the fact that somehow she had fallen deeply in love him, at least that's what he learned from the other girls. He believed it was because of the first day she arrived in the school. Her grandmother had just finished paying the two months tuition and was speaking with the director. As they talked, Taif wondered around the administration area. She then entered an area where there was an elevator. She leaned against the wall next to it. Sitting across from her were two girls sitting and eating their lunch while whispering to each other and looking at the awed stranger as they laughed. She didn't care in the least. In her eyes she was American and they were just local girls trying to be cool and in a not so cool desert.

"Excuse me is something funny," she asked in a pushy voice.

The girls just stuffed their face with food, not saying a word but giggling uncontrollably. Like the girls that sat giggling she wore a hijab, but not in the hijab way. On that day she decided to funk it up. Her hijab was actually a long red scarf worn loosely across her head. To match she wore a long sleeve white T-shirt, and over that T-shirt she wore another short sleeve T-shirt with an embellished picture of harriot from the Adams Family on it. To match the top she wore quarter length black baggy shorts, and to top that off knee high red, yellow, orange and green thick-stripped socks supported with black low top Nikes.

"Sorry to burst your bubble, but this is a new style from America," she said with a smirk.

Hearing her accent the girls stopped their giggling and stood in awe. A tiny girl fair skinned with brunette hair finally spoke up.

"You're from America? My mother is from America, she said with an excited smile.

It was all confidence from then on out. In -fact she was so confident that while proceeding to tell her fascinating story of being a Moroccan American, she leaned a little too far to the left. She hadn't noticed, but her scarf got caught in the closing elevator doors and as it went up. The higher it went the tighter it wound around her neck, and she began to choke. Terrified the girls just stood in shock as Taif screamed for help. Fortunate for her Salem happened to come walking by and with no one to help him he pulled out a pair of scissors from his bag cut her loose and pulled her to safety. Now at any other time her incident would have caused her to be the butt of the joke for her remaining two months in school. The only thing that stopped this from happening was the fact that most of the girls had a big crush on Salem, including the two girls that stood and watched in shock as Taif began to choke and because of this Salem's actions were not just good samarian, but heroic. It was from that point on that Salem became the object of her affection. It was even rumored during that time that she swore that if her parents ever thought of marrying her off to any cousin; it would have to be Salem.

284

This thought bought him to the present. Tip toeing away from the door he quickly exited the building.

The morning was warm and as Salem cooled off with quick shower, he remembered that he hadn't spoken with Mitch. Punching in the last number on his cell he quickly realized why he hadn't call, but it was too late to hang up.

"Uhm, Mitch, he asked.

Someone picked up, but there was no answer on the other side.

"Hello," Salem shouted.

Five seconds later he could hear the gurgling growl of Mitch's morning voice.

"Yea," Mitch said.

"It's Salem man, he replied.

"Oh shit," Mitch yelled.

Stumbling out of bed he clumsily stepped across his ten year old nephew who refused to go home with his mother the day before. Supporting the phone with his right shoulder he rushed to the bathroom splashing some water on his face. Quietly leaving the room he ran into kitchen where he knew his nephew couldn't hear him.

"Man what the hell happened," he asked whispering.

Feeling that the splash of water wasn't enough he ran to his room closed the door and went in to the living room. There he found his sister sprawled out on the couch. Dead asleep her lifeless body was propped in such a way that it looked like she was watching the still running television. Gently taking the remote from her hand, he ran to the kitchen. Putting on a pot of coffee he continued his talk with Salem.

"I blew your cover didn't I," he asked waiting anxiously.

"You couldn't have just called me before deciding to pay me a visit," he asked.

Pouring some warm milk over some frosted flakes, Mitch took this into consideration.

"Hey, it didn't hit me until I was standing in your kitchen talking with your dad," he said.

Pouring a cup of piping hot coffee, he then changed the channel on the television to VH1. Pressing the volume to its loudest while running out, just in time to get a glimpse of his sister waking up in what seemed to be a state of shock.

"Mitch you always playing! You know being scared like that can start my migranes up," she yelled.

Walking back into the room he stuck out his tongue and ran back into the kitchen.

"So you left fine ass Cherise to go to some other party without telling your boy. That's just wrong," he said.

"You know I can't seem to remember anything after falling out on your bathroom floor," he said.

Sitting on his brown stone stoop smiling at the return of the morning sun, he began giggling uncontrollably.

"Oh shit, are you sure you wanna talk about that," he asked.

Salem wasn't too sure, but it was either that or the underground party, where he had no clue on where to go on that subject.

"Go ahead, spit it out," he said.

"First of all you had her eating out of your hands, and then you just let it slip. Why man, why," he whined.

He looked up to Mitch especially when it came to girls.

"First of all Joint just appeared out of know where. You

know that would even spook you. Second I was drunk out of my mind. I didn't know whether to kiss her or to run," he replied.

"Oh so you're liken this girl uh," Mitch asked.

"Come on she'd be a good catch..." Salem said.

Good catch, she's a great catch, but you led her on. She was standing there waiting for your lips and in front of everyone you rejected her," Mitch whispered not waiting his sister to listen in.

Salem didn't know what to do. After what Mitch said he didn't even think he could look her in the face again. He asked himself how come he couldn't have been more like Mitch, who what have seized the opportunity and gone for it when he had the chance.

"That night was your lost and then to top it off you went into the bathroom and started crying nonstop man, nonstop. You were hollering some shit like "it's not me, it's not me." So I decided to save what was left of your manhood. I had to make sure everyone stayed away from the bathroom the rest of the night, which means everyone had to use my bedroom toilet. I'm still scared to sit on it.

"Was she there when I left," he asked.

"Not too long, she hung out with some friends and left just before Joint made the second scene of the night," he said holding his head as he spoke.

It wasn't important to him what Joint had done, besides he had the faint feeling that if Joint could he would get his cousin as far away from him as possible. Hoping off the train heading to Columbia, Salem had second thoughts about walking into the real world boldly. He always looked on the brighter side of things, and yea he had a nice job, a good place and some great friends, but what seemed more important to him was his personal life. He thought that at least after four years of no life in school, he could have one outside of school.

"Where are you man," he asked.

"Just reaching the library, Salem said.

"I think it's time for me to help you out," Mitch said smiling.

Salem had heard this before and he knew that Mitch had got him out some tricky situations in the past, but he wondered what was up his sleeves.

"What are you up to," he replied.

"Be patient, I'll give you a call later," Mitch said.

Before Salem could say a word Mitch was gone. He just wanted to tell him that he needed a day to himself, alone without Columbia's man of the year whispering ancient male proverbs in his ear.

It was like old times as he opened the door to the library. Mostly empty it had the musty smell of century old books, and what Salem considered the ambiance of home away from home. Picking up a book that he had on reserve, he took a seat close to the checkout counter. He never knew why, but since he was a child he could never fully stay awake. After just two pages of reading he would find himself fighting to keep his eyes open. The only thing that did keep him awake during studying was the sound of a television, and when he didn't have that the next best thing was a good seat around a load of people, which was all the television he needed. Unfortunate for him with summer well on its way and exams being over there were just no people coming through the door. His best bet was to stay close to the counter so at least the librarian could keep him going. This lasted all of twenty minutes, and before he knew it he was in dreamland.

It was around the 1920s, and Salem was walking into the office. He loved the fashion of twenties and in his dream he wore a Carolina Blue jacket, and the oxford pants to match. The suit accompanied a white dress shirt, and it was accompanied by slender silk black tie. To make the ladies swoon his look was topped off with a Carolina blue fedora to match. Casually pushing open the glass doors to the office lobby he two steps his way pass the door man, greeting him with a smile and a nod. While walking through the office hallways, his hands in his pocket and his

hat tipped slightly to the right, he gave winks to the female

assistants. Reaching his office door where his name was

inscribed in gold, he gave the plaque a quick buff before

pushing the door open where Mitch sat on top his desk

marveling at the video inspired model of a structure that

both he and Salem were working on. Relieving himself of

his jacket he hurled it behind him, where it landed on his

Josef Hoffman sofa in leather burgundy. Giving Mitch a

high five he sat at his mahogany oak desk, decked out with

lion claw English desk legs and adorned with a colorful

Victorian lamp. It was an accessory that was never used,

because the window behind him was so huge that there was

no need for it. Turning towards it he took a few minutes to

look out on to the world. Satisfied he took a seat in his

chair. Covering his eyes with the fedora he supported the

back of his head with his arms, while putting his feet up on

the desk revealing his two toned patent leather shoes that

were tan and black. Closing his eyes he imagined himself flying like a bird. Swooping from his office balcony to where ever, he was interrupted by the sound of a familiar voice.

"I'm so sorry Mrs. Carter. I almost forgot about those," Cherise said.

Salem's magical flight was interrupted and the realization of whose voice it was startled him, causing him to fall back wards out of his chair. On his hands and knees he crawled to the corner of his desk to get a peak at what was going on, on the other side. Too low to anything, but the legs, her toes did the talking for him. They were painted a pale pink, matching the beaded flip-flops that kept them clean. His eyes moved from her toes to her legs, he had the urge to touch them, but restrained just the same.

"Well, this will be my last time on campus, unless you count the party. I'll miss you Mrs. Carter," she said as she hugged her good bye.

Moving closer he caught a whiff of her rose scented perfume. Frustrated he dug his nails into the carpet. Definitely not wanting to be seen he abandoned the hand and knee position scooting himself towards the back legs of the desk where he sat. If it were possible he would have chosen to blend in with the furniture.

"I don't see anyone here. Has anyone come in the past half hour, "she asked the librarian?

Grinding his teeth and squinting his face up as if he had accidently sucked on a lemon, he cursed the day he had Mitch. He should have known. Hearing her footsteps he jumped back into a crawling position, hoping to make it back to his seat.

"Salem, Salem are you here, she whispered strongly.

Crawling like an infant after his mother, his knees were no match for her delicate quick feet. Reaching out for his chair he watched as she passed his desk, heading toward the magazine racks. Slowly slipping back into his seat, he pretended as if he didn't notice her rose scent that made him want to melt where he hid.

"So here you are? How come you didn't say anything earlier," she asked.

Straightening himself up in his seat, he looked over his left shoulder at the playful Cherise who smiled back at him. She placed her right hand on his shoulder as she moved to the front of his desk. Uncomfortable he held his head down not daring to look up. With no response Cherise planted both of her hands firmly on the desk in front of him looking him directly in the eyes.

"So I hear that's extremely important that we plan on doing a sound check," she said waiting for his response.

"Not knowing whether to smile or poop in his pants, he just sat there with a slight smirk on his face.

"Salem, the sound check," she asked raising her voice.

She looked agitated and he did not want to be the one to cause her any more pain. To tell the truth she seemed okay with the whole situation. Even though if it was possible he never wanted to mention it, but he knew it wasn't.

"Sound check," he asked.

Impatient Cherise crossed her hands and raised her left eyebrow.

"Checking the music at the party venue," she replied.

He though it must have been a part of Mitch's great plan, so he played along.

"Oh yeah, I told Mitch that since I was close by it would be good if we could hear what was going on, but I didn't want to bother you at the last minute " Salem replied.

"Mitch's girl friend gave me a call and she told me that you would be down here waiting, and that I should meet you. So what's the plan," she said with frustration in her eyes.

Salem of course didn't have a plan and his quick beating

heart felt like it would puncture his rib cage if he didn't come up with something soon.

"We should first call Joint to see if he can take a short test spinning while we listen," he replied.

"Relax, I called Joint, you guys better be glad he didn't already have plans. Please no more last minute stuff," she complained.

"Uhm, while we're waiting for Joint we can go and grab a cup of coffee," he replied questionably.

She agreed with him, but he could still see the disappointment in her face. He didn't know what else to say, but what he did know was that he wanted to kiss her right there and then. Finding it painful to sit much longer he pushed his library books to the side. Grabbing her right hand he led her out of the building.

"Why are you in such a hurry," she asked feeling like she was being dragged like some rag doll.

He didn't know if it was really the heat of the day or just the fact that Cherise made him so nervous, but by the time he turned around to answer her question, his curly hair had fallen limp just above his eyes and the sweat from his body flushed cheeks a rosy red. His flushed cheeks made him less intimidating than before.

"Never mind don't answer let's just get out of this heat," she fussed.

He didn't say anything. In fact he believed he deserved it. Not another word was said until they crossed the street to the coffee shop. Once inside he turned to look at Cherise.

She struggled to keep a sweet face as she wiped the sweat from her forehead.

"I'm sorry for dragging you like this. I think maybe it will be better if we grab cold coffees," Salem said.

Cherise accepted his apology, but had a question of her own.

"So what happened to you the other night? I didn't get it, I still don't get it," she asked.

He took a big gulp of coffee, almost choking in the process of quickly getting it down. There was no way he could tell her the truth.

"You know I should have bought it up earlier, but I was just embarrassed. I can't drink a lot and I took on more than

I could handle. The last thing I remember was running away from you because I was about to vomit. The next morning I woke up in the bathroom," he replied shaking his head at the disgrace of his lie unknown to Cherise.

Deciding to take the coffees to go, by the time Salem finished his explanation they were standing in the middle of the party room. Joint walked in minutes after they did and headed straight for where he would be playing. Hooking some equipment to the already placed speakers, he turned the volume up as high as it would go. Cherise's back was facing Salem as she looked up at the high ceiling that covered them. Salem felt awkward and placed his hands in his pocket while looking at the floor. Slowly turning around with her hands on her hips, she starred at the guy who caused her to sweat her hair out that morning.

"And that's it you just had too much to drink," she

screamed as the music began to blast in the background.

Pointing at her cousin he followed Joint to the DJ booth. Looking up at him with his white T-shirt and perfectly blown out fro Joint couldn't be anything else but cigarette bud. Joining him in the booth Salem smiled down at Cherise, he was safe in the booth.

"That's it," he yelled back.

"You know I didn't pay you any attention until that day in the book store, and now you've kind of grown on me, but I don't know," she replied with a frown.

Joint didn't say a word. He was enjoying the music too much and he thought it was better if Salem talked with his cousin alone. First getting an approval of the sound, he edged Salem out of the booth. Salem was waiting for it and hopped down to the floor. He walked past Cherise looking back at her to follow him.

"Salem we're you going to kiss me that night," she asked.

Cherise seemed pretty frisky, and moved closer to him. They had walked out of sight from Joint who was playing music and texting at the same time. It made Salem nervous and in his state for no particular reason he decided to grab a hold her hands. Cherise moved closer yet again. Before he could even think to respond to her question she lightly rubbed her right cheek against his. Her heart raced as she did so. Salem didn't move an inch; instead, he stood still, frozen in the moment. Cherise's cheek slipped from his and he found his bottom lip locked between the two of hers. He wanted to look in her eyes, but they were closed. He kept his eyes open. He wanted to experience everything. She held him tight, but still gentle. She was sensuous and with every move of her body she seemed to give more of herself to him. He cringed at the thought of the moment ending. Thinking back he remembered how excited he was at the fact that he grabbed her hand in the bookstore. It was what he had been waiting for. He then grabbed her by the waist and pulled her closer returning her kiss with a stronger more passionate one. He then wrapped his hands around her warm body brushing his nose against her's. Tilting his head down just enough to touch his lips to hers. Softly he passed against her clamping his lips teasingly on to her top lip. His eyes were still open and he could see how much she enjoyed the play. Bringing her lips together he gave her a soft peck, which led to another aggressive smothering of the two in a passionate embrace. The kiss seemed to last forever broken only by the voice of friend.

"Oh, man did I interrupt something," Mitch asked.

For a moment Salem felt as if his feet had left the ground, and with the appearance of Mitch he felt as if they had been suddenly caught in quicksand.

"Oh don't stop on my account. Sorry for the intrusion, but I thought you would have been gone by now. I was just coming to get a feel for the place," he said patting Salem on the shoulder, while pinching Cherise on the cheek at the same time.

Leave it too Mitch to lighten up any situation.

"So how do you like Joint's stuff," Salem asked putting his arm around Cherise.

"I love it, and while you were checkin him out I was passing out some flyers. I think we're going to have a lot of people coming. Also got a little hook up where WXYI will announce the party two days before it pops off.

"So we have the place, the music and the people. What else is there other than the volunteers for the connection booths? The school paper is going to put everything on line the minute people sign up," Cherise said.

"Well, I don't know exactly what you guys will be doing for the rest of the day, but I have things to do," Cherise said looking directly at Salem.

Taking out his cell phone he realized it was going on ten o'clock. Remembering that it was family day, he felt that it was better if he headed home.

"Yeah, believe it or not I should be leaving soon too," he replied looking at Cherise and hoping Mitch would get the hint to give them a few more minutes alone.

"I'll tell you what Cherise. I need to go into Brooklyn to pick up some things for my mom. If you like some company, I can head out with you," he asked.

Now usually Salem would be okay with the whole situation, but already wanting a few minutes with Cherise, it made him think Mitch was being selfish.

"I've never heard of you going into Brooklyn before, why now," he asked.

"Are you crazy the Bronx is like an old stomping ground for me, so mom wants me to go buy up some cheap souvenir," Mitch remarked shoving his fist into Salem's shoulder again.

Salem was jealous. He had to admit it, and there was nothing he could say or would say.

"I'm gonna tell you something. I know about Mitch, and I'm learning about Joint, but I still don't really know anything about you. So I thought maybe later if you are free I could come and see who Cherise really is," he asked putting his arm around Joint who had just joined the conversation.

"I think Slim's finally putting it together," Joint said sneaking up on the three.

"Let's see Joints going to see Trace, so Mitch, I'm great with you heading to the Bronx with me. Salem I really have a lot of work to do, but if I'm finish by seven I have no problem with you swinging by the circus round eight," she replied.

He was satisfied with the answer, but not with the fact that Mitch was still hitching a ride with her.

"Okay, that sounds good. I'll give you a call around eight thirty, he asked.

"Perfect," she said walking around all three of them and forcing them to join in on a buddy hug.

"Alright, let's go then. I have other things to attend to," Joint snapped heading out the door with equipment in toe.

While the other three took the train Salem thought it was best if he hailed a taxi. Sliding into the back seat just behind the driver, where he noticed the driver's short black hair. Looking into the rear view mirror, he also noticed that the driver had small beady eyes like the Arabs back home.

"Where to," the driver asked.

"I'm going to Astoria, and on that note are you emirate,"

he asked.

The driver looked back in his rear view mirror.

"Yeah, how do you know that, he asked.

"I grew up in Abu Dhabi, he replied with a smile.

Even though sometimes it could be frustrating with his family around, the unexpected feeling he received of seeing someone from home always made him wonder why they were there and for how long. Laughing the driver seemed to have the same feeling.

"Al Ain, U.A.E. s oasis," he said loudly.

"So what are you doing here," Salem asked.

"The same thing you're doing here. I'm enjoying life. Been here for seven years and you," he responded.

"Almost five years. Just finishing up school," Salem laughed back.

And that was that. Sitting back in the car the driver had him thinking, about an old friend Ali from high school, he was Emirati. They were in their second year, and one day Ali came into class with a brown leather bracelet. It had no colors and was made specifically for a male to wear. He picked it up on a trip to the states. Many emirates saw wearing jewelry as a woman's thing, and for a guy to wear anything resembling jewelry made others think of them as feminine, too feminine for a boy. It was a big mistake for him to make and by the end of the day, he had flushed the bracelet down the toilet, just as they had dunked his head in the toilet earlier that school day. Sometimes he didn't know what was quicker, the subway or the taxi, but before he knew it he was back home standing in front of his door. The aroma of fresh cooked pancakes and pepper filled omelets filled the air. Music played loudly and sounds of laughter lured him to open the door. His parents had finally made his place their make shift home.

"Marhaba, just in time for your breakfast, Mrs. Tamimi said, grabbing his right hand and leading him into the kitchen.

His father had just gotten out of the shower, and was splashing himself with some old spice. The family wouldn't start eating until he gave the word. It was their way, and as he sat down at the counter he watched his wife place three pancakes, one omelet and three slices of turkey bacon on each plate. Satisfied he stood up and placed a kiss on each member of his family including Taif. Sitting down again next to his son, the family followed suit. Salem watched as his mother marveled over her own cooking, by devouring each and every morsel on her plate. He then watched as his father examined every piece he picked up conspicuously, looking at it, and then his wife. He was truly amazed at the new techniques his wife was learning. He smiled at her, and she smiled back, it was as if they were openly flirting with one another. Not able to take much more he turned his attention to his sister and cousin. Since taking a seat they had been giggling like schoolgirls who were trying to keep a juicy secret.

"What's so funny," he asked.

The girls had it all set up from the moment Salem walked in. They wanted to make sure their plan was concrete and Mrs. Tamimi wouldn't change her mind at the last minute.

"You know it's going to be so hard to find the perfect dress for your graduation. It's not like home where you have dresses that cover you so we really need to look," she spoke loudly.

The two older Tamimis were so busy flirting with each other that they let anything fly.

"You too sure aren't going by yourself, Salem is still going with you right," Mrs. Tamimi asked looking around for a quick second and then returning her flirting eyes to her husband.

"Of course," Salem said shaking his head.

"Let them go. They hardly get out as it is, huh. Just get up early and spend the day doing what you need to do," he said, feeding his wife piece of pancake.

The girls kept their giggles to themselves and everyone went their separate ways except for Salem. The food was so delicious he had to ask for seconds. Sitting at the table alone, he began to wonder if his father had been snooping around his room again. Putting his plate in the sink Mrs. Tamimi announced that after the Today Show that they would watch some movies. He had at least an hour and half to himself. Walking over to the couch he gave his mother and father a kiss. On the way down the hall he peaked in on Lamya and Taif who were looking through some magazines while sipping some tea. Taif gave him a thumb up while Lamya ran up to whisper something in his ears.

"Salem, remember I have my second interview, so interview, and then shopping," she whispered.

He gave her an uneasy smile and slipped into his room. He hadn't thought about it before, but even without his family there he had chosen the smallest space in his room. Usually he felt snug, but this visit it felt small and claustrophobic to him. Closing the door he flopped belly first on his bed. He could hear the family within his walls so he decided to listen to some Mimz. Turning onto his back he looked up at the ceiling. He wanted to check on his box, but Cherise popped into his head. He had kissed her or she had kissed him, either way it was a good morning, but even her kiss couldn't keep his mind off the box for long. Slipping off his bed he listened to make sure no was near. Opening the closet door his clothes were neatly pressed and hung with care, some by him and others by his mother. Unknown to her they hid what lied beneath them. Digging deep he grabbed the box putting it behind his back and slowly creeping he turned the lock on his bedroom door. The box gave him comfort. Removing his pants and shirt he was left with just his briefs and boxers. Jumping on to the bed he opened the box. Exhaling in relief it seemed as if nothing had been touched. Closing his eyes he grabbed a pair of white and pink strawberry infused panties and rubbed them across his face. Like a greedy child in a pool of gum balls he took a strong sniff of its scent and as he rubbed it across his face he couldn't help but to clinch its sweet material between his teeth. As he did this he stared intently into the box focusing intently on some white panties trimmed in black lace with a tiny black bow to make the panty complete. Not satisfied he dug deep within the box. Throwing the white panties across the room, he grabbed a black pair, another with laced design and a simple pink hipster. Lying back on his pillow he relished in happiness with the treasures that surrounded him, until there was a knock on his door.

"Yeah," he yelled.

"It's your mother. Open the door, she demanded.

Rushing to put the articles back into the box he tripped over his words.

"Okay, okay I'm coming I just have to put on some," he responded with a pause, not wanting to say another word for fear that he may say the wrong thing.

"Are you okay? Are you getting sick or something," she asked.

Rolling his eyes while banging the back of his head repeatedly on the pillow, he was frustrated.

"No, I was just waiting to watch the movie and I thought I'd get relaxed," he said.

Jumping into some basketball shorts he leaped off the bed, and unlocked the door with a pretentious smile as he stuck his head through only enough where Mrs. Tamimi could see his face. Paying him no attention she pushed the door open looking suspiciously around the room. Giving her son a motherly smirk she sat on his bed beckoning for him to do the same. Salem loved his mother and at any other time he would have welcomed the company. Putting her arms around him she gave him a kiss on the cheek.

"In two weeks, we'll be on a plane back home, and I just imagined us all going home on that plane together," she said with a face ready to wrinkle up in tears.

She was sad, but there was sternness in her eyes that made him move away a little. He knew she had more to say, and he was waiting for the axe to fall.

"This is going to be good for all of us. Just think of it as the next step up. You can even have a larger wedding for Lamya in Morocco," he said.

Twitching his face in disbelief at what he had said about Lamya's marriage, he was even in more disbelief that his mother seemed to shrug the subject off.

"Is something wrong," he asked.

She smiled at her son, but not in her usual way. She took a hold of Salem's hands, holding them within her own. He had grown nervous at that point and didn't know exactly what to do.

"You and the girls are going out tomorrow. It's nice you're spending all of this time with them," she said keeping the strange smile on her face.

"I kind of feel bad. I think I should have been spending more time with the family, so of course I'm going to hang out, he said, not giving her a clue that he was nervous has hell.

"I know both of you are so use to having your freedom, especially when I was sick, but I just don't understand why your sister seems so overly excited about tomorrow," she asked.

Like any other son he knew how to charm his mother.

"Why wouldn't she be excited? She's helping Taif improve on her look. What could be better," he replied with that boyish smile she loved so much.

Mrs. Tamimi couldn't help but laugh at her son's comment. She had to agree something had to be done about Taif's clothing.

"You know you should be thinking about marriage yourself," she commented.

He shook his head in regret that she even decided to bring it up. Though he didn't like it, it did give him an excuse to take his hands away from her. He knew how to get her off the subject and he wanted to be cruel and honest at the same time.

"Since you bought it up, how would you feel if I was to marry someone other than a Moroccan, he asked.

His mother's puzzled look made him chuckle all over on the inside, but he kept a straight face. She wasn't sure what to say, but his future wasn't as urgent, as what was on her mind.

"Stop being silly, and if you do plan on doing something like that I do hope that she is worth it, she said.

He was stomped and hoped that she wasn't thinking she was calling his bluff. He couldn't find it in his heart to sympathize with her.

"Of course she's worth it. She even has your qualities," he said with a huge smile.

Laying her head on her son's chest she decided to change the subject back.

"I want you to call me at least every three hours. Just in case your father and me decide to join you. It's a family outing and if that's so then we may meet up with you at some point," she said looking up into his eyes.

"Sure," he said moving back more.

Mr. Tamimi knocked on the outside of the door, just before peaking inside.

"Oh, have I walked in on one of those mother, son moments," he asked walking in without a care.

If someone wanted to know nosey, Mr. Tamimi should have been the go to man. Of everyone in the family he wanted to know what was going on at all times.

"She just a little upset," Salem replied.

Mr. Tamimi could see the glossy look in her eyes, but like his son he wasn't sympathetic. To him his wife over reacted to everything, and somehow he knew it was one of those moments. Reaching out for her husband's hand he reluctantly gave it to her.

"So what's wrong," he asked.

She didn't open her mouth. It was always her way of

telling her son to speak for himself, about himself. Besides, she didn't want her husband to know about her worries with Lamya.

"I told her that maybe, just maybe that I might not marry a Moroccan woman. I mean who knows, Salem replied shrugging his shoulders.

For a moment Mr. Tamimi didn't say a word. In-fact he averted his eyes looking anywhere, but at either of them. Expecting her husband to give her some support Mrs. Tamimi yanked at his arm for some sort of reaction. Finally he looked at the two of them.

"You know, being our son and growing up around two beautiful women, whether she is Moroccan or from New Zealand, I'm sure he knows what he's doing," he replied winking at his son.

Wanting deeply to get out of the situation Salem stood up pulling his mother with him. Grabbing his father by the back of the neck he gave them a group hug.

"You see dad knows how I am. And if you think about it we are talking about things that haven't exactly happened yet. So, why don't we talk about this when it's actually relevant, and with that I need to go to the kitchen," he said.

Walking out of the room his father walked with him massaging the back of his son's neck.

Standing very close he whispered in his ear.

"I know you were just trying to annoy your mother. You will marry a Moroccan right," he asked giving his son a thumb up as he headed to the bathroom.

Salem just smiled refusing to give him the thumbs up. He couldn't promise anything to any of them, and he thought giving him the thumbs up would just be giving him false hope. It was too early to call Cherise, so he decided to see what the girls were up to.

The door was half open, so he invited himself in, but as he saw the intense look in Lamya's eyes, he just want to walk right back out.

"So you were talking with mom and dad ugh," she said in a questionable matter.

"Why are you looking at me that way? Yes I was talking to them, but it's because they forced themselves into my room," he replied.

And what were they fishing for," she asked.

Salem felt as if he were being interrogated for a war crime he obviously didn't commit.

If you're asking then you know what she was at least fishing for," he replied.

"Yeah, I know because she has been looking at me so strange today. Either she's going crazy or she knows something's up," Lamya complained.

"Exactly, she knows something is going on and she is not happy at all," but the good thing is that she doesn't want dad to know she's feeling that way," he replied.

Both of the girls sat at attention.

What do you mean," Lamya asked.

"She kept asking about you going to get clothes for Taif and why was it that you seemed so extra excited over it. Which leads us back to the question of when are you going to tell them," he replied in an angry agitated whisper.

Frustrated, Lamya held her arms high in the air. Grinding her teeth she planted herself on top of the dresser. Salem was used her reactions. Her motto was, "Just let things fall into place, and they usually will." He really liked seeing her squirm, and he wondered what she was going to do, but as he starred into his sister's eyes a growing sense of helplessness seemed to heighten, while Lamya searched for answer he could hear his mother in the kitchen. It was time for lunch and he knew it would be another two hours before they would start up a movie. Holding his hands out and shrugging at both the girls he backed out of the room slowly. He decided that if it were only a few minutes he had to find some refuge somewhere else. His mother was still upset about their talk, so she ignored him as he slipped out the apartment door. He needed some since able people, so he decided to pay a visit to his neighbor Alison. She was the only white American on the floor, and for that matter the whole building. Her apartment was the only door that was the keeper of a magnetic white board decorated with cute blue squigglies on each corner. On that day the board had the message:

Called you twice, came by once, won't come again, Greg.

He couldn't help but to smile, because by the read of the note Alison was up to her old games again. Knocking once with a pause and twice without, he knew she would answer. It was their secret knock.

"Well, it's about time you came for a visit. I thought friends were supposed to check up on each other once and a blue moon," she said rolling her eyes while walking back into to room.

Though she talked as if she was someone's mother, she only had Salem by a year. He could tell that she had been laying down by the way her curly hair stood up on her head, as if she had just been shot with some electricity. She had an attitude, but he didn't care. It was the way Alison was. Walking in behind her he could see that she was not alone.

"What, Alison I must be dreaming. Cause we ain't seen your ass for a minute," Renee said as she hopped up off the couch.

A close friend of Alison's, sometimes they seemed inseparable.

"What's up girl? You know where I live. All you have to do is knock," he replied giving her a hug and jumping in the seat where she was sitting.

"Yeah, right, you've been giving us the cold shoulder since your parents came, she said flopping down herself with another glass of wine.

Their personalities were as opposite as night and day, and he often wondered how they met and befriended each other. Alison was the heartwarming mother figure, with cold Irish American blood running through her veins. Sometimes this coldness showed up in her ever-changing moods. Renee on the other hand was African American. Once someone met Renee, there was no forgetting her. She was about five feet eight inches tall and around three hundred pounds of unadulterated, intellectual fun. What made Renee even more interested is that such a big girl had such a light voice with the dialect of a Wisconsin white girl. The twist to this is that she had a singing voice to rival Ella Fitzgerald, and when the music came out, so did the attitude. Accepting a glass of wine from Alison, he watched Renee as she set up a game of scrabble.

"Yea, if I introduced you to them, you would never get rid of them. Trust me they would have some reason to bother you every day. I'll introduce you before the ceremony. Is that fare?

"It's okay baby. Mama understands your situation, Alison replied finally putting a smile on her face.

"So what's the dibs? Give it up. What's going on over there," Renee asked.

"Nothing much," he said keeping a tight lip.

Renee knew there was something up. It was how they met. Taking the same English class they met while sitting in the back of the class together. Anytime he was having trouble he would out of know where start talking to her before and at the end of class about his problem's, usual dealing with other friends or class. He looked annoyed, and she sometimes hated how he seemed to hold almost everything that bothered him on the inside. If it weren't for that, she would have stuck to having one major crush on him.

"That's it," she asked.

"Alright, alright, my sister has decided that she wants to stay here. She went job hunting, got an interview and has another one tomorrow, "he replied sitting up to take a sip of his wine.

"You need to tell that bitch to get her life together and stop dragging your coat tail," she said slamming her glass on the table.

"Looking agitated Renee rolled her eyes at Alison, who thought Renee could sometimes go a little over board without knowing the whole story.

"So what you're saying is that her coming here could mess up the good thing you got going on," Alison replied.

Seeing the light Alison pointed her finger at Renee and gave her a wink. They then reached across the table giving each other a slap handshake as they giggled in self-gratification.

"You've got it, but what can I do," he asked.

Annoyed with what they saw as lack of backbone in

Salem they looked at each other and then him without a word. Taking the final drop of his wine he signaled for Renee to give him some gum. Shoving four pieces into his mouth he raised his hands in the air, a hopeless expression to his situation.

"I'm not doing anything. What am I suppose to do? Tell her to take her ass home. I can't do that. I told her that I didn't think it was a good idea or that I would really like to be the only Tamimi here, but that's as far as I go. Could you tell one of your family members that? I know you couldn't," he replied.

He was right and they knew up. They could talk all the big talk they wanted to, but family was family and to turn your back was just wrong.

"Anyway I have other things to worry about, like going

and meeting a friend of mine tonight," he said giving a sneaky smile to the two.

Renee was not good at being patient, and sitting up in her seat she knew he had more to tell.

"What do you mean," she asked.

"Her name is Che-ri-se," he said teasingly.

Renee's eyes opened wide. If he was talking about, whom she thought he was talking about, to her it was like history in the making.

"No, the assistant teacher," she screamed.

Salem shook his head in agreement. There was nothing else for him to say. It may have taken him four years, but at least he did it.

"Damn, I thought you'd never get the balls up to spit it out," she replied.

Pulling his cell phone to check the time, lunch was about to start.

"Their gonna be looking for me. I gotta go," he said.

Bringing out more snacks they both looked disappointed.

"What, you're just gonna leave like that. Everyone is coming over," she complained.

"Yeah, everybody excluding Greg. You sleep with a person one time and they think they own you," she said popping a Doritos in her mouth.

"It's family guys. I have to go," he replied.

"Alright baby, you gotta do what you gotta do," Alison replied.

Lying back on the couch Renee could only go with the flow.

"Yea, come on over later when you can't take any more of that shit, she said taking a puff from her a cigarette.

Giving them the piece sign he waved good-bye and saw himself out.

Lunch consisted of American hoggies, beef kabobs with salad dressing, mixed with cucumbers, and carrots. Lays potato chips made the meal complete. Forced to listen to his dad talk about all the plans he had coming up, Salem looked across the table at Lamya who sat happily enjoying her hoggie. Even though his face read angry all over she seemed to pay him no mind. He just wanted her to speak up, because it wasn't his responsibility. After lunch like any emirate family they decided to take a nap. Not wanting to even see his sister he gladly slipped back into his room. Those days it seemed as if his bed had become his comfort zone. As soon as his head hit the pillow he fell into a deep sleep. Dreaming again he was seated at his office desk slaving over some construction plans, when suddenly his parents burst through the door. Their faces were contorted with frowns and tears that seemed to flow continuously.

"Do something, do something," they whaled.

Behind them was his boss screaming at the top of his lungs.

"Get them out of here now," he screamed.

Then beyond his voice came the whining words of his sister.

"Salem, tell them I have the right to do whatever I want. Salem, Salem, Salem, she shouted.

The last Salem was accompanied by an aggressive shake to his body. He opened his eyes only to see Lamya standing over him.

"What," he screamed.

Covered from head to toe she was disappointed.

"You missed prayer you idiot," she said pulling the pillow from beneath him.

Since their arrival Salem had done little or no praying at all. It wasn't as if he prayed that often anyway, but at least he would think about it. Forcefully grabbing her by the hijab he whispered angrily in her ear.

"You better tell them about this job thing, he said moving her aside so that he could get up.

He was starting to feel guilty about the whole situation, not for him or his sister, but for his parents. If Lamya were not around they would be on their own. It was as if they didn't have enough extended family that had already deserted them for the states, and he knew nothing was considered dearer to them than their children. Walking into the living room he picked up the prayer rugs that had been left on the floor. Taif was setting the snack table with a big bowl of nachos with dip followed by popcorn and some kit kat bars. He wondered how no one in their family was obeist. It had to be a miracle; because with all the junk they ate each of them should have been at least around two hundred pounds. Plopping down on the couch Salem poured himself a glass of Pepsi. It was tradition. He was always the first one to seat himself for the big movie, and usually the last one to get up after gorging on snacks. A knock at the door bought him an extra treat. The family had ordered Rizzo's Pizza and burgers from Jackson Hole Burgers. His family took movie night seriously, and they pulled out all the punches that night. The first film of choice was You Again; Mr. Tamimi thought that the family needed a laugh. Watching the film Salem pictured Taif, who was stuffing her face with a big juicy burger, as being Marni. She was the main character of the film that wasn't so popular in high school. It was Taif all the way he thought and he purposely focused on the television screen not wanting to burst out into laughter because of his thoughts. As Salem tried to hold his feelings in Taif identified herself with Marni as well, like Marni she would change her life and show them all not just how successful she was professionally, and personally. Yes indeed, she thought it was time to lose some weight. And while Taif hesitated picking up just one more fry, Lamya hoped that in the states she would be just as successful as Marni. Unknown to the girls Mrs. Tamimi noticed the smug looks on both of their faces, and in her the gut of her stomach she knew they were up to no good. Mr. Tamimi could feel something was going on too, but he didn't care. He figured it was family and family would always have tension at one point or another. He looked around the room at children once crying for their mother's milk now making their way in the world. He knew that before their trip ended there would be more change, and whatever it was, he was ready to welcome it.

12~

PASSION GROWS

By seven they had watched two movies and Mr. Tamimi was setting up for the third one. At six thirty the time with Cherise had been confirmed and Salem was getting ready for the night. He wanted to go retro that night. He chose a black puma t-shirt with the logo written in burgundy on the front. To match he wore beige and black, tweed designed, slim fitting slacks. The shoes were Puma, brown and beige. He had a different mood going on that night. Retro was usually reserved when he would hang out with the alternative group, the ones who seemed to wear retro as if it were their second religion. After helping his family to clean up and looking in the mirror one last time he was off to see Cherise.

The sky was clear, but the night was buzzing with life. Taking out his phone he gave Cherise a call.

"Hey, are you here already," she asked worriedly.

"No, no. Just letting you know that I'm on my way now. Is Mitch still around," Salem asked.

He hadn't met a girl yet who couldn't resist Mitch, whether he was trying to get them to pay attention or not.

"Uhm, no actually he helped me with some groceries earlier and he was gone. He's a little bit of a busy body isn't he," she asked while laughing.

Taking a seat on the train a broad smile over took his face.

"That's Mitch, so since your finish being the practice house wife, what's on the agenda for tonight," he asked.

"House wife, I hope that's not what you think, cause this girl will never be a house wife, and the agenda. Remember you invited yourself over," she said still laughing.

Her words hit home because what she didn't know was that his mother was a housewife, but he understood where Cherise was coming from.

Walking down the hall into the living room she kicked her roommate Storm in the back of the knees, causing her to fall on the couch. Putting her hand over the receiver and then on her hips she gave Storm a look that read no love here.

"Get your stuff off the couch. I told you someone was coming over," she said with what seemed to be a sneer.

"Cherise are you there," Salem asked.

"Sorry, the phone slipped. Are there any movies or snacks that you like specifically," she replied.

Motioning for her roommate to beat it, she flopped on to the couch. Grabbing the remote she hoped to find a good movie.

"Okay, I thought you had changed your mind for a second," he said.

Talking over the dishes that were being washed in the kitchen, she watched as Mark peaked his head out of the kitchen door.

"Sorry about the dishes," Mark whispered.

At the same time Rico stuck his head into the living room from the hallway to say good-bye. At least one person was leaving for the night she thought.

"Ha ha, no way, one more person want do us any harm," she replied.

Salem was relieved.

"Whatever you pick is fine with me. I'm a snackaholic anyway. Is it okay if I stop and pick up something to drink," he asked.

"Hey, now you're talking, how about some tequila, and I promise this time you won't get sick. I'll talk to you when you get here," she giggled.

Hanging up the phone she pushed her way into the kitchen grabbing Mark by the ear and yelling for Storm.

"Where are you Storm," she yelled.

Leading Mark out of the kitchen, through the living room, into the hallway and up the stairs, she found Storm, snacking on one of Cherise's pizzas while searching google for art supplies. Storms eyes never left the lab top screen.

"What," she replied.

"What, Salem is coming over. Don't you guys have some where you may want to go," she pleaded.

Under her breath she gave Cherise a long-winded no. Mark on the other hand reached deep into his pockets and pulled them inside out.

"Listen Cherise, I'm broke. While you're graduating we have another two quarters of school to pay for," he said rubbing the top of her head.

Exaggerating the last of his words, she invaded Storm's room flopping on to her bed.

"What are you doing, " Storm asked annoyed at her roommate's intrusions.

Feeling defeated Cherise lied back down looking up at the ceiling.

"Ugh, I don't know." she sighed.

Storm stopped what she was doing and joined Cherise on the bed.

"You know if you weren't working so much, maybe more girl on boy action would happen and you wouldn't be so hard up right now, she replied giggling.

What was she suppose to do? She couldn't disagree with Storm and realizing that she didn't have much time left she jumped to her feet. Giving the two a nose salute, while sticking her tongue out at them she slipped out of the room.

"Well, real mature Miss. Leflore," Storm yelled.

Running down stairs she popped another pizza in the oven while grabbing some chips and putting some fries in a skillet. Finally popping some popcorn in the microwave, she was satisfied. She was a healthy eater and having

Salem over gave her the excuse to eat like a pig. As Cherise

nibbled on some chips, Salem finally reached Brooklyn.

Taking a short walk through little Odesa, the feel of

Brooklyn took over him. The sidewalks were filled with

various vendors and as he walked passed roaring roller

coasters, and roller bladders, the environment lent him a

playful spirit. Sprawling through some of the booths

leading out of Odessa, he found a vendor who sold roses.

He wanted to give her a dozen black roses, but that was for

Russian women, not American. He thought they were

sexy, but decided to take a single pink rose instead. He

made his way from Odesa to Bedstuy. Cherise lived in one

of the brownstones between a pharmacy and a small

market. Hiding the rose behind his back, he knocked three

times on the door before she answered. Holding his breath

he braced himself from the time the door cracked until the

end of the night. Checking himself out one last time from

head to toe, he looked up to find a tall, quirky, blond guy at the door. Pausing just before pulling the rose from behind his back, he didn't know what to do next.

"Hey man welcome to the layer," Mark said holding his hand out for a shake.

"Uh, I'm sorry I must have the wrong," Salem said, but was interrupted.

"Nah, you're in the right place. My little sweetheart is right around the corner," he grinned.

Motioning for him to come in Salem followed him suspiciously into the kitchen. Entering the kitchen first, Mark grabbed Cherise by the waist, who was putting some dry dishes away.

"Hey sweet heart we have a visitor," he said.

Before she could see who was in the kitchen he gave her a hard kiss on the cheek, while he looked out of the corner of his eye at Salem. Caught off guard Salem almost dropped the bottle of tequila he bought. Startled and realizing Salem was standing there Cherise angrily pushed Mark out of the way.

"Mark, that is not funny," she yelled.

Pushing Mark clear out of the kitchen, she pulled Salem inside instead.

"Ass hole she yelled," more agitated that Mark stood laughing to tears in the next room.

Cherise was starting to blush and to make her feel comfortable he handed her the pink rose that had begun wilting in his hand.

"Ah, thank you," she smiled.

Rubbing his forehead making sure no sweat showed, he allowed Cherise to lead him out of the kitchen into the living room. There they found Mark, as red as any jokester who had been successful at a prank. Behind Mark, a black haired girl with round rimmed glasses pulled her hair back into a pony tail. Wearing a t-shirt pulled over a long sleeve shirt and some pre-washed jeans with holes, she looked more like a high school girl than one in college.

"So you're him," she asked.

Measuring him from head to toe she walked a circle around him as if she was getting ready to perform some type of ceremony.

"Yeah, I'm Salem, and you are," he asked.

"The artsy roommate who hates new people walking into her life via other roommates," she said sarcastically.

Cherise gave both Mark and Storm an unwanted look.

"Okay guys, I can take it from here, and you can go and find something else to do," she replied.

Pointing towards the couch she offered Salem a seat.

"I like your friends, but how in the world did you guys meet," he asked.

Walking over to the couch she didn't know whether she wanted to grab a seat next to him or take a place on the floor.

"You know their friends turned roommates and now maybe ex-friends," she replied taking a seat on the floor.

"So what's that family of yours been up to while here, she asked.

"Planning parties and their future from my success," he replied.

Looking back at Salem from the floor she gave him a wink and pulled out season two of True Blood.

"Are you a friend," she asked.

"Yes sir," he bellowed.

As Cherise slipped the DVD into the Xbox, Salem slipped down from the couch on to the floor and crept up behind her. He was so close that he could smell the faint scent of perfume on her neck. It made him want to get closer and he wondered if the perfume was a hint as to how Cherise was thinking. Taking his right hand he used his middle and index fingers and ran them playfully up the spine of her neck. Jumping in surprise she turned and gave him a slap on the shoulder.

"I was just trying to keep myself busy until you were finished." Salem replied.

Feeling guilty of having hands he jumped to his feet. He had always been respectful of women and he wanted to make sure he was respectful with Cherise. He decided to plop back down on the couch, and feeling more comfortable Cherise decided to do the same. He couldn't help himself, and grabbing her by the waste she found herself not on the couch, but on the lap of Salem. She was

okay with it and playfully rubbed the back of his head
finally slipping down onto the couch.

"What, you're leaving me," he asked.

"No, I just thought it was about time for some
TEQUILA," she sang.

"Then, let me go get it," he replied.

He gave her a quick kiss on the cheek and jumped up.
While Salem poured them tequila with ginger ale, she
tested different seating positions that she thought would
look cute when he returned. Putting the drinks and snacks
on a tray he grabbed the rose that Cherise dropped in a
slender vase by the sink. Walking into the din he put the
tray down on the coffee table that sat in the middle of the
room. He placed his glass on the table and personally

handed Cherise hers. Accepting the glass he then took the rose and handed it to her once more. She accepted it and gently ran the stem across her lips. Still standing, leaning over he took the rose and slowly moved in for a kiss. They were so close, but as he went in for the kiss, he was knocked back off of his feet onto the coffee table, startled by the sudden screeching sound of an electronic guitar sliding across the hallway floor with its owner in tow.

"What are you doing," Cherise yelled once again.

Cherise had a temper and though she seemed to be a pro at controlling it, the guitar situation was just too much unexpectedly. A black guy with a curly Mohawk poked his head into the doorway leaving couple in pose with a shaky grin. In female skintight black skinny jeans, a white t-shirt and a black leather jacket, he looked like he was ready to play some more.

"Erick," she shouted.

Erick unlike everyone else in the house was musician, at least half of the time. He usually kept to himself choosing to practice cords instead of wasting vital time hanging out in the television room. As he spoke he didn't exactly look at Cherise, but instead he kept his eyes on the stranger.

"Ohhh, you have company. What's his name," he asked.

"I'm over here Eric, and my frightened friends name is Salem," she replied with attitude.

Reluctantly looking at her he squinted his eyes at Salem as if expecting for him to say something.

"Sorry, so nice to meet you Salem. I didn't realize anyone was down here. It was so quiet," he replied trying his best not to look at Salem, but not being too successful.

"Well you would know if you would came down and socialized more," she replied.

Eric had heard it all before and Cherise's visitor was not going to make a difference.

"I have work to do Cherise. It's not that I'm non-social. I'm just busy. Get that through your head and we'll all be a happy family," he said walking over to Cherise and giving her a kiss on the cheek.

Cherise pushed him away playfully knowing that he was only telling the truth.

"Hey like I said nice to meet you Salem and sorry about the interruption," he said once more as he ran and snapped up his guitar disappearing back down the hall.

He had to admit; he had met some interesting roommates before, but noon as interesting as Cherise's, especially Erick. Thinking that the night was turning into a disaster it took Cherise a minute to relax again.

"I know by now you think this place is a circus, but I swear, it's usually not like this," she said.

Digable Planet played from the film and Salem pointed toward the couch leaping and stretching his body across it as if he were at home. Cherise was in thought mode, wondering if he was just putting on an act, or really okay with the whole situation. Shyly she dropped to the floor again. Her back was to his and he rolled his eyes almost into the back of his head out of frustration. It was his fault; he thought he needed to learn how to be aggressive in the right way. To be closer to her he laid his body on the opposite end of the couch and resting the back of his head on his arms, he ran his eyes down the back of Cherise's neck. Stopping at her back he noticed a small mutli-colored beaded necklace. Between every fifteen or twenty beads laid four small piece signs. The necklace was so tiny someone would think that it was part of the top of her shirt. H couldn't help it, no matter what he focused on his thoughts were still in the gutter and all he wanted to do was straddle his legs behind her and massage her shoulders while they talked about the movie or some other trivial subject. His graphic thoughts led him to imagining himself slowly slipping his tongue across the lobes of her ears, exhausting thoughts forced him to collapse back on to the couch.

"What's up with you? You're pretty quiet back there," she asked pushing her back against the couch.

"Oh naw, I was just trying to figure out where you got your furniture from. I really like it," he replied.

Her eyelids shuttered back and forth as she looked back at him.

Dragging his hand across the arm of the couch, the texture was tough, but worn. The couch was pale green along with two more chairs making it a set. He thought that probably in the early sixties it would have been a stunning decor. He was taught that the color of green represented renewal, growth and harmony. He took it as a sign and leading his hands from the couch to the back of Cherise, he started to play with her hair.

"Have you ever worn your hair long," he asked.

Turning upside down on the couch he laid next to her

looking up into her eyes. Taking a hold of the back of her head he pulled her down just close enough to give her a smooch on the lips. Each kept their eyes open for different reasons. He wondered if she was enjoying it, and she wondered if he could be a player in disguise, slowly closing her eyes she decided not to think and just live in the moment. As she closed her eyes he clutched her bottom lip, while grabbing her by the waist and pulling her completely on top of his body. He could feel the rhythmic change of her heart, but failed to notice the same within himself. He felt no more than he did during their first kissing encounter, but yet he still yearned for more. Turning her over on to her back, his lips moved from her bottom lip to the top, as he lightly ran his hand across her defined shoulders, down her arms, and up again across her chest to her neck.

"I'm starting to think you kiss as good as you look," she

whispered.

Running his fingers through her hair he was glad that she started a conversation.

"That goes both ways," he replied.

Sliding off the couch and sitting up he pulled Cherise with him. He couldn't see anything behind, but Cherise could, and the first thing she saw as they sat up was Erick leaning against the living room door way.

"Uhm, sorry to interrupt this love connection, but before I'm allowed to leave the rest of the crew, they wanted me to join them in a little Brooklyn night viewing. You guys interested in join us," he asked.

Salem saw Erick's sudden appearance as a way of

getting him away from his precious roommate. And what bothered him even more than that was the strange feeling that every time Erick opened his mouth all of his comments relevant or not seemed to be directed towards him.

"So, you wanna go and join them on the roof top," she asked.

He didn't like the fact that she had interrupted his thoughts, even though she couldn't have the slightest idea of what he was thinking or what she interrupted.

"Rooftop or not quiet boy," she asked again.

"Why not," he said holding his hands high into the air to give her roommate a sign that he was very frustrated.

"Alright guys come and grab some of this stuff so we

can continue our snacking up there," she yelled clapping as if it were a signal for the rest of them to come out of their hiding places.

The other two roommates came out of their hiding places like mice out of wall holes. Even though they were annoying he couldn't help but feel welcomed by them. With snacks and a few chairs in place, Salem took his spot at the edge of the roof. Closing his eyes he breathed in the fresh night air. A slight breeze took him back to Dubai on the rooftop of his friends place in Karama. It was the night before he would leave U.A. E., heading off to college. The breeze was nice as he stretched his arms out wide so that he could feel it flow between his fingers. Karama was like his home away from home and other than his cousins one of his closest friends Sheikh always welcomed him. He was Bengali and though he was born in Bangladesh his whole life was spent in Karama. That night was his second going away party one because it was in Dubai and two because most of his Arab friends and cousins wouldn't be caught dead in Karama with Bengalis. If it wasn't for Sheikh's friendship he didn't know if he would actually have had the guts to go off to the states by himself. Salem could feel Sheikhs eyes on him and the hugs that he received from the other guys just seemed like a formality. He looked across the rooftop at his old friend, no hugs were needed, and he could see how Sheik felt through his eyes. Sheiks eyes also bought him back to the present. He grabbed Cherise from the back and bought her close to him. Resting his head on the back of neck he closed his eyes in comfort, but the comfort took him back to that Karama roof top where Sheikh's eyes seemed to grow more intense. Sheikh was a dear friend, but in that moment he hoped the tight grip on Cherise would somehow take the memory away.

"Hey boy, loosen that grip a bit. I'm not going anywhere

unless you want me to," she said.

13~

SELFISH DEEDS BAGGED AND HOOKED

The next morning he awoke to the face of his sister standing over him with a simple look planted on her face.

"Hey, get up, we have an hour to get out of here," she whispered to him.

Whipping his eyes he soon realized that his sister was not just ready to go, but really wanted to play the part. He hardly recognized her. Her hair was nicely pulled back into a respectful bun. Her eyebrows had been neatly shaped and lightened, but slightly covered with black round rimmed glasses that made her look more distinctive. Even her makeup was toned down. Though he was annoyed with her he couldn't help but to laugh out loud. Her new look made him think back to one of his female professors who had a habit of bringing a Betty Boop coffee cup with her to work every morning that read." DARK head girls have the most fun."

"So what do you think," she asked.

He was speechless and even if he could he wouldn't say a word. Giving her a thumb up he anxiously watched her leave the room. She was right, they had to get out of the house right away or their mother was going to wake up to a very rude reality. After getting dressed he met the girls outside of the apartment building. He was in for more than one surprise. Though she was on the thick side, Taif stood before him in a tight light blue pencil skirt matched up with a long sleeve white ruffled shirt. The outfit showed that his cousin had curves. Taif knew he was looking and as she walked down the apartment hall in front of him she couldn't help but turn around and give him a sly wink. Seeing everything Lamya rolled her eyes, pulling them both into the elevator.

"I think we should just take a taxi into the city," Salem said.

"Well, since we're taking the taxi, why don't we have a power breakfast before her big interview," Taif replied.

She was just as excited as Lamya. The night before she spoke with Lamya, hoping her cousin could put a good word in for her as well. If the second interview went as well as the first one and with her cousin's charming personality she had the potential of making even more money with this company and dressing up for the part couldn't hurt a potential opportunity either.

Grabbing a taxi Salem finally felt comfortable enough to confront the two girls, who he was beginning to think we're going nuts. They were just to cool about the whole situation.

"So whose idea was it to come as you please," he asked.

One girl sat on each side of him and as he waited for an answer they pointed at each other, and since no one owned up to the idea they stayed quiet the rest of the way.

Ordering some coffee, eggs and turkey bacon Salem didn't know whether he was angry or impressed with them.

"Okay, who ever came up with the idea you both decided to go through with it, but what if someone saw you? He looked at both of them and they both looked back at him clueless, but still enjoying their food. He tried once more.

"Lamya, let's say we walk in there today and you get this job. Then what do you do," he pushed.

Lamya opened her eyes even wider. It was as if the words her brother spoke were poison. She thought since birth she had been living the life they wanted for her and whether she told them right off or at the last minute she figured the response would have been the same. Yeah her brother may have had some tension over the whole situation, but he was the brother. She looked at him as he talked and enjoyed a nice piece of juicy turkey bacon. Of course he could sit on his high horse and preach all he wanted to, because he was free to do whatever he wanted. He had experienced life, but she hadn't. Even an arranged marriage would be worth it if she got to live a little before being tied down. Calming down she pinched her brother on the cheek. Her decision required her to be more of an adult than a selfish brat. Taking her glasses off, she held both her brother and cousin's hand.

"You know, in a way we're all in the same boat. Salem you're doing something that our parents would rather you not do. Taif, you obviously have a change in heart about your life style, and I'm just doing the same thing. The only difference is I'm the second one in our family doing it and I'm the girl. Everyone just isn't bread to follow the straight and narrow, and I'm part of that select few," Lamya replied with a smile.

It seemed as if Lamya was finally waking up. Relieved

and without thinking he grabbed his sister's and Taif's hand. She had been as quiet as a mouse and as he clinched her hand she in turn clinched her lip. It revealed a chipped tooth, which made it hard for Salem to contain his laughter. It had been that way since Valentine's Day in elementary school, and Salem suddenly remembered why. After the elevator accident Taif had become pretty low-key personality wise and the four eyed gullible doll face had become a bullying tyrant. In the two months that she was there she made a name for herself and was becoming a U.A.E. legend. On Valentine's Day while Salem was playing soccer with his classmates in the school courtyard two boys from a higher grade decided to play keep away with their ball, angry Salem jumped on the back of the boy who took the ball. Unfortunately for Salem he was light and the bigger boy slung him to the ground with little effort involved. There was no supervisor around at the time and the only one who saw the incident was Taif. She had been standing around the corner enjoying a chocolate croissant sandwich. She loved to watch Salem when he was in play mode. He seemed like a super hero to her and she could just imagine how strong he would be when was like eighteen. Salem was at his happiest when he was playing football and Taif loved to see that gorgeous smile on his face. On the other hand his smile disappearing by the hands of two large bullies, made her want to shove her croissant sandwich right into their faces. Marching across the courtyard she watched as one bully grabbed Salem's arms and the other his feet. Picking him up off the ground they pulled him towards a pole, where the object of the game was to tear Salem's body apart by straddling him between the poles. Not being able to watch any more she tossed her sandwich ran up to the boys, and grabbed one by the hair and the other by the ear. The boy that she held by the hair swung his arms wildly and with one clinch of his fist slugged her right in the mouth breaking off a piece of one of her front teeth. She hardly flinched, and instead seemed to get angrier. Giving him a kick in the stomach he fell back first to the ground. Still holding on to the ear of the other boy she stepped back jerking his ear downward so tight that he fell to his knees in pain. Still not happy she jumped on his shoulders and shoved his face into the pavement. She then went up, picked up her half eaten sandwich and shoved it into the face of the other boy. Not saying a word she picked up the ball, walked over to Salem who was still sitting on the ground and dropped it into his lap. Walking away she gave her cousin a naughty smile and headed straight for the director's office. With the sound of Taif's voice the memory was behind, but the comedy of it still lingered.

"You're right, we all have our objectives and yes I do have mine too. You think you've had it so bad. At least you were living in a country where most girls had to act and dress in the same way. Imagine me in a freaken free country where I still had to cover twenty four seven. It excluded me from the cool girls. I had to hang out with asthmatic, winded Wendy who hadn't even bloomed at sixteen. While the other girls were wearing miniskirts, putting on makeup, and kissing the cute boys, after school I was hoarded back into a small apartment each and every day, hoping Wendy wouldn't need more than an inhaler. The only time I got out was on family movie weekends where I was always embarrassed because somehow I would always run into one of the other girls who were out on fantastic dates with their awesome guys," she said taking her fork and sticking into the restaurant table.

After her speech she grabbed a hold of Salem's hand with the tightest grip he had ever had from a girl. Starring both of her cousins down she had one thought. No one would succeed if she couldn't. Her stares made the siblings uncomfortable and in-turn convinced Lamya that it was time to head towards the interview.

"So are we all finished? I want to make sure I'm there at least five minutes before hand," she pushed.

Sitting in between the two girls in the cab he laid his head back on the seat looking up out at the morning sky. He had to give it to them they had guts, and he believed that they probably had the balls too. Being dropped off right in front of the building Salem left the girls to handle their own business. He knew he would have to stay in the same waiting area and he just couldn't take having that creepy feeling again. He decided to keep to the ground floor grabbing a cup of coffee and donuts from one of the cafes. He understood the importance of physics, but he couldn't understand how in the world anyone in their right mind could spend their days trying to solve mysteries of the world, that he believed would stay mysteries. White coats passed in and out of the shop. He had seen his sister in the white jacket many times back home, of course accompanied with a hijab. He looked at the clothes he was wearing. Sporting some jeans and a simple white the thought that clothing all boiled down to sex. People wore clothes because it made them feel good and sometimes made others feel even better. Married, single, gay or straight clothes had the ability to turn people on. His culture and religion hid sex. America sometimes kept sex a conservative subject and at other times over played it as a free for all at all times. In Europe no matter how savvy or conservative they thought themselves to be, Salem believed that they just over did it all together. His thoughts turned back to his sister. He was undressing her, and he didn't feel guilty about doing it. He took down the bun in her hair, letting it drop to her shoulders. Taking off the frames he imagined her lips pinker. The sophisticated suit she wore was replaced with a woven laced chiffon black dress worn just above the knees. He placed her dull patent leather conservative shoes with high heel Jimmy Choos that made her calves seem to whistle. That was it even his sister could be sexy if she wanted to. Pronouncing the word s-e-x slowly within, he gripped the corner of his bottom lip with his teeth and his thoughts went from his sister, to Cherise. Her body he thought was fantastic and the clothes, Cherise new how to wear the clothes. She was never vulgar or sluttish, in-fact even with the sexiest of dresses, she seemed to maintain an indescribable innocence, even when most of what she wore would catch many more than just Salem's eyes. Those clothes, it was something about her clothes that made him just want to violate her innocence and make it as dirty as possible.

Of course glorified thoughts like anything seem to fade away when problems arose, which is what happened as

Salem received two taps on his shoulder. Both Lamya and

Taif stood behind him with the biggest grins on their faces.

He waited for either of them to make squeak, yell, or just

say anything, but they said nothing.

"Okay, I give up, but I guess since you too can't stop

smiling, somebody must be getting something," he said.

Taif, not Lamya knelt down, gave him a kiss on the

cheek and grabbed one of his hands.

"In less than forty five minutes, we were both offered

positions," she shouted.

Salem felt that even though the words came from her

own mouth, she couldn't believe it. As he looked up at his

sister, her face read the same, shaking her head in

agreement with Taif.

"It's true. Their gonna sponsor me. I have to go home for a month or two to sort out the paper work, but I'm in. They're also re-hauling their financial branch and they were looking for someone with Taif's knowledge. Looks like we could be colleagues," Lamya squeaked trying to hold back her excitement.

They both grabbed a chair and sat next to Salem. For a few moments they sat still in silence. Finally Salem spoke.

"Okay, so I guess it's time to celebrate this news, or push it under the rug like it never happened," he asked.

Both girls looked at him as if he was crazy to even think of sweeping such an opportunity under the rug.

"Come on let's catch the train. I don't know about you,

but I need to get ready for a party," Lamya said.

The girls shopping venue of choice that day was the Manhattan Mall. Since being back in the states it was the first time that she had been to the mall. Taif on the other hand hated going to malls. To be honest most people her age would hate shopping too if they had to chose from what Taif always labeled the dull and the drab items. But putting into consideration that taking on the new job could bring new things, a trip to the mall didn't seem all that bad. Salem knew that the girls wanted his help in picking out items that they thought would make guys heads turn, but the more he thought about their destination, the more he felt that it wouldn't hurt him to join in on the fun himself. Getting off the train a worried brother couldn't help but to pull the girls aside.

"What Salem? Com on let's get started," Lamya

whined.

"So you actually want go ahead and start shopping without letting them know what's going on," he replied.

The two girls looked down at the ground simultaneously as people passed. Grabbing the hands of her brother and cousin she dragged them to the side of the walkway just before the mall entrance.

"You know I could go home with mom and dad tomorrow. I could also keep the job I have, marry the man they want, and the next day end up dead run over by a bus. So not only would I die young, but hopeless, because I'm sure I wouldn't be living a happy life. At least if I can make a few of my own choices life would seem like it's so much more worth it," she said putting her hands on her hips as she talked.

"Nice speech," Salem said clapping his hands.

Fed up with Salem's whole attitude about the situation Taif gave him a push hard enough to knock him into a passerby.

"Listen we decided that it would be best for Lamya and me if we went ahead and let our parents choose our husbands, but only if they were westernized. We get our way, and they get part of theirs. Most of the Arab guys here don't get married early and it gives me Lamya a chance to live our life just a little and then be packaged," she said.

"And that's it? You think their just gonna go for that," he asked starting to believe that they were two of the most stupid girls he had dealt with in a long time.

He knew that it would work. An arranged marriage was

one of the biggest deals for women of their culture. Their parents could be strict, but he knew as well as Lamya did that for her they would all but roll over and play dead. He found the idea to be kind of cold and calculating, but he also thought when there's no other way out, then what else could they do.

"I'm sure it's gonna work," she replied.

Grabbing a hold of her brother's neck she planted a lipstick kiss smack in the middle of his forehead. He stayed quiet and watched the both of them carefully. Their eyes were honest, more honest that they have been since the beginning of Lamya's arrival back.

"Well then if you're so sure, then why wait any longer? Why don't we get started on this shopping spree with a clear conscious," he asked.

It seemed a little harsh, but it was the best idea. First of all if they told them after returning from the mall it would seem as if they didn't care at all. If they did it while they were already out, Mrs. Tamimi would be sure that they had all been in on some big plan from the start, which would have been true. What Lamya didn't want to do was be stuck at home with a sit down talk with her parents.

"It's best to do it now. Otherwise I don't think they will ever trust me again. Just promise me that you will plant yourself in the apartment for two straight days, just in case," she winked.

To Salem's knowledge neither parents trusted either daughter too much. The best way someone could tell that they were family was by the negative track records they held in and out of school. Lamya had not been an angel all of her life. It was the reason Salem thought she had the guts to do what she was doing. Walking into the mall the three found a quiet coffee shop where they could give their families a call. Taif was the first to make the call, but saying and then doing were too different things, and as her father picked up the phone she wanted to faint.

"Uh, hi daddy, I didn't wake you up did I," she said nervously.

"It's after twelve, why would you think that I would be sleep. How is your day out with Lamya and Salem by the way," he asked.

She took a deep breath before she opened her mouth. She knew that her parents expected for her to stay in the house with them until she was married. Though she followed their strict rules she could be a hard one to control. That's why they looked at her staying home as their safe net to keep her in place until she was married.

"Actually, the day is going really good. I got this great opportunity to take another job offer with great facilities even better than what I have now," she said.

Her father was always looking for more opportunity for his daughter. She was successful and he believed the more successful she was the more successful her future husband would be. He listened intensely on the phone with a huge smile on his face while he stared at his wife who sat right beside him.

Taif knew what he was thinking, and knew that it was the exact moment to spit out the news.

"I decided to take the job because it pays so much that

I'll be able to move and share a flat with Lamya," she said so fast that her father almost missed her words.

Her father's smile was replaced with distress. Taif's mother knew something was wrong and took the phone from her husband.

"What are you doing now Taif," her mother asked in angry suspicion.

Again with one of the happiest voices she had, in a long time she said that she was moving in with Lamya. Before her mother could get out of her mouth that there was no way she could be moving in with a cousin who was leaving the states, her voice was drowned out by the voice of Lamya. Shocked that Lamya was actually making the call and not having her brother do it, she accidently hung up the phone on her mother.

"Hi mommy, can I talk to both of you? It's really important and I want you both to hear it at the same time," she said.

Both Taif and Salem moved closer to the phone.

"This morning I snuck out with Taif and Salem to go on a job interview. One reason was to do some shopping, but before the shopping I had to go for an interview," she said quivering as if she was going to cry.

"A job interview in the states, I knew you were up to something Lamya, but I didn't know you would go this far. I don't know what's worst imagining you running off to get married or this," her mother said shaking her head.

Lamya was actually doing it, and she seemed quite

convincing.

"You mean my job in Abu Dhabi, the job that I would have to quit when you decided to move back to Morocco? That's the job you're talking about right," she asked waiting for a response.

She was right either way. Her whole world would change just because Salem would be able to provide for them. Salem hadn't thought about it before, maybe she was right. What difference did it make if she was going to be pulled up and uprooted anyway? He could hear his mother putting on a fake cry while screaming the word why over and over. At the same moment their father grabbed the phone taking over the conversation.

"You have a job here? It takes a lot from someone in your field to be able to come here and actually got a position. You had a great position back home so it must be something else. But what will you do here? Salem is not going to always be there to catch you if you fall Lamya," Mr. Tamimi said sincerely.

Lamya shook her head in agreement. She understood that from the beginning.

"It's a good position daddy. Taif and me have decided to move in together and Salem will be right here in the city with us without me bothering him all the time. It will also help set me up for my wedding. I still want to be married, by you, but at least let me have four years of freedom. You can even get me engaged now, but he has to have a western background, and other than that I wouldn't care, honestly," she replied.

With those words the moans of her mother's heart ache

ceased. Her father didn't say anything for a while. He knew it was coming, and if he had to have it come through the hearts of his children, he was okay with it.

"Daddy, are you okay," Lamya asked.

He looked over at his wife as he responded to his daughter.

"So both of our children will be leaving us for a while, but it's for a good reason, and unlike your mother we should be celebrating and thanking Allah for our good fortune," he said reaching over to give his wife a comforting hug.

"So everything is okay. We can talk more later if you want to," she replied.

They had nothing else to say. Lamya closed her cell

phone and slipped it into her purse. She hadn't said goodbye yet, but she could feel that a piece of her heart had been taken from her. She was doing a good thing, and she knew that she would keep her word on the marriage, but it didn't change the feeling. She looked across at Taif who couldn't seem to contain herself.

"So how were your parent's," Lamya asked.

It was then that she remembered that she had hung up on them.

"Oh, you know, they'll be alright by the time I get home, I guess. Doesn't matter, what's done is done; she said shrugging her shoulders as she headed into the mall.

Salem didn't say a word. He just followed the young

princesses and watched as they reveled in their own glory.

14~

DEMONS DANGLE

Saks was the first official point of business. Lamya had been in her field for two years and had saved up more than a few pennies to spend. Party or no party, staying or leaving it was her goal to pick up a few things that couldn't be found back home. Unlike Taif, Lamya was much smaller in build and when in a department always darted toward the junior department with no urge to look anywhere else. The object jeans and the labels were True Religion and Seven. Salem walked the floors as Lamya and

Taif disappeared. Just the sight of clothes gave him more pleasure than one of his mother's best dishes. He wanted to go off on his own, but thought it would be better to at least know where the girls were. Seeing the hand of Taif turn a corner of the dress section he figured Lamya went in the opposite direction. Like their personalities, their taste in clothes was totally different.

"Hey Lamya, where are you," he quietly yelled.

"I'm here," she said waving her hand over a clothes rack.

He followed her to a back rack and noticed an employee dressing a manikin in a mini skirt and a pair of dojo low rise, wide cut jeans. He knew exactly what Lamya would look good in and with the thought beat her to the destination. Usually he tried to hide his real love of clothes from the girls, but in that moment he felt free to express himself for the sake of their perfect look.

"Okay, if you're picking jeans make sure they don't pick you," he said.

Looking over her shoulder she rolled her eyes at his remark. Since they were small kids it was always the same. While she was the math whiz into the Discovery Channel and PBS, he was the popular good looking one, always drawing pictures for the girls and showing off his great football moves. She hated when he gave her advice on style, unless she had directly asked him. Holding up a pair of Seven Dojo, Salem showed his pearly whites that seemed to shimmer at his sister as he smiled. Looking at the jeans she had no choice but to agree with him. Without saying a word she grabbed the jeans and headed for the dressing room.

"You have the jeans but grab some shirts to try them on with," he yelled.

He followed behind her and waited outside of the dressing room for her.

"So Salem, I want to stay here and work for a while, but what is it that you want," she asked.

"Why, what do you mean, he asked.

Pausing before she entered the dressing room she turned, pinched Salem on his cheek and just stared at him for a moment. She wanted him to say something, something fundamentally, important. She wanted him to say something that she had never heard from him before.

"What is it that you want Simi? For example I never

knew that you wanted to be an architect. In-fact I'm sure that none of us knew what you wanted when you started school. Why is that, because the only reason I can figure out is that you never really say what is on your mind, not what's pertaining to you," she said in an almost somber manner.

He didn't know what she was talking about. He always spoke his mind when he needed to and that's all that counted. He pinched her back on the cheek harder than usual and held a tight smile on his face. From the corner of his right eye he saw Taif waving for them to wait up for her. To avoid anymore questioning from his sister he waved for Taif to come over, while urging his sister to finish changing.

"Okay, okay you guys need to get moving because speaking my mind right now I think I want to check some stuff out too. Go and try on the jeans and let me know what you think," he said.

Literally backing out of the situation he did a skip and a hop away from the area darting toward a green fighter jacket that he spotted just walking in. It was his size and he immediately had to try it on. Looking in the mirror it went well white T- shirt, Khaki pants and black converse. Walking around the men's department he thought back on Lamya's question. Brushing his hands across some Sean John jeans he figured he would buy at least one pair. In his mind her questions kept repeating. Strolling on past the jeans into Dulce and Gabbana, on his way to Verace he noticed a couple around his age deciding whether or not to purchase a Polo Ralph Lauren shirt in peach. The girl was sold, but it didn't look like the guy was feeling it. He imagined him and Cherise looking for that shirt. He thought he probably wouldn't have picked the shirt either;

instead he would have gone with a simple white T meshed with some Vineyard Vines patchwork twill shorts he had passed earlier. Grabbing a white T he decided that he needed to help the couple out, while making sure the guy kept his dignity. Along with the white He quickly searched in the polo section for some twill shorts, not exactly vines, but he picked would certainly do the job. Throwing the shirt across his shoulder and holding the pants up to his waist he walked right in between the couple. Posing in front of the mirror he gave himself a big smile, shook his head in agreement and walked away. It always worked, and as he went to hide behind some racks, he proved to be successful again. Taking the hint the guy grabbed a white T and looked around for the shorts in his size. Clinching his fist in victory Salem victoriously threw the outfit aside. Eyeing a Diesel Black Gold contrast blazer he slipped it on while grabbing another style of blazer from the next rack. Checking himself out in the mirror he could hear Taif whispering his name softly across the room. He only wanted fifteen minutes, and with these girls he couldn't even get that. Reluctantly he walked towards the voice and as he came up on a Royal Under Underground Hoodie Blazer, he threw everything else to the side he had collected and through the hoodie over his shoulder. It would be a keeper.

"I'm coming," he whispered back.

Rushing to the dressing room he noticed that Taif's hands were still empty.

"You were so right about those jeans. So, if Seven is her lucky number, do you think that you can find mine some where out here," she asked while batting her eyelashes.

"Alright, let me check out Lamya first" he replied.

It had been some time since he had offered to do something for Taif. Stopping in her tracks she turned suspiciously getting a good look at her cousin's face, which never told her anything, she always had to ask. She heard Lamya earlier, and like his sister she had her own questions. They weren't kids anymore; they should be able to talk like adults she thought. Salem kept following and around the jean section past the shirts, in the back corner stood Lamya. At seeing them she held her hands high. She wore a pale pink sleeveless Taffeta Bow Blouse that went perfect with her jeans. Salem couldn't take his eyes off of her arms.

"The arms are a little floppy, but that's okay" he remarked laughing.

She paid him no mind, to be frank Lamya's arms were more developed than her brothers, and she was proud of them.

"So what do you think about the jeans," she asked.

"Seriously you look great," he smiled.

Lamya reassured herself by looking in the mirror once more.

"This is the outfit for the party," she decided in a matter of fact way while looking at Taif.

Lamya went back to change, and as she did Taif pulled Salem back onto the floor. She searched through the items with her eyes, but seemed over whelmed with the choices. Pushing her towards the skirts Salem picked out a La Via 18 Jaquard Matelasse skirt. It was black and made it easier for him to pair it with something else. He looked for the perfect blouse in the sea of clothes and was able to find the perfect silk chiffon denim print blouse.

"Hey, I know this seems to be over whelming, but snap out of it and try these on," he said.

Passing Lamya on the way to the dressing room, Taif's hands full of goodies almost made Lamya want to look a little more.

"Wow, I like it," she said squinting her eyes at her brother.

She didn't want to wait around and signaled that she would be at Cafe SFA where they could meet her. Salem found her move to be the Lamya he knew. Why should she wait around on Taif when her outfit was already set? Holding his hands up for an explanation as she disappeared around the corner, he realized that he would be by himself with Taif. It didn't take long for Taif to change and when she stepped out of the dressing room she looked like a different person. She was hot, she knew it, and she knew her cousin who was standing alone knew it. Grabbing his face and giving him a big kiss on the cheek, she wished she had made the move and kissed him on the lips instead.

"I'm starting to think that you just might be a genius. Salem, this outfit is awesome. Get me some heels and I'm ready," she almost screamed.

Putting his hands on her shoulder he tried to calm. He tugged at her blouse to adjust it and had to admit that she looked amazing too.

"Why is it that you haven't got married," he asked.

Taif had waited for that question for what seemed to be all of her life.

"Because I've been waiting for you," she said while trying to press the wrinkles out of her skirt.

One thing was for sure is that Salem would never let that happen. He appreciated the compliment but decided to get himself as far away from the subject as possible.

"Really, other than me with all of those big fish out there, why aren't you married," he asked again.

In her heart she knew that he wouldn't be the one either, but it never hurt for her to keep trying.

"Look at me. I may talk the talk, but I haven't, you know walked the walk. Come on my firsthand account of any male action has only been through the experiences of my experienced girl friends. Plus I feel like I've been in a cage all of my life, and being married right now would make it even worse, unless you waited for me. I'm totally with your sister. I can be engaged no problem, but give me a couple of years to at least spend time with me, to figure who I am away from my parents expectations. So your question about me just leads me to you. Forget marriage how come you don't at least have someone in your life," she asked sincere in the questioning.

She didn't know it but he had someone on his mind and in his life.

'It's not like we ever hang around each other you know. I f you were so interested in meeting guys you could have took the effort and hung out with me and some of my friends. You know I wouldn't have mind," he replied.

It was Taif's family that Lamya stayed with when she was in the states. Many times they had invited Taif to join in on their weekend escapades and most of the time she had refused. She was going through the phase of being the good Muslim girl. In reality she was punishing herself for letting Karem Tibbs, Marshall Pierce, and Cole Brandon get to second base with her, when she didn't get any satisfaction out of it at all.

"Well, yeah, but I would see you around with your other friends and usually you were alone," she said.

"Don't worry, I have a life and have had a life, " he replied turning and looking at more jeans on the rack.

He always answered questions this way as if turning his back on the person talking to him would stop them from asking more questions.

Taif didn't know why, but turning his back to her just made her enquire more. There was another reason she never really pushed the issue of her attraction to Salem.

"So what's your type," she asked.

Salem paused going through the jeans. It was a good question. He had never thought about it before.

"Good one. I don't think I have a particular taste," he said.

"You know I kind of figured that. Don't know why, but I got you," she said.

Salem felt that he had to explain himself even though he didn't have an explanation. It made him think or rather Taif made him think.

"I don't think I look as much on the outside as I do on the inside," he said surprisingly.

"You're a guy and you're saying you only look at the inside," she asked.

He didn't have to think about it. It was true. Cherise was the only one who attracted him with not only her inside, but first her looks. It's why he couldn't think about anything else but sleeping with her even though his first thought was to just to get to know her.

"Yeah, looks usually are not important," he replied.

Taif looked her cousin up and down. A guy like him didn't come around every day, and guys like him didn't look past a girl's big nose or beady eyes.

"You know most guys that make that statement don't like girls. They would rather play on their own team," she said with a wink.

Salem's face turned red. It was the first time Taif was talking so openly, and the first time he felt like really strangling her.

"Every guy is not the same you know. If you meet the right person instead of psychologically hiding in la la land you'll find out what I'm talking about." he replied.

"Salem I didn't mean anything by it, I'm just going with how I feel. So you're not gay, and you're not shy. I've bet you've had a lot of adventures then," she asked.

She wanted know even though she thought she had it all figured out.

"You know your friend Shaikha," he asked.

"Shaikha, Baloushi," Taif asked.

"Yeah, ask her what she thinks about me other than the fact that I had to keep away from her after she started stalking me. This stays between me and you okay," he replied.

Taif considered herself five times better looking than Shaikha and instantly felt jealous that Shaikha got a taste of her dream man. Her first instincts were to call her up for a mall visit so she could beat the hell out of her, but her second thought was that it was best to just let sleeping dogs lie.

"Well, if she was that satisfied we better keep it to ourselves. We wouldn't like such a juicy cat to get out the bag, would we," she replied with a wink.

It was with her own response that she realized she had to start seeing Salem not even as her cousin, but instead her brother. It was probably due to the fact that her last remark made him frown up as if Iron Man had just struck him in the stomach. It sort of bought her spirits down. She hadn't had a date in a while, and realizing that she couldn't even bag a cousin just made the situation all the more dire. She began remembering the last real attachment she had to the opposite sex. She was sixteen and her best friend Alia was moving to Chicago. Alia had a brother, freckled face Asif, who was just a year older than his sister. He had a big crush on Taif. The day before leaving he rushed over to her place to say good-bye without his sister. Taif hated him, but on that day he bought with him a single rose, her favorite chocolates and a small silver canteen of his parent's best tequila. It was the end of exam week and her parents were away being a part of a three-day wedding ceremony in Jersey, trusting to leave their daughter at home for the first time. Lured by the chocolates she offered him to come in and watch television with her. Stuffing herself with chocolate she decided to take a swallow of the tequila, and after three shots decided that if she ever drank again she would make sure that tequila would be her life time choice. They were both buzzed and the boys buzz gave him the guts to give her a kiss on the lips, the kiss in turn gave her the need to try French kissing for the first time. They found themselves two hour laters wrapped in her mother's Persian rug within each other's arms naked and embarrassed. Though it would seem that the two would have had sex, unfortunately the boy had an immature penis, barely allowing him to hold it to pee. It was after that experience that she went through a short phase where she believed beyond a doubt that men were just put on earth to carry things, and just the perfect girl could satisfy those lustful urges. Her reality was not pretty to her at that moment, and heading back to the dressing room she quickly changed hoping that meeting up with Lamya would change her mood.

The main part of their shopping goal was done and Salem thought it would be a good gesture to let the two busy bodies meet Cherise, so he gave her a call.

"Hi, what are you up too," he asked.

"Nothing, just doing some odds and ends," she giggled.

"Could you come and maybe hang out the mall for a few? I thought it would be nice if you met some friends of mine he said winking at the girls who had leaned across the table trying to figure out who he was talking to.

"Okay, is it okay for me to bring a friend along," she asked.

He would have preferred that she came alone but what could he have said?

"Of course," he replied.

Hanging up the phone he gave the two nosey girls a smile.

"Who was that," Taif asked almost blown away for fear that Salem was getting ready to prove that he was social with someone.

On the other end of the phone Cherise thought the mall visit was a good idea. Throwing Erick a bag of open chips she rushed him to put on his shoes and join her. Running upstairs she threw on some brown fatigues, a sleeveless white fitted T-shirt and some flip flops for ultimate relaxation.

"So Mr. Silence what do you think about Salem," she asked.

Looking like her evil twin he decided to wear sneakers with his fatigues.

"There's really not much to say seeing that most of the time I just saw him with his tongue down your throat," he said with a sneaky smile.

"Erick, you know that's not true," she replied.

"Well, you didn't even introduce us to him properly. What does he do? Where in the world is he from by the way," he asked.

"Well, he's from Morocco. He's not a future architecture, but a fresh out of school architecture that already has the job," she replied.

"Hey, whatever makes you happy. I just hope this one doesn't lead you down the love express for a year and then break your heart afterwards like the last one, that's all," he said opening the door for her.

"You know I must be the only one in the world who has four roommates that are literally like my second family," she replied.

"Let me ask you something. Why do you keep going after these artsy guys? I'm an artist and I know how I think and there aren't many guys that are too different from me no matter what way they swing, especially the guys. We're like little boys that never grew up. We live in our own made up world of art, and we really don't care about what others think."

"What, you'd rather me go back to your cheating brother, " she asked.

"This has nothing to do with my brother," he said trying hard not to laugh.

"Whatever you meant, I'm just saying I can't stay alone forever. It was time for me to go on with someone else and Salem came along at the right time," she replied.

Mentioning Salem's name made Erick pause. Catching the taxi he thought back to the night that Salem came over to visit.

"So what do you know about this guys past dating history? I mean do we know anyone he's been with before," he asked.

"Damn, what kind of question is that? I try to make it my business not to ask about their past business. It kind of makes things run a little smoother. Beside what do I care he's not with whoever anymore he will definitely be with me," she said with wink.

Erick didn't say another word, instead he took a white hanker chef out of his pocket laid rested his back on the seat and covered his face with it. Taxi time was always naptime where Erick was concerned.

Finishing up their coffees the Tamimi's decided to take a run of the main mall before the others arrived. Having already chosen their outfits they had time to relax and just fool around. Express for men was their first stop. Skipping

the women's department they directed Salem to men's

section. Right away Salem was attracted by a half bodied

black mannequin dressed in a beige and white sweater. He

wanted to collect more sweaters for work and thought it

would be a good fit in his wardrobe. Behind the mannequin

were two other guys. One was about the same height as

Salem and his back was towards Salem as he decided to put

on the same sweater. He wore True Religion jeans making

it the perfect match. There was a mirror to the left of Salem

and the Mannequin the man took a look in the mirror. The

reflection revealed a dark haired man with a close shaven

beard to match. His complexion was olive, but his facial

features were broad, and chiseled between high sunken

cheeks. Salem watched as he put his hands in his pockets

turning from one side to the other, while looking back at his

friend for advice.

"Feel my speed, you cookie stealers," the man with sweater said.

"That's no cookie stealer, and if you really want people to feel your speed, you best not get anything from express. Everyone will be wearing it," his friend remarked.

Listening closely to the conversation Salem barely noticed Taif tapping him on his shoulder.

"So, thinking about getting that sweater or not," she asked.

Turning to Taif he watched out of the corner of his eyes as they spun around excitedly in front of the mirror.

"No, just looking around," he said.

Wanting to escape Taif for a moment he walked to the back of the store looking at a jacket that was clearly not his taste. Hearing Lamya's voice he sought her out and signaled for Taif to follow. He needed a new scene and decided to lead the girls to Puma. Though he considered himself a slave to Adiddas, Puma always had an item that would blow his mind. As they walked up the display window seemed to be alive with the new items that decorated it. It was either that or the DJ that stood in between them blasting some Kid Cuddie, while he sported his on Puma ensemble. Two disco balls flashed colored fluorescent lights above them, drawing people like magnets to the store. This was something new for Lamya. Four years ago she probably wouldn't even have known what Puma was, and then there she stood watching a DJ play the latest hits in a retail window. She pushed through both Taif and Salem as she rushed to the door, fighting to get in like she had a back stage pass to the Black Eye Peas. She seemed so excited about the store that it gave Salem an idea. Skipping the men's section he pretended to browse the women's bags and shoes. He watched as Lamya eyed the various choices of baby blue track pants racked with pale purple and white dry fit shirts. Picking a rack opposite of hers he grabbed two sweat suits, one black and the other burgundy. He handed the Black to Taif and the Burgundy to Lamya.

"So, why don't you try these on and show um how we do it back home," he asked.

Grabbing a pair of shoes the girls dressed quickly and came out to show off to one another.

"Hey, let's g practice our moves for party night," Taif said.

Pulling Lamya towards the retail window Taif danced provocatively as someone like Taif could, while her cousin Lamya moved side to side shyly because her brother was present. Salem followed them to the window. He watched as the girls giggled about a half monkey half man tattooed on the right shoulder of his arm.

"Why do you have this funny tattoo on your arm," Lamya asked.

The DJ was waiting for it. His tattoo had become like its on conversation piece without him even having to try.

"You really want to know," the DJ asked.

"She didn't ask to be funny. She really wants to know," Taif replied with an attitude the DJ could respect.

"It's a symbol of life for people like me," he replied.

"People like you," Taif rebutted.

"Ha ha, yeah, at night I'm the DJ girls love to flirt with. During the day I'm the guy that everyone likes, and I mean everyone. Sometimes I just can't figure out which way is straight being pulled from all sides, if you know what I mean," he winked.

Taif was revolted by his response, but Lamya on the other hand couldn't keep her eyes off of him afterwards. Like the Tattoo he had a funny look to him, but one that made people not want to look away. His nose was not long, but slender and sharp on the end. His nostrils were not big, but turned up almost into his cheeks. His lips were short and thick. They were almost red in color standing out in comparison to the brown skin that he had. His rosy high cheekbones led straight to his eyes that were slanted and grey in color. The ends of his eyes led to his wide loopy black curls worn short on his head just covering his ears which were pointed in shape. As Lamya swooned over him he watched her brother looking out the glass door. People rushed in from outside as the DJ decided to let the record spin by itself. Jumping off the corner of the stage he used Salem's shoulders to hop down.

"Life is for living, not hiding in the shadows. Besides that tail will show sooner or later," he whispered to Salem as he sprinted out the door.

Just like that he was gone. Lamya watched him intensely, but never figured out where he went, and as he disappeared Cherise appeared around the same corner the DJ turned in to. The look she was sporting was different than Salem was use to. He liked it. Smiling from ear to ear, she guessed right away that the two girls that stood excitedly near him had to be family.

"Hi, I'm Cherise. Nice to meet you," she said.

Pushing Lamya out of the way Taif grabbed Cherise's hand.

"I'm Taif and who exactly are you," Taif replied crossed.

Grabbing the arm of Salem and locking her arm within his, she gave Taif a heart-warming smile.

"I know Salem," Cherise expressed as she looked up at him.

To Taif, Cherise seemed sure of herself and she hated

her for it. Walking around her slowly she looked her up and down. Her smile revealed sparkling white teeth. Her shoulders were slightly muscular and tight as if she worked out every day, and she didn't have a piece of hair out of place. She was perfect Taif thought. She also thought about Timbaland's single "One and Only," where the bridge went, "Wipe that smile off your fucking face." A sudden since of glee came over her at the thought and as she stopped in front of Cherise again and she gave her what she considered her most unfriendly smile to date. If she couldn't say anything out loud, at least she could think it.

"So your Salem's girlfriend," she asked, still hoping the answer would be no.

Cherise looked over at Salem. He nodded his head in agreement to Taif's questions. This in turn made Taif feel like an idiot seeing that it was her nosy question that seemed to have sealed the fated deal.

"Ha, we knew something was up. Especially when you would disappear for a day or two," Lamya replied.

"Actually I was just hanging out with other friends most of the time Lamya not Cherise," Salem replied.

He wanted to stop the missing in action conversation from continuing any further.

"Oh, you mean your friend Mitch," Lamya asked.

Mitch was certainly Salem's boy, but when he heard his name coming out of his sister's mouth, he immediately got angry. The only thing his mind went back to was his dream.

"You met Mitch? How," he asked with a snapping

voice.

"What's wrong with you? I didn't actually meet him, but when he came looking for you that morning he had breakfast with dad. I just peeped my head out of the bedroom door to see what was going on. From what I saw he's the typical Salem type," she giggled looking over at Cherise.

His anger slipped away as he loosened the tight grip he held on Cherise's hand.

"What Lamya means to say is that we know about most of the friends Salem has," Taif said.

Wanting to walk right out of their lives of all of them, Taif turned to leave, but was stopped by a guy he walked right up to her and grabbed her by the waist.

"Hi," the man said as if he knew her.

"Uh, Erick why do you always do that? Hey you guys this is my friend Erick. Erick this is Salem's family," Cherise said.

The tuff boy look of Erick's drew Taif right back to the group with a smile larger than the round rimmed glasses that sat on her face.

"Erick huh, I think it's nice to meet you," Taif replied.

Moving away from Taif Erick walked up to Cherise and put his arm around her waist and with that Salem's energy went from red bull running to crappy brown. He wondered of all friends why did she have to bring Erick along. Embarrassed at his unusual mood Cherise pulled away from him. Disgusted that he was even present Salem felt it was time that they make a move. Taking Cherise's hand he pulled her away from Erick and led the group towards Bloomingdales. It was a place he hoped all the girls would enjoy, and he thought if Erick were any kind of gentlemen, he would just have to roll with the rest of them.

It didn't take long for Cherise to take Salem's mind off of Erick. As the girls ran in different directions Chersie turned to Salem and Erick

"I hope you don't think you were going to sneak away did you," she asked giving them a sneaky smile.

Erick wanted to sneak away as Taif snuck up behind him and grabbed him by the hands, while Cherise draped both of them with women's scarves. Satisfied with their creative art Cherise gave Salem a kiss on the cheek and the two caught up with Lamya, who was checking out purses.

From afar Salem could see that the items were colorful and extremely shiny. Gold bracelets and necklaces were their next focus and as they adorned themselves Salem imagined the three of them dancing to the music of the Nut Cracker with their stage being Erick's nuts. The thought gave him extreme pleasure as he imagined Cherise floating through the air bouncing harshly up and down on the tips of her toes, while grinding her nails in the flesh of his scrotum as she twirled effortlessly in a sheer pale pink dress draped in gold earrings and bracelets. He began to sway in rhythm with her dance, until Erick tapped him on his back.

"You know what I just realized where I know you from," Erick said as he pointed at Salem.

Annoyed that he had ruined his divine visual, he couldn't keep his mouth shut a minute longer.

"What are you talking about man," Salem asked.

'Hell Bent, you were there with a group of friends of mine the other night," Erick replied.

"What, Hell Bent, what is that," Salem asked.

Erick gave him devious smile. It was as if he had discovered some dark deep secret and couldn't wait to use it against him somehow.

"Hell Bent? There is an underground club, literally in the tunnels of the subway. There's no way you could forget going anywhere near that place," Erick said.

"Oh, I never knew the name of the place," Salem replied.

Erick shook his head.

"I know you were too clean cut to actually be true," he replied.

"What do you mean," Salem replied.

Erick looked him straight in the eyes, looking for any type of unusual movement that may have signaled that he was lying, but he couldn't find it.

"So you really don't remember anything? You were pretty quiet when you got there, it was after the juice that you just went wild man," he said laughing.

The conversation had become weird for Salem and with every word that came out of Erick's mouth it didn't seem to him as if it would get any better.

"It was late night and I was out before that. It's hard to remember anything," Salem replied.

"So you wouldn't know if you were doing things that you usually wouldn't ha," Erick asked.

Salem was speechless.

"I don't know, but I do know that you don't know me or what I would or wouldn't do," he replied pushing his finger into Erick's chest.

"Calm down, I guess that mean you remember them all giving you group kiss good night then, uh," he asked pushing for an answer with a dirty smile.

"WHAT," Salem replied sheepishly.

"Yeah, man. I guess the pink fuck got you real good uh," Erick asked.

"The what," Salem asked again.

"The juice man, you don't remember the juice I handed you," Erick's smile widened.

And then it hit him. He looked at Erick closely. He didn't remember his face, but he did remember his dirty smile.

"You're the bartender," Salem asked.

"Yep, bartender by late night, rocker in the early night. You see the juice usually brings out those things people just don't want others to see. From what I saw you were a changed man that night," he laughed.

From across the room Lamya yelled for the guys to join them. Salem stared at Erick intensely. He was afraid that maybe he had made out with another girl that night.

"If something went on I can't remember, and if I can't remember it couldn't have been that bad. So if you think you have something on me you don't. I was just getting to know Cherise that same night. So if you don't mind, instead of haten, can't you just let things go," Salem asked aggressively.

Erick was beginning to believe him, and wanting to tell him something else he reached out to grab a hold of his arm just as Taif interrupted.

"Okay you guys seemed to be getting too comfy here. Let's go see if we can grab something to eat, and Erick you can tell me what your favorite foods are on the way," she smiled grabbing her cousin's hand and looking back, giving Erick an open mouth wink. It was beginning to become her signature flirt move.

"Food sounds really good about now," Erick replied passing both Taif and Salem to search for a good place.

Salem watched as Erick walked away. He noticed that he was a little shorter than himself. In- fact he seemed so short, that he imagined picking him up with just two fingers, balding him up like a piece of paper and throwing him in the nearest trash can. The thought put another smile on his face as he followed in line with the rest of them.

Grateful that the smell of piping hot chicken gave him a since of comfort, he sat next to Erick who was forced to sit next to Taif, while Cherise sat in between the girls. The food came fast and grabbing the first piece Salem took his time biting into the moist fried thigh that almost burned the tips of his fingers. He closed his eyes for the first bite, and as he opened them to spectate on the second bite he could feel Erick staring at him.

"So you and Cherise are actually a couple of some sort now, and you're not dating anyone else," Erick asked Salem.

By that time the question was out of context to what everyone else was talking about at the table. Silence swept among them and Salem felt uncomfortable.

"Yeah, why are you asking," Salem replied.

Though she thought it was a good question, she also wondered what business it was of Erick's.

"Oh, I don't know. You know how us guys always seemed to have something we're hiding," he replied.

The curls behind Salem's ears seemed to tighten, as he grew red with frustration.

"Unless there's another one of me running around somewhere, no I'm not SEEING anyone," he replied with a forceful voice.

Erick didn't say anything instead he nodded in response to Salem's remark, but stared at Salem's sister as if he still had something to say. Salem still couldn't figure out what exactly Erick was getting at, but the look he gave his sister made him more than a little anxious. He began to go over the events of that night again. They were scattered. He remembered snippets like raising his glass in a cheer to new friendships. From the ringing of the glasses, the sound bought back a flash of him singing and dancing on a stage. He began to remember that it was a slow melody with a dark tone, and then that was it. He remembered waking up and stumbling out of the place. He felt as if he was stuck in some sort of time warp. Realizing where he was he noticed that he was the individual of interest at the table. Cherise seemed to believe him, but he felt in the pit of his stomach that the Tamimi doublement twins thought other wise. Luckily Lamya broke the silence.

"Anyone up for a movie," she asked.

"I'm up for whatever. Maybe another activity will melt some of the ice forming here," Taif replied clutching her bottom lip while looking over anxiously at Erick.

"Alright, I was just trying to be a good friend that's all. You never know what's in a person's collection box," he whined.

15~

SUSPICION LINGERS AND TEMPTATIONS

AWAIT

That night the three Tamimis decided to take their

resting place on the couch. Lying on his back Salem dared

not to move for fear that he would wake the others. He

needed sometime alone. With his hands behind his head he

looked up at the ceiling. Closing his eyes he went back to

the night of Hell Bent again. The same memories seemed to

run through his head over and over again. He became

frustrated by the fact that he couldn't remember anything

else, and refusing to accept the fact, he quietly got up and tiptoed away from the girls. He thought back and he remembered anytime he had gone out in the past, the next day there were remnants of his own goings on. He remembered one night drinking so much that the next morning he woke up with one of Mitch's ties tide around his head and someone's jeans wrapped firmly around his waste. There had to be something in his room he thought. Digging through the closet, looking under the bed and eventually checking the contents in each and everyone of his shoes, he had begun to give up. Time was ticking away and still he had found nothing. Sitting on the bed he thought for a moment. He could hear someone walk into the bathroom. Footsteps could be heard passing h is room and continuing into the kitchen. Frantic he began to look into the pockets of the pants he wore that night. Reaching deep he grabbed his wallet. It was the one place he would shove every, and anything as long as it would fit, but he couldn't find a thing. Finally he grabbed his wallet and started to check any place he could slide something in, but still he didn't find anything. Getting ready to put the wallet away, he thought that he would check the small front pocket sewed into the wallet. He felt it from the outside, but it felt empty, still he decided to reach inside and surprisingly pulled out what seemed to be scrap papers and some business cards. The scrapped papers revealed numbers of former classmates and a few club girls who he never got around to contacting. And then after flipping through what he thought was his last business card, the back revealed that there was a slightly smaller card stuck to it. It was designed with a black background, which contained red writing reading Hell Bent. The words were designed to run down the card like drops of blood from the fangs of a vampire. Detaching it from it's mother card, the back of the card had a white background with basic font in black, informing of the days and times of operation. At the bottom was the title bar tender and the name Erick B. Underneath his name written in black ink was a personal number. He could hear footsteps down the hall. Clearing the throat to adjust to the morning air Salem knew that it was his father. Reading the number over and over he quickly checked his phone to see if any of his saved numbers matched up, but had no luck. From the kitchen he could hear the water running and the smell of coffee forced him to inhale the fresh scent. He decided to shove the cards back into their former place leaving the Hell Bent card on the top of the pack. The number was in his head and all he wanted to do at that point was make a call, but had know idea what he would have said. After the scent of coffee, Lamya's voice screeched past his ears like finger nails across a chalkboard. The call would definitely have to wait.

After a day of lounging and more family visits with the news of the girls future plans, Salem's place was busier than it had ever been. By three Taif and the guest had left. It was only the four Tamimi's at that point, and three of the four were literally worn out. This didn't stop them from nagging Salem, and finally he felt that he needed some fresh air. Salem told the family that he had to make room for any of Lamya's things that needed to be stored while she returned to Abu Dhabi. He gave a call to Alice wandering if it was okay for him to drop in, but she was out with Renee. She always thought of Salem as the brother she never had, and the brother she never had to be obligate to cater to, so any time he asked she was ready to oblige giving him permission to do as he wanted that day, as long as he locked up afterwards. Alice didn't party much, but when she did, her speed for fun was alcohol central. The reality was that memories of this fun were sometimes left behind, along with her purse and the keys that resided in them. It had gotten so bad that many of the other tenants in the building began to believe that she was some sort of vagrant. At one point she was caught sleeping in front of her apartment door. The surrounding tenants called the police, and clapped as she was awakened and taken down town to be booked. After that she was forced to leave an extra key with someone she could completely trust, Renee and Salem were just those people.

He hadn't been alone for some time and unlocking the door to Alice's place seemed to lift his spirits. He was always very careful when walking into her apartment. She kept it spotless and always seemed to notice when something had been taken out of it's original place. He felt a little uncomfortable even flopping onto her couch though he knew that was probably the safest place for him to hang. He just wanted too breath, so for about fifteen minutes he sat thinking of nothing, just enjoying the silence, and then he thought about the number. He decided that he didn't want to sit down to make the call so he went into the kitchen. While her living room was dressed with brown leather couches, and leather end tables to match, her kitchen was like visiting a farm wife's kitchen in Kansas. He hated it, but he did love the island. It was something about having a center in the place where you were nourished. Marble pound cake sat on the kitchen counter. A piece had already been cut, so he didn't think it would matter much if cut himself piece. Hoping up on one of the island stools he pulled out his phone. Trying to think of what to say whatever the scenario he paused. Nothing came to his head as he took the card out of his wallet. He already had the number in his head, but figured he would take the card out just incase. Flipping the card on the counter once or twice he decided to dial. Listening to the phone ring one, two and finally three times, a familiar, yet unfamiliar voice picked up on the other end.

"Yeah, who is it," the voice asked.

Salem was silent for a moment. He didn't expect anyone to pick up so fast and still had no idea of what to say.

"So are you gonna say something or continue letting those well paid minutes slip away," the voice asked.

"Hey, so I don't mean to rude, but this is Salem Tamimi. Do I know you," he asked.

"Uhm, I just gave up on you calling all together. What, did you just happen to run up on my number somewhere? First you leave without even a good bye and now you have no idea who I am," it figures the voice replied.

"The voice was genderless it seemed to Salem. He didn't want to make anymore mistakes yet he couldn't figure out whether it was a male or female.

"I'm so sorry, but the only thing I can remember is going to the place and waking up the next morning alone trying find my way back to the surface," he said.

"You don't remember," the voice asked.

"No, nothing," Salem replied.

"In the background he could hear what sounded like soft music and other people talking.

"And do you want to remember," the voice asked.

Salem really didn't want to know anything other than the fact that not only was the number someone's other than Erick's, but Erick's number was on the phone too. Being puzzled before now made him feel like a fool.

"Yeah, of course," he said.

"Then okay. I really can't talk now, but why don't we meet up some time," the voice asked.

He was clueless to what would happen, but had no choice. He decided that Times Square was public enough. He didn't know why, but he thought the night before graduation would be the best time. Wrapping up the plan he could hear a key being put in the door.

"So I'll see you Friday at the square 12 noon, okay," Salem replied.

Hanging up the phone he felt as if he had butterflies in his stomach. He had to ignore it. What ever happened now was pretty much out of his hands.

Alice walked in as motherly as ever. Even though they were around the same age Salem couldn't help but to think of her as someone who some where had to be hiding a couple of crumb snatchers. He told her once what he thought, and for two weeks every time she would get drunk she would bring the subject up giving him an evil eye that was never forgotten. It got so bad that it made him feel guilty enough to make out with her one night. That turned out to be a bad move, because as son as Alice realized it was Salem she was kissing, she nearly knocked him across the bar. Her smile walking into the apartment took his mind off of the left-handed hook she planted on him. It was the day off for Alice and she was satisfied with hanging with her day with Renee, whining about her men problems.

"So are you here because you love me too much or because your family is driving you up the wall," she asked.

Still having the feeling of butterflies in his stomach, Alice's voice made him feel better.

"You got it," in a small apartment it gets a little bit cramped sometimes. Plus I needed to speak with Cherise," he said.

"Huh, huh, so your over here talking up a little some thing, some thing," she laughed.

Sarcasm was the way that Alice communicated best. She was always real, but it was as if sarcasm was a mask for something else.

"Yeah, and too bad I just got off the phone with her. So you'll just have to wait to see what you're missing next time around," he laughed back.

He knew how Alice loved her space, so he thought it was best that he headed out.

"Well, I was just getting ready to leave, so you can have your girl layer back," he said.

"No problem, you know you can come over anytime, unless I'm sleeping. A girl needs her beauty sleep you know," she replied.

Heading out the door he stopped for a moment.

"Why is it that you guys don't invite me over more," he asked.

"I don't know. All you have to do is invite yourself. I didn't know you were that big on hanging with the girls. Don't fear though, because if you're serious, Friday night is scrabble night at my place," she replied.

He had opened his big mouth, and he was in whether he wanted to be or not. After closing the door he knew that in less than a minute Alice would be on the phone to Renee, letting her know about the new development.

16~

Communication Keeps Inner Harmony

It was Wednesday and graduation day was near. As the days grew closer he could see that the smile, which seemed to be glued on his mother's face grew dimmer. He knew that most of this had to do with him staying behind, and add that with the news of Lamya, it had to be a double heartbreak for. Before he walked back into the place he figured that it would be smart to actually check the storage, while moving boxes around he received a call from Mitch.

"Where the hell have you been man," Mitch asked.

The sound of Mitch's voice put a smile on his face. It felt secure hearing from here. In the weeks earlier he thought it would good to keep a little distance, and for a moment Cherise gave him the perfect excuse. Unlike Mitch he didn't have much time to play around and would have to focus on his new job. Everything seemed to come easier for Mitch and sometimes his good friend would forget that everyone wasn't really created equal in the intelligence category.

"The same as you man. Catching up with family and trying to get this girl," Salem replied.

The player of players was always ready for any conversations when it came to women, and he had a special interest in how Salem was doing with Cherise.

"Ahh shit, so is there any action at all going on man, or are you still just trying," he asked.

"I'm saying we spent some time out openly with my sister and cousin. I have to admit I got a kiss in here and there. I think it's going good since she agreed that we could start calling each other a couple," he replied laughing.

"It's good it's okay for someone," Mitch sighed.

For Mitch that meant one thing, the excitement over his present love interest had dried up. Since freshman year Mitch had two problems when it came to women. One was that he was like a magnet and women attracted to him like flies, and two, Mitch would hide the fact that though he acted as if he was player, in reality the guy had a heart of gold. The problem was to cover the fact when it came to women he would choose the worse of the litter. For instance, before Michelle, he dated a girl named Sadie. She graduated the year before and paid for her education by stripping. He loved the fact that he could go and see her at anytime and everyone knew she was his. The headache would come in when they went out during the day and guys would come up to her expecting her to give them an afternoon lap dance. Michelle was another story though. She was perfect. She worked a nine to five, and went to classes at night when it was possible. She cooked for him, and even ironed his clothes so that everyday of the week all he had to do was wake up and jump into them.

"What's wrong man? Michelle really seems to have your best interest in heart," he replied.

"You think? Anyway I broke it off. It's done, over," he replied.

"You know Michelle is good for you. She's an engineer

man and she graduated in three years. I mean I could do without that white accent, but other than that she's perfect! What else is there," Salem asked.

"For her not to force me to meet her parents and not to talk to me as if she were my parents. You know those small things that make you think you're already married without that certain certificate," he replied.

"Is it really that bad? It's not like she can make you do anything. It's all up to you," Salem said.

"You know, I've been thinking how it is that I let the guy who gets the least booty give me any advice. I'm not scared of marriage. I think when it's time it's time, but for some reason even though she seems to be the perfect package. I really don't think she's the package for me. I can't even see her having my kids, and I thought you were supposed to see that shit. Trust me she ain't the one," he said.

"I'll tell you what. Let's do it like we use to, just with some extra people around us," Salem said.

While talking on the phone with Mitch, Salem received a text from Renee:

"You got your wish B-i-t-c-h, tipsy scrabble at my place, nine tomorrow night."

"What you got up your sleeve," Mitch asked.

"I know it's not your type of thing, but I just got an invite tomorrow night to some friends gathering. It's called Tipsy Scrabble night," he said almost hating to say it.

"Are you kidding me? For real, scrabble night," Mitch

whined.

"Hey you know it's not called Tipsy Scrabble for nothing. Two or three of them are good friends. They might not be your type, but you may just surprise yourself. Plus I haven't met their extended group of friends yet, it might be worth the hang," Salem said.

"Fine, but what get's my mind off of this situation now," he asked.

"Don't you have some game or something you can develop," Salem asked.

"I got a little somethin, somethin I'm working on, but you know I can't create when stuff like this is on my mind," he said.

"Just kidding man, I know. Come and hang out with the

family. We'll be waiting," he said.

"That' my man. I'm heading over now," Mitch said hanging up the phone before Salem could say good-bye.

Stepping back out of the closet he was amazed at how much work he had gotten done. He walked back into the apartment, but promised himself that he would avoid all contact with his mother and let Lamya deal with it. What Salem didn't factor in was that Lamya had so much on her mind, that the fact that her mother was throwing a hissy fit didn't bother her at all.

An hour before Mitch was to come Salem looked around his place. For the past several weeks his apartment was more like home than home itself. The idea was to hide any traces of home, by turning it back into a bachelor's pad. Rearranging the furniture and giving it that sloppy feel,

Salem was feeling comfortable again. He told his family who would be visiting and from that point on his mother fluttered around the kitchen nervously. It wasn't Mitch that made her nervous, but the tight connection that he and her husband seemed to have after his first visit. It wasn't that she didn't like Mitch. In fact she thought that he seemed to be a pretty nice person. The thing that bothered her was that he was western and her husband seemed to drool at anything western. He had already asked Salem if it were okay for him to join in on the fun, and of course Salem happily said yes. Slamming a bowl of Doritos onto the kitchen table, she took a peak into the living room where her husband and son seemed to be lovingly setting up the PS3 system. While Mrs. Tamimi was struggling with her own special demons, Lamya was finishing up filling the empty space with items she would need on her return from the U.A.E. She looked a mess and locking the storage door she hurried back to the apartment to make herself look at least presentable.

"So you're sure he's staying for the rest of the night," Mrs. Tamimi asked.

Both men could hear the tension in her voice, but neither of them seemed to care. To them she was always the same when it came to the east colliding the west. Even being in another environment wouldn't do much to sway her stubborn ways.

"Yep, he's a good friend and it's kind of this habit that we have," Salem said without turning his head.

Mr. Tamimi was excited and still fiddling with the system, he dared not to look back at his wife, but Mrs. Tamimi could read him like a book and all the happiness he showed was like a bee sting to her heart. He knew this, but didn't really care. During his life he had done a lot of settling down for her and thought, maybe just maybe it was time for her to stop being so guarded, and open up for him.

An hour later there was a knock at the door. Usually Mitch would just walk in, but with Salem having family over he wanted to give the best impression he could. A week earlier Mr. Tamimi purchased his first pair of kaki colored parachute shorts, with a white short sleeve polo. Slipping into his Pacific Sun Wear flip-flops he ran to greet Mitch at the door.

"What's going on Mr. Tamimi. Long time no see," Mitch said giving Mr. Tamimi a manly hug.

Trying to register what Mitch said, he just smiled, returned his hug and welcomed him inside. By the time the door shut Mitch had already charmed Mrs. Tamimi with a gift of a single red rose. While everyone else seemed to know his or her places when it came to Mitch, Lamya didn't have a clue. She hadn't really shared the same room with a male that wasn't some how connected to her family, she also wanted to be modest, but not boring. She decided to wear some black scrubs and a long sleeve grey t-shirt underneath. As she walked out into the living room, though no one seemed to have anything to complain about, her mother was keen on reminding her where her place was in the family.

"Lamya can you come and help me with the food please," Mrs. Tamimi said solemnly.

Walking into the kitchen she wandered if her mother was as angry as she looked.

"What, why are you looking at me like that? You know

this is the life your going to be leading one day. You might as well get use to it now. Just finish putting the food on the table and go ahead and join the rest of them," she huffed as she spoke.

She may have agreed to have an arranged marriage, but she didn't agree that it would be any eastern bullhead with the intention of locking her away for life. She knew what her mother was thinking. Imagining her daughter in the states wearing clad dresses and going out with every cute face she saw. Lamya gave her mother a reassuring smile, but as she left to join the others, she couldn't help but think that her mothers imagination was right on point.

"I'm going to visit your aunt for while, you're welcome to come along," Mrs. Tamimi said with a luring voice.

Lamya's smile grew larger as she stopped, turned and

gave her mom a hug. She showed concern on her face for her mother, but she wasn't going to miss boys' night in for nothing in the world.

"Then if your going, you better hurry and get dressed," Lamya said as she hopped across the couch joining the others in the living room.

Not at all surprised by her daughter's response she rolled her eyes and stomped out of the kitchen, thinking it was better than jumping across the couch herself and choking her daughter until she turned blue in the face.

Lamya had heard a lot about Mitch, and what she heard seemed to ring true. Mitch sort of reminded her of Salem accept he was maybe half an inch taller and muscles in all the right places. As she sat down she pushed the snack bowls closer to the middle of the table. Mr. Tamimi watched her carefully hoping no one would notice. He was nervous about her being around, but at the same time proud. He had two sisters of his own and what he always wanted for them was to be more confident individuals. Looking at his daughter she was doing what he wished they could have done.

"Mitch, this is my daughter Lamya," Mr. Tamimi said.

For Mitch looking at Lamya was like looking at Salem with a wig on. The only difference was that Lamya was hot.

"I've heard so much about you Lamya. Nice to meet you," he said getting a closer look as he reached across the table for a handshake.

Mitch was lying the most Salem ever said about his

sister was how much she annoyed him. But then, she smiled before letting his hand go, and it made him remember. It was his junior year as an undergrad and he was at an end of the year party. It was around 1 p.m. and he was ready to go home. His head had been spinning for two hours, due to what he blamed on too many alcohol mixes. Stumbling towards the door he slipped falling to the floor. A girl calling for a friend named Simi stopped, knelt down and asked him if he needed a hand. He took her hand and she gave him the most beautiful smile he had ever seen. In return he couldn't help but to give her a peck on the lips. With Salem right across from him he felt uneasy, and then he thought, he knew some of his family after all. Pinching her middle finger before letting go, he hoped she remembered that he did the same the night that they accidently. With that pinch some how, Lamya thought back to the same kiss from the same face, on the same night. Salem was deep into one of the games and didn't have an idea of what was going on. Mitch flopped back onto the couch and nudged Salem in the shoulder.

"You guys look like twins," he said uneasily never taking his eyes off of Lamya.

Mr. Tamimi burst into laughter.

"Yeah, everybody says that, but they also say that I look five times better," Salem replied.

A burst of laughter filled the room as Mrs. Tamimi headed out the door. Saying good-bye their laughter bought out anger she had never felt before, or was it just jealousy? She wasn't sure, but what she was sure of is that she was glad to be leaving for a while. She also hoped that in her absence their fun would be stopped some how. As the door slammed behind her Mitch received a phone call from

Michelle. He obviously didn't want to talk, but kept a smile on his face because of Mr. Tamimi. Salem had given his family a rundown of what was going on, and so realizing that the call was probably his girlfriend, he thought he would try and help out.

"So what is it, the pressure she's probably putting you under, or maybe the fact that you want to say yes, " Mr. Tamimi asked.

 Choosing not to say a word Salem was both surprised and impressed with his dad.

"I've known her for two years, but we've only dated for six months," Mitch replied.

All of the sudden Lamya wanted to know everything about his relationship and wished that Taif had stopped calling her so she wouldn't miss a word that came from his mouth.

"Two years knowing her and you were with her for six months? Back home that's a ticket for marriage, that is as long as your family doesn't find out you've been seeing each other from the beginning. Does your family know," Mr. Tamimi asked.

"Yep, they love Michelle," Salem replied.

Mr. Tamimi smiled.

"Okay they love her, but you don't," he asked.

Mitch gave them all a faraway stare for a second.

"Yes sir, I love her, but not enough for taking my focus

off of my job right now. She demands too much attention. I need at least another three years, and then I would be ready," he replied.

Lamya's eyebrows rose high on her forehead. Sitting back on the couch Mr. Tamimi seemed to juggle the situation in his head. Though Mitch was the same age as his son, he saw Mitch some how as being more mature. Sitting forward and resting his elbows on his thighs, he looked Mitch straight in the eyes.

"No, you're not in love, but you do care for her," Mr. Tamimi replied.

"Yeah, we click, but we don't click. I wish we did but she knows it," he replied.

It was a simple straightforward answer that made a lot

of since, and one Mitch had already reckoned with. Lamya grabbed her dad by the neck and gave him a big kiss. Her father was talking about love, and not just to the guys, but also in front of her. Speaking out loud about the problem made Mitch come to the realization that it was better for them to go their separate ways right away instead of letting the problem linger.

Six hours later Mitch couldn't have been any happier. Mr. Tamimi was off to bed and Lamya was in her room on the phone. It gave them the chance to walk around to the corner store and pop open two cold beers. Mitch was glad that he stopped by and as he laid spread out on his back the next morning in the middle of Salem's living room, he found himself anxious about the night that lied ahead. Giggling to himself quietly, what Salem didn't know, was that until just three years ago he was the king of scrabble in his dormitory building. The only reason he wasn't king anymore was because he didn't want any girls knowing that he was a scrabble nerd. Nope, he was all about the ladies.

17~

BUSY MINDS NEED REST

As Mitch left Salem could here the door close, as he lay in the bed nervous of the morning to come. He couldn't believe that it had slipped his mind until he received a text on his cell phone. It read...

"Don't forget Times Square at noon."

It was nine o'clock when he received the message, so he had more time to think. He really wanted to know who the person was, and all he could do was run the strange voice through his head over and over again. He was the type of person who loved surprises, but he tended to hate secrets, that may or may not in the end make him smile. The anticipation made him fidgety, so he reached into the back of his closet to grab his shoebox. Throwing the box on the bed he jumped up and locked the door. He didn't need any more surprises. Pouring his collection onto the bed, he sat with his legs spread open, slowly he pressed his hands down upon his white sheets letting his fingers glide in and out of the pile that laid before him. Playing with them he would hold them high dangling them in the air or twirl them across the sheets watching their colorful designs against the white background. It had become a ritual since he landed in the states. They came from girls that he knew, dated and didn't know, and though he didn't do it everyday day from each article he had a memory. Reveling glee he could hear the shuffling of his mother's feet as she readied herself for the morning breakfast. Even though he knew the

door was locked he felt guilty. It wasn't because of his

hobby, which was something he never felt guilty about.

Instead he thought it was something that all men should

have the pleasure of doing openly. Looking at the rainbow

of colors that were spread across his bed, he had the urge to

slip into something more colorful himself. Choosing a red

Philadelphia 76ers jersey, the number 42 was matched with

some knee length khaki shorts a long with a plain white

pair of Adidas sneakers. Deciding to join his mother in the

kitchen, he rushed to the bathroom to wash his hands and

put some cold water on his face. Looking into the mirror as

water dripped from the tip of his nose, he wondered if

others saw what he saw in the mirror everyday. He wasn't

sure, in-fact he had never been sure, and on this particular

day he had a strong uncertainty about himself, one that he

couldn't seem to shake. Rushing into the kitchen he hoped

that his mom had made him feast, because he felt that a

long day was ahead of him.

It was five to twelve by the time Salem reached Times Square. He almost thought it was a mistake having breakfast with his mother alone. She made it very difficult for him to leave as if he wasn't going to return to his one and only place in New York. Mrs. Tamimi made pancakes again. Salem thought they were good, but he was getting fed up with even hearing the name. As good as they were pancakes had a way of making the person devouring them, want to devour something else after an hour of eating. Salem was hungry, so hungry that he text the stranger and asked if they could meet at McDonalds. Halfway through the line he received a text from his stranger that read...

"Called into work, you still want to meet?"

As he reached the counter, he thought that the ball had already been dropped and why should he stop its movement? He needed to know what the deal was, so after grabbing his tray and fighting for a seat he text back.

"Why not. Meeting some friends tonight. I'll text you the address later."

Three hours later he found himself back home just in time for a small dinner his mother whipped up for her two children amidst her inner turmoil. It wasn't as if she had given up, but she had given thought. The next day her son would graduate. She had to admit it, even though she was angry, she was somewhat proud of both of her children, even if the emergence of Friday made her uneasy. She watched her son as he walked through the door. He had given her the broadest, brightest smile, and though it was clear of guilt or worry, his smile some how made her heart race nervously.

"Well, that was quick. Go get dressed. This food just isn't for us," she forcefully smiled.

He didn't know how, but his living room had been formed some what into a formal dinning room, equipped with two portable tables, covered with a white laced cloth. His mother always had a knack for making something out of nothing. He liked the surprise dinner even if they had already had enough dinners to last another lifetime of visitors. As he walked down the hall he could hear Lamya on the phone with Taif. She had left the door open so he grabbed her powder sponge and slung it in her face. Running out of the room as she screamed, he passed his father in the bathroom who was trying to figure out what color Kaftan to wear. Rushing to his room he decided that he would surprise his parents at least once while they were visiting. Digging deep into his closest past his special shoebox, underneath his collection of T-shirts were two more large boxes. He grabbed the one closest to the floor, along with a pair of his slippers. He had two kaftans, one in off white and another in pale green. He thought the off white would go better with his beige and gold slippers, embroidered in gold. Spreading it out neatly on the bed, he ran back to Lamya's room, where she was still talking on the phone. Grabbing a pillow and throwing it at her, he caught her attention.

"Hey, where one of your dresses and get ready so you can help mom out, " he whispered.

Usually she would have retaliated with some harsh word, and a returned pillow throw harder than Salem would have ever imagined, but she got what he was doing. Life would change for the both of them soon; so they could at least act like a family for one night.

There was a harmonious feeling within the Tamimi household. It was the type of vibe, which seemed to be contagious. At least this is what Alice thought as she had a strong urge to knock on their door. The sounds of laughter, the smell of food and the music seemed to sharpen Alice's senses and just as her hand was inches from the door she also heard the laughter of Salem. He didn't sound like himself and though he laughed loud and spoke even louder his voice was shaky and the laugh half there. She couldn't put her finger on it, but her feelings must have been right on the button, because the urge she had just seconds earlier slipped away, and so did she.

It didn't take Taif and other family members long to start knocking on the door. Everyone dressed traditional. Kneading some dough Mrs. Tamimi almost lost it when Taif entered the room. The last time anyone saw Taif in traditional dress was at the age of twenty-one. It was the night her then best friend was getting married, but Taif found herself dragging that best friend into the bathroom and shoving her head into the toilet. It seemed that her friend failed to tell her until she reached the house that the man she was marrying, was the very same man that turned down the Tamimi's proposal because another family claimed that the Tamimi's were trash. Everyone thought her actions were too much, but no one could disagree on how fabulous Taif looked in the Kaftan she wore. Even the groom to be couldn't keep his eyes off her as his soon to be wife and she fought. In pale burnt orange, trimmed in heavy gold she looked liked a Moroccan queen. Taif may have stepped to an American beat, but she seemed to dance elegantly to her African rhythm. It was just as if her body was made for it. As Mrs. Tamimi finished up with her dough, Salem seated the guest starting with Taif.

"I know you think I look good," Taif whispered as she

took her seat with a satisfied grin.

It took another thirty minutes before everyone was situated and the food was done. As the last dish was set on the table Mr. Tamimi entered the room and took his place at the head of the table.

"Everyone welcome to what I guess will be one of our last dinners her in America all together. I'm so glad we have been able to do this. So tonight enjoy the food. Take all of your worries and put them behind you, and let's have a beautiful dinner with beautiful people," Mr. Tamimi cheered with a glass of orange juice

18~

A TORMENTED SOUL CONFRONTED

It was scrabble day. Renee lived in between downtown Manhattan and Soho. To be more specific she lived in China town. Most people wondered how it was that a hearty black chic sticking out like a sore thumb found herself in China town. Whether others had asked or not, he had not a clue, but it was the first question Salem asked when he found out about it. The story went that she had a big thing for Jewish guys. Salem never figured out why, but it was obvious. Once in a blue moon she would have a fling with a dreadlock, wearing hippie that is until she couldn't stand either their smelly ways or the fact that sometimes they seemed just too into her. She didn't know how she was going to catch one, but what she did know was that in Manhattan there were more than 243,000 Jews, and within that group there had to be someone just for her. The two guys hopped off the train just before entering China town. Taking a trip to Renee's place was like taking on an unknown urban excursion. She lived on the lower east side. The Shanghai World Expo was going on overseas, but it also seemed to be going on in the states too, making the already crowded streets somewhat unbearable. A group of men passed by them dressed in Sapphire red robes, wrapped with royal blue belts. They held long totem poles covered in yellow silk, and at the top of the poles dangled green, yellow, red, and blue silk strips that tickled the tops of Mitch and Salem's heads. Salem hated large crowds and moved faster while Mitch seemed to drag behind entranced with the sights dancing before him. Proving that he knew almost all of New York, Mitch was stopped by a friend.

"Hey, what's going on man," Mitch yelled.

He made a jumping hi five with a Puerto Rican guy, while giving a hand shake to the guy's friend. Salem walked backwards gesturing for Mitch to hurry up, feeling a sharp object in the middle of his back, he abruptly turned to see what it was knocking a sword out of what appeared to be a half monkey half humans hand. Dressed in a yellow silk ninja suit with a black sash, his face was covered with reddish brown hair, so much so that the only thing noticeable was his pug nose and slanted eyes. He grinned directly at Salem as he hopped up and down making monkey noises that could have been mistaken for the real thing. His grin was distinct, and though Salem found him disgusting he couldn't help but to be pushed to grin too.

The man jumped higher and Salem followed in pursuit. He seemed entranced and as the monkey's tail began to wound its existence around his waist, he felt as if he was being sucked within the being itself. The tighter the tail wound the more free Salem felt. His body was weightless as if he were thrust up left floating in mid air. The half monkey half man grabbed Salem by the front of his shirt. Salem was so close he could smell what seemed to be the beings flower scented breath. Batting his eyes until his top and bottom lashes met, he whispered in Salem's ears.

"I think it's time that you let that tail show," the monkey man said letting go of Salem and then hopping away.

Salem felt a tap on his shoulder. Startled he found himself stumbling backwards trying to get his footing just before falling painfully onto the pavement. He could hear Mitch's voice, but he could only see a man standing before him disgruntled because he had torn off the tail of his costume.

"Wa`ngbagazi, I don't have a freaken tale now," the man yelled.

"Hey we ain't at the party yet man," Mitch laughed.

Giving him a hand Salem stood up looking for what he thought he saw earlier, but found only the cursing guy still looking back as if he wanted to jump him. He could see Mitch's mouth move, but couldn't decipher what he was saying. Still walking backwards he found himself up against a wall and when turning around he discovered that his clumsy trips had led him straight to Renee's place. Checking to see if there were any spots on his clothes he signaled for Mitch to follow him. They walked through an antique shop filled with gold Buddha; stone Buddha, colorful glass lanterns and timeless pieces of furniture that real collectors would die for. At the back of the shop were some narrow stairs leading to another area. He didn't know why, but each time Salem had to make a trip up Renee's stairs it made him feel uneasy as if he were walking through a part four of a Gremlins film. Mitch seemed to feel the same way.

"I thought you said this girl was black," Mitch whispered.

Salem didn't say a word instead he kept creeping until he finally reached her door. While it was dim and quiet on their side, a strong beam of light peaked through a small crack in the door. Following the light was the sound of people talking softly and music playing. The sound was welcoming to Salem it was something about Renee's group that made him feel good all over. With the back of his fist

Salem gave the door three solid knocks.

"It's open Bi-at-ch! Just come in," she yelled.

Making his final step Mitch wondered why he didn't turn back as soon as they entered the antique shop, until he heard the way Renee pronounced the word bitch. Gently he pushed Salem to the side. He then pulled his smile to one side of his face and gave Salem a wink.

"Let's go my boy. We've got some partying to do," he said.

The inside was nothing like the outside. It was as if they had walked out of China town, onto a page of American Living. Bamboo colored, wooden floors, were being trampled upon by an excited Renee and the rest of her crew. Alice sat on a dark brown rag rug with a glass of red wine while talking with Jenny, a vegan was swearing up and down that she could make any delicious meal vegan in seconds. Giving Renee a slapping handshake Salem introduced Mitch to the rest of the group while scoping the room. He saw the night as being an interesting one. Along with Renee, were Rob, Diesel, Keith, Jenny, Sparks, and Alice, and seeing the girls Mitch began to think of the evening as an equal opportunity playing field. Away from the shag rug, Diesel and Sparks set up a small round table where they planned on playing cards. Mitch focused on Sparks right away. Around five foot six, the half Korean and black girl had Mitch drowning in his own imaginations, but one was not enough. Making his eyes fish like a hand in a cookie jar he set his eyes on Jenny who had flopped down on Renee's brown couch to match the shag rug. In front of the couch was a small rectangle coffee table creatively painted brown with thin lined white designs giving it a bit of hippish appeal. While Mitch fished, Salem gave his hellos to Rodney who was in between the kitchen and the dinning room watching Diesel shuffle cards, while Sparks did what she did best, make sure all eyes were some where on her. She pranced around the room circling Diesel and talking across the room to Renee as to how she should paint her kitchen lime green to go with the curtains covering the two windows in the dinning room. All the while Renee stood looking into her floor size mirror hung on the back of her front door, fluttering her eye lashes as she smiled at Sparks remarks.

"Hey man what's going on," Salem asked raising his hand for a hi-five.

He asked the question, but already knew the answer. Rob was a young obviously lonely Vietnamese guy who believed that the only way to find happiness in his life was to meet another Vietnamese girl. For him this was difficult, because not too many girls were willing to get with a guy who refused to stop shopping at a thrift store even to buy socks.

"I'm cool man, tryin to find an outlet during the summer months," Rob replied.

Rob was a twenty-seven year old once nerd turned a mellowed sort of cool guy. Salem thought it was almost too much for the guy to bear. To have a second chance at coolness and still not be able to get the girl had to be a cruel life. Scanning across the room Salem spotted Keith putting in an Xbox game. Keith was the big guy of the group and big meant at least six foot seven. He should have been some type of wrestler, but instead he was a numbers pusher and was headed straight to Wall Street. Running away from Rob, Salem walked over, jumped up and gave Keith a shoulder message.

"Keith you know you can't beat Rob in Madden. Why do you even try," Salem laughed.

Keith and Salem's way of saying hello to each other was putting the other down when ever the opportunity came up.

"Thanks Salem, I guess that's why your bitch ass ain't over here playing," Keith replied while grinning back at him.

By this time Mitch was across the room talking to Jenny in what she believed to be a deep conversation, Mitch on the other hand was just bull shitting to get what he always wanted.

"Slim Sim, what's going on? The first time you've been to a scrabble party, you know I can't handle these girls all by myself. We gotta hold it down together," Diesel shouted out.

It was a man's comment, which would have offended any other girls, but this lot was special. They were totally confident and saw it as friends just shooting the breeze.

"Ha ha, the only thing you guys are gonna get around here is the smooth vibe we girls give off without you ever getting a chance to even taste," Renee laughed.

"That's all well and good if it makes you happy, but what I do know is that no one is getting out of here tonight without putting just one hand into poker game," Diesel rebutted.

When he played cards, the group called him a Paraná. He loved a game of cards and could talk almost anyone one into playing a hand, and then when he got you hooked, he was even better at taking your money. Renee didn't respond to Diesel, she was too busy scoping out Salem's friend Mitch. She loved her men, but was never one to go goo goo eyed over anyone, but at that moment her eyes were glued to Mitch, like Keith's were glued to the Xbox game. She figured she had to get Jenny away from Mitch, so as quick as possible she began to get the drink flowing.

"Hey you guys there's a lot of drink in the kitchen waiting to be ravished," she yelled.

For Salem and Mitch the night started out with one, then two, three, four, and some other lost of count beers. By eleven o'clock they had finished the beer and took a breather to start on the wine. While Renee smoothly worked her way into a conversation with Mitch, Salem received a phone call.

"Hi, is it you," the voice asked.

"Yeah, it's me. Are you coming," Salem asked.

Two games of scrabble already won by Mitch made it harder for Renee to contain herself. Rubbing Mitch on the top of his head she couldn't help but to bud in on Salem's conversation. In her mind the more people meant a longer party, and longer party meant more scrabble with more of Mitch.

"Hey who ever you're talking to invite them over. We can do with a few more scrabble players," she shouted.

As Renee rubbed Mitch's head, Mitch looked across the room at Jenny. Renee was pissed and rolled her eyes at her new playmate. Mitch knew what the deal and flirted with Renee a little longer to keep the friendship vibes flowing. Needing a breather Renee focused on Salem.

"So is this that new chic you've been blabbing about," she asked.

Resetting the board for a third game of scrabble, she looked across the table under eyed at Alice. By that time Alice was on her way to nights-ville while Keith sat behind her giving her a back message as Rob looked across the room at him in envy.

"Hold up now, hold up. Renee, are we really gonna meet this girl," Alice asked.

Salem's eyes went from left to right as he listened to what the two girls had to say.

"Nah, this isn't Cherise. Come to the party tomorrow night and you'll meet her. I actually don't know who this person is," he replied nervously realizing what he was saying. Picking out letters for the board, Alice cocked her neck back like a rooster ready to strike.

"Sounds like some one has been doing a little too much ecstasy," she said.

"Ecstasy, sounds more like some white powder to me," Renee laughed.

The two laughed back and forth at each other like cackling old ladies sitting on a porch trying to pass the time.

"Okay I'll text you the address and I guess I'll see you when you get here," he said returning back to his conversation on phone.

"So who the hell is it," Mitch asked.

Waiting for his turn at scrabble he looked at Jenny with his hypnotic Mitch stare while he waited for Salem's response.

"Yeah man, it's not your girl, but it's someone, and you have no idea who it is? This shit is interesting," Diesel remarked.

Diesel had a knack for being sarcastic and usually Salem would find himself caught up in his remarks, but that night he decided to ignore what ever he spit out.

"I guess you guys will just have to wait and see," he said then feeling a little uneasy.

By the end of their fourth game of scrabble there was a knock at the door. The group was moving from one table to the next in order to start up their first game of poker.

"Alright pretty boy, you got some guns in scrabble, but let's see what you got in poker," Renee remarked.

As Renee went to get more drinks, Mitch insisted on giving Jenny a hand with the popcorn. Sparks had given up her venture of trying to get Mitch's attention, and wanted to make sure that Mitch understood it. Renee and Alice were talking about their problems with men so she decided that it would be best time to get her point across.

"You are so totally right. I get so tired of some guys who think that every girl is into them. It makes me want to puke." Sparks said adding to the girl's conversation.

Creating an engaging moment with her fingers, she walked closely pass Jenny and Mitch and took a seat next to Diesel, one guy that she always knew she could get attention from. Not wanting to hurt her feelings as Jenny took popcorn Mitch walked up to Sparks, held her by the waist and gave her a kiss on the back of her head. Eyeing his poker hand Rob looked up wondering how Mitch did it.

Seeing the two embarrassed Keith so he decided to put on some music that bumped to make sure no romantic hanky got started. As others played games and mingled there was a knock at the door.

"Get the door Bitch, it's your company," Renee yelled.

Salem had almost forgotten and as he jumped up from the poker table he nearly poured a glass of wine onto Spark's shorts. A little off balanced after the drinks he tripped over Renee's shag rug. Grabbing the knob of the door as he fell, it opened like clockwork. He remembered that the voice seemed male or female, but he for some reason didn't expect for a male to be standing at the door. The guy obviously worshiped black, and as he looked up pass the chain dripping black leather pants and to the see through black cotton t-shirt, he quickly realized the guy was Asian. With long black hair that fell perfectly to his shoulders the stranger smiled at Salem. Not knowing what else to do Salem thought the next best thing was to smile back and shake his hand. As the stranger reached to greet him he noticed that he paraded a two faced tattoo on the back of his left hand between his thumb and the index finger. One side was animal like while the other revealed the stranger's face, which was dark and shadowed while the animals face was playful and bright. The sound of the subway came rushing back to him. The walk through the tunnel seemed so real that for a moment he thought that he was taking the walk again, and then he remembered that the face of this stranger sat at the same table as his host.

"Ssssssalem, mommas waiting to see what her baby has bought home," Alice shouted.

Salem heard her, but it didn't register. He was too focused on what was in front of him.

"So are you gonna invite me in or what," the stranger asked.

He invited him in, but no one had seen him yet, so he whispered for him to act as if they didn't know each other.

"I don't know you, and you don't know me," he whispered.

Walking in the stranger followed the sounds of conversation and laughter. Holding his arms high in the air and showing the piece sign with each hand, he gave everyone a smile and a hello.

"Hi, I'm a friend of the owners down stairs. I'm his cousin visiting from Cali. He told me that the tenant here could probably introduce me to some good people. I'm sorry to disturb your party here," the stranger said.

"Uhm now mama thinks she may have to know your name," Alice remarked again.

"My name is Jin Jin," he replied.

Renee welcomed not only the Jin but also his look. The conversation quickly moved from what he was doing there to where he got his clothes. Putting on a show Jin Jin grabbed a chair from the corner of the room, turned it backwards, and straddled his legs across it before sitting.

"Hey, Jin Jin, you're not gonna be a choch are you," Renee asked looking under eyed at him.

"Slow your roll girl. You got to know me before you judge me," Jin Jin replied.

With that he gave her a wink and held short

conversations with the rest of the group. He then stood up and shook hands with all the guys. He was cute, and Sparks didn't like the fact that She couldn't go a second without getting even a small glance from him.

"So which guy are you interested in? It's got to be your flavor at least for the night," she insisted.

You know my flavor of the night is you and me sandwiching someone way hotter than you to at least get me going," he replied as Sparks stormed out of the room.

As the night went on the drinking grew more intense. Salem didn't have too much of any conversation with Jin. He was too busy either talking with the girls or trying to get Mitch away from another future girl friend mishap. The last hand was played two hours later and by that time Jin had Renee spread out on the couch in a deep conversation about the social state of New York. Wasted from the exhaustion of it all fifteen minutes later Renee closed her eyes falling into a deep sleep dreaming of kisses from Mitch. At the same time Mitch decided that it would be good for him and Jenny to explore the antique shop down stairs, if it was only to get away from Salem. Rob and Keith decided to go back to their video game, while Sparks and Diesel stood on the sidelines to wait their turns. For Salem it was all about the munchies. No one had any idea of how this guy stayed so slim, but what they did know was that if there were any more snacks left in the room Salem would be the one to finish them off. Jin watched as Salem walked to the kitchen. Alice's attention was on Sparks who was up next to play the game. They were game rivals and Alice wanted next game bad.

"Hey Diesel, is it okay if I take your turn. Me and Sparks have some unfinished business to handle," she asked putting her hands on her hips and waited for anyone to tell her no.

Slowly removing Renee's head from his lap Jin slipped off the couch and headed towards the kitchen.

"You know you and Renee have been such a good host. What can I get for you another drink, some food," Jin asked.

"Well, since you asked that way, I could use another dose of that red wine," Alice replied devilishly.

"Yeah, I think I'll have a little of that too. I mean we don't want any excuses as to why one of us won and the other one gets left in the dirt," she replied with a smirk so large Alice wanted to choke her.

With Alice's approval Jin made his way to the kitchen. Towards the back of the kitchen there was a small laundry room, where Salem knew Renee stocked up on extra goodies for her guest. Reaching across the dryer to uncover the goodies, Salem felt a sharp tap on his lower back. Standing up with a bag of chips in his mouth and a fresh bag of double stuffed Oreos in his hand, he was surprised to see Jin standing there.

"What's going on? I see you're pretty good at making yourself at home," Salem remarked.

"I don't think you invited me here to talk about how well I socialize," Jin replied.

Just like everyone else he was drunk and had forgotten the real reason that Jin Jin was there. Setting the Oreos aside he let the chips slip from his mouth and struggled to open them while keeping his balance.

"So how come you didn't just tell me your name over the phone," Salem asked.

Jin relaxed his back within the frame of the door. He looked up at the ceiling smiling, while shaking his head in disbelief of Salem's question. Gesturing for Salem to come closer he grabbed the back of Salem's head pulling his face towards his lips. Jin then clutched Salem's top lip with his teeth. Astonished and frightened Salem pushed him away, but not before Jin grabbed him by the waist pulling him close to him and then walking him back against the washing machine. Salem was confused he didn't want to raise his voice and have someone walk in on them, but he also didn't want Jin touching him. Though Jin seemed to be thinner than Salem he was solid and had a grip that was hard to shake. Jin easily over powered Salem and with no more strength he fell limp in his arms allowing Jin Jin to push a kiss on to him. He then began to unbutton Salem's shirt and just as he was to massage his chest Salem fought back again pushing him against the wall. This was about the time that Renee stumbled into the laundry room looking for the same snacks that Salem had picked up. She watched the two tussle and from her point of view Jin definitely a choch, because only choches could attack another person knowing that the room was spinning in their heads. Cocking her head back she turned towards the kitchen counter and clumsily poured herself another glass of wine, while lighting a cigarette to go with it.

"Geez, you know if you're gonna swap spit like that, you could at least take time out to make sure the Lays bag was closed," she complained.

Salem was embarrassed, and seeing Renee with strength or not, he shoved Jin against the wall punching him in his stomach. He head continued spin as he tried to focus on Jin. He looked him over closely realizing for the first time since he met that guy that night, that he had the body of a man, but a face that was undeniably beautiful, not handsome like himself, or cute, but beautiful. Jin Jin looked right back at him with a smile that 007 could have killed for.

"What's the matter? You're not into me anymore," Jin Jin asked.

"What do you mean in to you," Salem asked.

As he spoke he could hear Renee close the kitchen door. He felt trapped, not wanting to go out, and certainly not wanting to stay in.

"You're still out of it? Come on, me and you man, in the back room of Hell Bent. Nothing's coming back? Come on man, you're like my Shiva," Jin Jin smiled.

He didn't like where the conversation was going, and frustrated pushed Jin against the wall again. He began to felt uncomfortable in his skin, and he didn't like it. Pointing his finger at Jin Jin he dared for him to make another move. He just needed one excuse for trying to put the guys head through a wall, and he might have just done so if Mitch and Jenny hadn't walked into the room. Renee was behind them signaling Salem that she tried her best to keep them out. Salem quickly composed himself keeping a distance between himself and Jin Jin.

"Hey, Mitch where have you been, you know there's no party without you," Salem asked.

Mitch could see that something was not right.

"I was just checking out some of those antiques down stairs. Everything good," Mitch replied.

"Yeah, yeah. It seems that Jin Jin was telling me a little something about Cheries's past. It may not be as good as gold, but it's okay," he replied.

Jin gave a nod of the head and a smile. Not wanting to make things seem even more awkward, Renee headed back into the din, and grabbing Mitch and Jenny by the shoulders she led them both out of the kitchen. Salem was about to follow as Jin gave him a whistle.

"You know it really wasn't my plan to cause a seen. I just thought the phone tag was just a game. That night at Hell bent you went to the bathroom and never came back even though you said you would. You just disappeared," he said.

"I woke up the next morning in the club on the floor. That's all I remember," Salem said walking away.

"I don't think it's good for me to be here anymore. I'll

call you," Jin shouted back.

An hour later everyone was clearing out of Renee's place. Salem was the last to leave. The rest of the night and the next day would be for the girls. Both Sparks and Jennifer were already in deep sleep, so Renee and Alice decided to walk Salem out. At the entrance of the antique shop sat a wooden statue of a fat Buddha smiling down on what looked like a half man half monkey. What Salem admired most about Renee was that she was like a walking encyclopedia. Ask her almost anything, and she was bound to have some knowledge about it.

"Hey during the parade I saw a guy dressed something like this statue. You know anything about it," he asked.

Taking a puff of what had to be the final of a third box of cigarettes, Renee gave Salem a peculiar look.

"It's funny you asked. The Chinese believed in this monk Xuan Zang during the Tang dynasty. He went on foot from China to India to find some holy books. The Chinese created some mythical stories of his travels, and one was about the Monkey King. This kid was like good, but was always tempted into wanting to do something bad, but he helped the monk through his journey" she replied.

He had enough adventure for one night, and though he wanted to hear more the nine drinks that he had earlier just wouldn't allow him to. Making sure the girls locked the door behind him he set off for home.

19~

A STATE OF PRESENCE

It was the day of graduation and even though he knew it was a done deal somehow he was still nervous. Sitting up in his bed he discovered a baby blue box with a dark blue ribbon wrapped around it. It was placed in front of his closet door. Crawling to the other end of his bed he unwrapped the box and found a brand new three-piece suit. Salem had so many clothes for all types of occasions that he never really thought it was important to get anything special for his walk across the stage for the second time.

His mother usually was off the rector in the worse way when it came to choosing clothes for Salem, but for once she was right on the money. Stumbling to his feet, he was in the same clothes he had on the night before. Removing his shoes and pants he looked in the mirror at himself. The suit was brown with a bronze tone to it. Quickly trying it on he also put on the slim black tie that went along with it. It was perfect. It didn't seem as if anyone was up, so he decided to give Renee a call.

"Hey, I know it's early, but can you tell me more about that statue you have down stairs," he asked lowering his voice.

"Are you serious? You're calling me this early to ask about that," Renee replied.

"Yeah, have I ever bothered you before at this time? I

know how you are, but I'm just curious that's all," he said.

"Is this about that dude Jin Jin, because if it is it's okay. I'm not going to say anything. You didn't even seem like you were with it," she said.

"No, I don't know. I just want to know more I guess," he expressed.

"Alright, alright," she said struggling to sit up on the couch.

"You coming to my ceremony today," he asked.

"Hell yeah, you know I'm gonna be there," she said.

Grabbing her I Book she Googled Monkey King. Reading through it she looked for what she thought was relevant Salem.

"He was something like a deity. Get this he was born of a stone, but graced, was pushed to grow through the wishes of heaven and the fruits of earth. I guess you could say even though he wasn't a man and not really a monkey he was accepted for who was born to be. He had this special power where he could transform into seventy two different things," she read excitedly.

"So a man who was monkey who could change shapes," he replied.

"Yeah, but even though he was different, he was treated the same, and because he wanted to learn about himself and the world, it was like he was more confident or something," she exclaimed.

"Do you think I'm different," Salem asked.

"What do you mean? You're like so many people I've met. I don't see any real difference Salem," she replied.

"I mean I'm different, but I never thought it mattered. I still don't think it matters," he replied.

"You ain't any different than anyone else. But get this the thing he could never totally change into was a human even though he was half human. It seems that no matter what he did, his tail would always show. So if you say you're different and your trying hard to hide it, sooner or later like that tail it will reveal itself," Renee laughed.

"So since we're being open and you could step to Cherise and that Jin, then motha fucka how come you couldn't step to me," she asked laughing.

She wanted to get him to loosen up and say what was on his mind. She always knew there was something, but could never truly put her finger on it. Salem said nothing on the other end of the phone, but he wanted to. He trusted Renee, never knew why, but he did, and then he heard his mother walking down the hall.

"Hey, thanks. I've got to go I can hear the others getting up," he said.

By eight am he had showered and fixed himself some breakfast. He desperately needed some time alone. His mind went back and forth to Cherise; he needed to talk with her.

"I wish you were with me last night. I had a lot of fun with Mitch and some other friends of mine. How were things with you," he text.

He was anxious for her response. The hall light was flipped on and he knew in a few minutes he wouldn't have any piece.

"Hi cutie. My night was turned upside down. I wanted to give you a call, but I had family show up that I didn't know I even had. Right now it's like a family reunion up in this place, lol," she text back.

"Well, I guess we'll just have to wait for tonight. Don't forget the plan or you may just loose me in a sea of other hungry girls, lol," he text.

The toilet was flushed and the shower was running. Lamya was knocking on the bathroom door asking Mrs. Tamimi to hurry. Salem tapped his fingers on the counter impatiently. He wanted one more text from Cherise before the craziness started.

He hoped that Mitch had informed her about the plans. The night before he got the idea of inviting Salem's parents to his house for a small party his mother was throwing for the rest of the family. Salem accepted knowing that his parents would be family and then would have to go back to the apartment alone. The plan was for him to drop his parents off at Mitch's place and they would all meet from there and be on their way.

"Good morning habibti," his mother sang as she came around the corner.

The light on his phone flashed red. It was Cherise's text.

"Don't worry fly boy. I've got the plan on lock down. Can't wait to see you," she text.

Salem was satisfied and grinned ear to ear at her response.

She held her breath as she pushed the disconnect button on her cell phone. She wanted to tell her mom what was going on, but for some reason felt that it wasn't the right time. While Salem's mother fixed her husband breakfast, Cherise's mother ran around in a silhouette slip looking for the right tie to go with her son's suit. While Salem got ready to the mixed language of French and Arabic coming from his father's singing, Cherise listened to the rhythmic accent of her family's southern drawl. They talked about her childhood, and what a beautiful person she turned out to be. Two families in two different worlds they thought separately as they both prepared for their special day.

It was tradition that all ceremonies for Cambridge graduates be held in the Senate House. Salem kept this a secret from his family, just to see the surprised looks on their faces. As they drove up to the house Salem quickly jumped out of the front seat to open the back door. Mr.

Tamimi's eyes opened wide with excitement, though he looked a bit confused.

"Where are we," he asked.

"Graduation base, other schools envy us because of it," Salem bragged.

In awe Mrs. Tamimi put her hands over her mouth. She looked as if she wanted to cry, but as she watched other parents pass with their heads held high, she kept the tears back. While Lamya was proud of her brother, she was also jealous of him. She couldn't hold it in. There were no other words to express how she was feeling. Salem looked back at her with a smirk that made her want to kill him.

"I could have graduated from this place too, if anyone would have allowed me," she said with puffed lips.

Her brother was enjoying every minute of it. Lamya begged her parents to let her attend Berkley or Cambridge, but Mrs. Tamimi thought a girl going by herself was just too much. Rolling her eyes at her mother she stumped up the stairs owning her space, as if it were her ceremony she was attending.

"Maybe if you would have actually applied to the schools, mom would have changed her mind, he yelled back at her racing ahead to get ready.

He didn't have time to change at home, plus he thought it would look pretty weird for him to be driving in his gown. Rushing into the bathroom crowds of future alumni stood talking. Mitch caught eye of them and rushed his family up so that they could meet the Tamimis.

"What's going on man? This is all she wrote. We are

finally here," Mitch smiled.

Salem was fixing his cap and gown in the mirror. He could see the proud look on Mitch's face, and it made him smile too.

"I don't know. It just struck me right now that it's real, ready or not," he replied not looking at Mitch, but still starring into the mirror.

Gripping his friend by the shoulders Mitch made him focus on his image in the mirror.

"Look at you man. It's time to make some things happen. In two years you and I will stand in a mirror like this again. Imagine what we will see," Mitch replied.

Salem looked hard it was the first time that he hated the

fact Mitch was touching him. He wondered if Mitch saw what he was seeing. For four years they were the dynamic duel. Mitch had become Salem's Sheik in the states and as he looked at their reflection in the mirror instead of Mitch he saw Sheik.

"Salem come on out here your family is waiting for you and Mitchie you come on too it's time to find your seats," Mitch's mother yelled.

As they walked into the main room Renee and Alice showed up. One standing on each side of Salem, they both gave him a kiss simultaneously on the cheek. While the Tamimis looked alarmed Salem signaled that they were just friends.

"Go get em graduation boy," they both yelled like young cheer leaders on a football field.

"So that's your family uh," Alice asked giving Mr. and Mrs. Tamimi a wink.

"Well, who else would it be? He looks just like them," Renee replied rolling her eyes.

"I'm glad you guys came. I'll see you tonight too, right," he asked.

He knew that they wouldn't say no, and before they could embarrass him with a hell yeah, he pushed them aside to finally meet up with his family, while Cherise searched for him within the crowd. The Tamimis, Mitch's family, and Renee and Alice all took their seats together. Cherise's family sat with her roommates. After the ceremony both Salem and Mitch found themselves shaking hands with people they didn't even knew they knew.

"So I heard, you're the man with the plan. Tell me can you introduce me to some hot chicks," the stranger asked.

Turning around he was met with a guy about his height and his shade of color. He wore thin silver framed glasses and had curly jet-black hair that he wore cut close to his head. From Salem's view the stranger didn't look like he needed much help in the female department.

"Well," the stranger asked again.

Salem didn't know whether to offer him a few numbers or just run away, and just as he was about to choose the second thought a familiar voice caught his ear.

"Hey don't be alarmed. It's just my little brother. Salem, this is Stephen, or Stylo, and Stylo this is Salem.

"Nice to meet you Salem, what it do? I should have introduced myself, but I was just acting a fool. You know, having a little fun," he said.

Giving a sigh of relief he shook Stylo's hand and turned to greet Cherise who looked fantastic even if she was hiding everything behind her robe.

"Well, hello to you," Salem smiled.

He tried to contain himself as he watched her family walk up behind her, but he felt that if she weren't near his heart would just stop. He didn't know why ignored the feeling and went on as if everything was okay.

"Hello, I don't believe I know who you are," Cherise's mother said.

"Oh, I'm sorry, mom, this is Salem and Salem this is my mom and the rest of the family," she replied.

It wasn't as if her mother didn't have a clue, but she wanted to hear from either her daughter or the guy. Salem's heart skipped a beat. Her voice was soft, but stern, and her face was welcoming but weary of his presence. She was lighter than in complexion than Cherise, but wore her hair short and natural. Though she had what seemed to be pure silver streaks in the front of her head, she looked surprisingly young for her age.

"Hi, it's very nice to meet you. I'm Salem Tamimi," he replied.

"Just Salem, or Cherise's Salem," Mrs. Leflore smiled.

Salem smiled nervously, and that was all Cherise's

mother needed to see.

"Mom I'm going to the graduation party with him and a few other friends, the one where Joint is playing tonight," Cherise said.

The introduction of her family made him jittery. It wasn't that he didn't like it, but it was new and a-part of that so-called real world. He quickly shook hands with everyone and slowly backed himself out of what could have turned into an uneasy situation. Giving Cherise a nod and smile he excused himself to catch up with his family.

There was a lot happening that Friday. The Graduates hardly had time to breath even though they had been through it all before. The rest of the day was all about family and celebration. The Tamimis were excited about celebrating with Mitch's family and so they decided that they would contribute to dinner by making a Moroccan dish. While Mrs. Tamimi prepared the food, Mr. Tamimi finished packing their things. It was a possibility that their outing would be an all nighter, at least that's what he hoped, and he wanted to make sure if they were short on time that they would just be able to pick up and go. While Lamya graciously helped her mother in the kitchen, Salem fussed back and forth with his father about which shorts were more presentable for a fifty three year old to wear to a dinner. Back home Mr. Tamimi had a habit of sporting shorts around the house. His runway favorites were white retro tennis shorts for bed, thigh high running shorts during the early part of the day and sailor length shorts for the rest of the afternoon. None of these were appropriate for an evening with Mitch's family.

"It's not like you're going to play tennis and it's nineteen seventy. When you sit down in shorts like those things can happen. Like things can fall out," Salem said.

"I've seen plenty of men wearing these shorts. What about in that James Bond movie," Mr. Tamimi asked.

"That was James Bond coming out of the sea or something and that was before the 90's. Styles have changed since then, Salem fussed.

Mr. Tamimi held the shorts high in his hand observing the look that he so much liked.

"If there are new styles, then how come they keep making these," he replied.

It was almost too much for Salem to bear without wanting to take his hands and end any future embarrassment by taking his father's life. After five minutes of fussing he talked his father into wearing some white Addidas sweats with a blue grey t-shirt to match, the shoes of choice, white Addidas of course.

"You see, you look really good. If you started lifting some weights mom would have to work hard to keep the girls off of you," Salem said trying to pump his father's ego up.

Mr. Tamimi gave his son's comment some real thought, and as he did for just a few seconds he felt funny from the inside out. The image of young girls surrounding him and his wife know where in sight made him feel as if he were walking off the edge of a ledge without realizing it was the edge, but being happy he didn't realize. With a strong smile on his face he took a seat on his bed.

"Sit down. Let me talk to you for a few minutes," he said to Salem.

Reluctantly Salem sat down as Mr. Tamimi put the rest

of his American items nicely beside him in the suitcase. There wouldn't be much use for most of them back home.

"I don't know why Salem, but all of your life, I've felt in some ways you were unhappy. That's one reason your mother and me allowed you to leave home. You know I've always told you to look on the bright side of things, no matter what the negative may be. Since you've decided to stay, you can really make a life for yourself here. That's all I've ever wanted for you. I may not have shown it, but back home is so different from here. Everything is just too black and white there, what can you do," Mr. Tamimi asked as if expecting Salem to give him the answer.

Though they could almost talk about anything, the two Tamimi men were not very affectionate with one another. It wasn't that Salem had a problem giving his father a hug once and a while, but it was his father who was just the opposite. It had been that way since his birth. He knew his father loved him. It was in his eyes anytime they were face to face. But that night it wouldn't be the eyes that did the talking, but instead his father's actions. Grabbing his son by the neck before he could get up and walk away, he gave him a hug that seemed to make up for all the past years of hugs lost. Needing more than he realized, he returned his father's hug with a massive clinch that made it almost impossible for his father to breath. Feeling safe Salem closed his eyes and opened them as a five-year-old boy. He had been running on the Corniche and simply fell and scraped his knee. His mother rushed to his side and caressed him. Resting his head on her shoulder he could see his father run up behind them. He was worried about his son and seemed as if he wanted to hug him too, but never made a move to do so. The five year old closed his eyes as his mother embraced him, and when he opened them again it wasn't his mother, but his father who was holding him.

For all of the memorable moments that he had shared with his mother, he was sure she wouldn't mind this one trade off, just once.

"Oh my gosh did someone die," Lamya shouted sarcastically.

Lamya finally had a lot to say and she needed to say it behind closed doors. Not only was she getting ready for the party, she was also getting ready for her trip back to the U.A.E. She planned on leaving happy, tired and clear headed about her decision. Though her parents agreed, she believed she had to tie up a few ends with her brother. Pulling him to his own bedroom she closed the door and immediately opened his closet.

"So what are you going to wear tonight? You already know what we're wearing," she smirked.

Salem wanted her nowhere near his closet, but on the

other hand he had no idea what he was going to wear.

"You know there is a thing called privacy," he replied.

Picking her up and almost slinging her over his shoulder, he decided to playfully body slam her on to his bed. It was something that they had done since they were kids. The light hearted play put the spring back into Salem's step, and the step made Lamya feel as if she could spill her guts to him.

"Okay, okay stop playing and listen," she giggled.

Sitting on the floor he laid his head on the side of the bed to listen.

"So, this is it. I know I'll be back in about a month, but there are those what if's, if you know what I mean. So if it turns out that for some reason it's difficult for me to return, you have to do your best to get me back and I'm mostly referring to mom and dad," she said.

She grabbed her brother's hand and squeezed it so tight he just wanted to pull away from her.

It was already in the back of his head even if he hoped it never came down to that.

"What do you think, that I would just say, 'Oh she can't make it' and just throw my hands up? I hope you know me better than that," he replied.

Though sometimes she didn't act like it, Lamya was a little more sensible than her brother. Her fears were always thought out well.

"I know you know your responsibilities, but you're

starting a new job. By the time it's time for me to return, you're going to be knee deep into it. Think about it. It won't be easy," she said regrettably.

"Well you're right about that, but you know family comes first with me. You can't let things that haven't happened worry you," he replied reassuringly.

She could only believe him as she kissed her brother on the top his head.

"Now let's say I get back here. I still haven't searched for a place. I mean Taif is going to work on it too, but just for back up. Don't get me wrong Taif can be okay with choosing some things, but I think you understand where I would be comfortable and most happy. By the way unlike this place I like to be in the mist of it, like Soho or Manhattan," she implied.

He started to believe that it would be the best prank ever to set her up in a place like Renee's, she knew his sister would die of culture shock. Wanting to laugh he decided to give her a wink instead. She knew it was time to let the subject go. Taking a breath she took a long look around his room. It was the first time she had did so since being there. There was a desk that sat on the opposite side of his bed. As she looked up above it she noticed an intricate model of what she saw as a futuristic building that would probably put the city of Shanghai to shame. Placed on a stand that protruded from the wall, the structure was made of pure glass. It's exterior rose to a ninety-degree angle. The glass was strategically cracked in specific areas giving someone standing below it the illusion that it would shatter. It was impressive, and beside the structure was a plaque that read Student of the Year Pritzler Architecture Prize. Made of glass like his structure it gave off an air of prestige without her completely understanding its significance. But as quickly as the plaque caught her eye, it was lost in the discovery of what surrounded it. From that point on sketch after sketch plastered his wall to the point that Lamya thought it was just some expensive comic wallpaper he bought. All the sketches were in black and white of different shades. Each sketch of structures like the Eifel Tower, the Burj Al Arab and the Oriental Pearl Tower were given the feel of a dark comic strip with a slight touch of Hollywood glamour. Between the buildings were other sketches of Iron Man, Emma Frost and Blade. It was an amazing piece of work that even captured her imagination. Salem sat watching as she looked around his room. Too much to take in she sat on his bed. Laying back in amazement she was only met with more of his work. Starring down at her was not a sketch, but a painting. It filled all most the entire ceiling leaving just enough white space on all four sides that created a natural frame. The colors were bright, but soft, and knowing her brother even though she didn't know art, she would have bet that he used waters colors. The painting was set in a snowy area, and on the ground warriors from hell held spears in the air, while along side of them, the army of heaven flashed lightening toward the heavens as arrows followed. Their target sat on a white cloud above them. It was human like, but it had neither face nor an actual body, but more of a shadowy shape. It's back was turned on it's enemies as it looked up holding a staff in its hand aiming it towards the heavens. It was amazing, and she wanted to know more about it.

"Where did you get this idea," she asked.

"In my dreams, since we were kids," he replied.

As he talked Mrs. Tamimi walked into the room.

"I was thinking earlier this month, I bought some white pants and a beautiful Hungarian blouse. I thought I would wear it tonight. What do you think," she asked.

Her eyes lit up and her face was flushed red, tickled with excitement.

"It sounds good. Are you excited about going," Lamya asked.

"Yes, I really want to go," she expressed.

The siblings were hoping for a positive answer. In fact they hoped that they enjoyed themselves so much that they would forget about them for the night. She was in a good mood and it showed as she scanned both of her children.

"So what are you to doing? You should be getting some rest before going to dinner," she said.

"I was just making sure that while I was gone Salem didn't forget about me and promise to stay close when I get back," Lamya said.

Mrs. Tamimi caressed her daughter's cheek while taking a place on the bed between her and Salem. Reaching down and putting her fingers through Salem's hair, she was amazed at how thick it still was. Looking up in to her eyes, Mrs. Tamimi saw not a boy, but a man. A man that she felt was some how at a stand still in life. He was there but not there. It was probably the reason she thought that in the last couple of days each time he entered the room, her heart seemed to slow as if frightened of something, but then she figured what was too be was too be. Smiling she gave him a kiss on the forehead. She would be leaving tomorrow and such little time had to be spent wisely.

"You decided to get this job Lamya. Semi still has himself to worry about. I know how you do things. I don't have to worry about that. My only concern now is matching you up in three years to a nice man," she said with a wink that made Lamya cringe.

Mrs. Tamimi looked back over at Salem and grabbed his hands. He didn't pull away even though he had a strong urge to. He figured it would be the last night of her trying to get in to his head. Pulling her son closer he looked up into his mother's eyes once more.

"Any decisions you make are yours and yours alone. You're in the real world now. These sketches and paintings are just that, sketches and paintings. Taking a step off the paper is your real challenge," she said.

She pointed up to his painting on the ceiling as if she knew something Lamya didn't.

"He'll be fine, besides he'll have me to deal with if not," Lamya replied.

Mrs. Tamimi gave her daughter a kiss on the forehead and just smiled. Salem was surprised that she even noticed the painting.

"Okay, whatever you were talking about please stop. You have to get ready and so do we," Mrs. Tamimi replied rushing out of the room to try on her shirt.

"Hey, you didn't tell me what you were wearing. Come on, you've got to look good tonight, so what do you have in mind," she pushed again, while pushing her mother out of the room.

He didn't want to go the closet right away. Instead he collapsed on his bed. He knew he wanted to feel comfortable for the party and even more comfortable for Cherise.

"I'm not sure," he replied trying to shoo her out of the

room so he could have some privacy.

Grabbing his cell out of his pocket he decided to give Cherise another call. She picked up the phone on the first ring like she had been waiting for.

"Hey, I'm glad you called. Since my cousin is DJing this thing I have a little dilemma. Every time I go to one of his shows, we have a competition of who will be dressed the flyest. So we both have to look good Salem," she said anxiously.

Thinking for a moment he did a mind shift through his closet passing jeans, short sleeve shirts and blacks slacks.

"Okay, so how does a nasty grey suit with a soft pin stripped pink shirt, dawned with a white collar and silver cuffs sound," he asked dramatically already knowing the answer.

He winked at his sister who had refused to leave the room. She was excited about the whole dressing her brother thing, until it sounded like he was going to look better than her. She slipped out of his room thinking her only hope was to make her face look like a goddess. Closing the door behind her Salem was free to get ready.

"Hey, let me get ready so we can actually get together. I'll see you at Mitch's soon," he said.

She gave him a soft laugh on the other end of the phone and hung up. The suit he had in mind was James Bond chic, with a touch of Mr. Ripley classic and sophisticated. It was brand new; he bought it over the summer during a school trip to France. It was the first time he had put any real money down on something like a suit. He and a few other guys took a walk down Rue d' Antibes and he happened to walk into a particular shop, which featured only a few suits. This particular suit sat assembled in the back of the shop on a mannequin with breast. The group was attracted to the obviously unusual sight, and no one more than Salem. The breast actually made the suit look alive in a comedic kind of way, and if they had imagined like he did, they would have seen how great the suit could look on the right body. His only thought was that the suit would make him infamous not only in France, but back in the states. Reaching for the shelf at the top of his closet, he pulled down a large gold box with black writing on the top. He never did get to wear the suit in France, but a person could still become infamous for their last night among the college crowd.

"Are you ready, because I am," his father asked.

Mr. Tamimi was shouting on the opposite side of

Salem's bedroom door. He grabbed the items in the box,

and hoped for a night that would make him forget his father

was ever on the opposite side of his door.

20~

ENCHANTMENT OVERTAKES RENUNCIATION

CONQUERS

With the families of Salem and Mitch hanging out like they had known each other forever, it was time to hit the party. Mitch rented a car for the night wanting to get away from the everyday public transportation. Cherise and her brother showed up just as the others were heading toward the car. It was perfect for Salem. He didn't have to explain anything to his parents. Taif and Lamya felt free for the first time ever, and couldn't wait to get the night started. As

Cherise walked up Salem felt as if he had finally out done Mitch. His girl was so hot she was getting delayed movements from those passing by and Salem could hardly keep the smile off his face. What made him even happier was that their obvious differences made the perfect match like fava beans and cumin. She was wore a lighter shade grey than he wore. The design was a classic one, dipped with a little futuristic flare. The outfit was sleeveless. Her collar was thin and stood straight up touching the tip of her chin. Just below the collar the material spread apart shortly leaving an oval opening where the top of her chest was slightly exposed. From that point on the dress fit snug around her body until it fell halfway through her thighs where it was still fit but material changed to medium sized pleats that fell just above her knees. Her shoes like his were a grey color. Instead of flats she wore heals. They were high enough to give her height, but thick enough to allow her to dance the night away if she willed it. She was accessorized with what looked like platinum on the ankles, ears and waist. For Salem there was more than enough to see, and still too little to brag about, but just enough to make others imagine. Her hair was pulled up tight, spiked at the ends to give her a Mohawk style, which went well with the aggressive runway makeup that put the icing on the cake. Taif walked up to her, looked close in her face, and waited to find just one blemish.

"Damn, fuck the models. Tyra has nothing on you," she expressed walking away without taking her eye off the only girl she thought could ever take Salem from her, or for that matter Salem would have as his own.

Taif had a way of surprising everyone around her especially those who were closest to her. Her mood changed like a chameleons and when she wanted to express herself people would see sides of her they never knew existed, anywhere. Lamya tried hard to take her eyes off of Taif, but found it almost impossible. Focusing on Mitch instead she had to look away. Each time she saw Mitch he was usually in some sport shorts and baseball t-shirts, but stepping it up for the party he was looking too good. He didn't wear a suit like his Salem, but decided instead on some black wide legged slacks with a Sean John short sleeve button up. Just to make the ladies swoon he wore a fedora to show off when he decided to do some two stepping. Lamya had to look away and needed another distraction.

"Let's go. I don't want to waist anymore time here," Lamya expressed.

Salem wanted to say so much, but with her brother there and everyone ready to go, he said just enough for the both of them.

"I'm speechless. Break me out of this spell please," he yelled with a smile.

The car ride seemed pretty long with everyone excited to reach their destination. Salem sat up front with Mitch while everyone else squeezed together in the back seat. The music was loud, but not loud enough to stop the girls from talking the ears off of each other. As Mitch talked trash Salem received a text.

"Pushing me away doesn't mean that you can get away."

It was Jin, surprisingly Salem had forgotten about him, a memory wiped clean. It came back in a rush after the text, and it gave him a scare. Salem listened to the voice of Cherise as he sat and thought of a response. Other than almost making him loose face in front of his friends, Jin never gave him any more information about the club. But then Cherise asked a question that would change his mind about Jin.

"Hey Salem, Erick asked about you. I don't know why, but he is really interested in getting to know you. He's coming tonight. Talk with him, please," she asked

Salem shoved the cell phone into his pocket, but not before telling Jin to meet him one last time. He was deep in thought and hadn't realized that they had reached their destination. Knocking on the passenger window Cherise stuck her tongue out and made funny faces. Jin didn't matter, Salem knew what he wanted, and sticking his tongue back out at Cherise, he was positive she wanted to him too. The time was ten and as the group walked into the building they could hear music, but not the banging sound of Cherise's cousin. He wasn't on yet.

"Ah, you know what this means sis. Joint may be having a little trouble finding something to wear," her brother laughed.

There was a black curtain that divided the partiers from those just arriving. As if reading each other's mind both Salem and Mitch hesitated at first deciding only to stick their heads through the curtains instead. As their eyes scanned the room, the two could hardly contain themselves. Mitch stepped to the side holding the curtain back for Salem to enter. Even though the night was early, at least a hundred people were already crowding the floor. Surrounding the crowd were tables sponsored by different clubs of the university so people could join the schools Network of Opportunities program created by Mitch and Salem. Professor Chow had been on his game and not only did he do what was asked of him, he put in a little extra choosing the treats of the night. He had exceeded their expectations and he knew it as he pranced about the dance floor with his wife. They thought the place looked spectacular and as Mitch walked in with the rest of the group he look up at the ceiling which seemed to be looped end to end with black silk fabric. The fabric seemed to be endless, running down the walls of the room parting in the middle forming frames, which surrounded large rectangle mirrors on all four walls. Hanging from the looping black fabric were three-dimensional mirror like structures of various sizes that gave off soft

white light from within. The fourth framed structure was not just a mirror, but also the DJ booth. It paraded from the wall opening up to reveal Joint just entering the booth to show off his skills. On the sides of the booth facing the crowd were two white roman columns connected by glass barriers that protected the DJ from being bombarded with too many request. On the top of the columns ran more black silk fabric, which covered the DJ and his surroundings. On the remaining three sides of the booth wall on top of the black fabric ran column after column of tiny shiny silver beads. It seemed like Joint was going to be the university prince performing on his own personal thrown. The place was perfect. Raising his arms high in the air Salem made one huge spin on the floor as if he were in the middle of an amazing concert and couldn't get enough of it. Mitch was speechless and as Professor Chow gave him a slap on the back, he could only turn, shake the man's hand and give him a massive hug.

"You are shitting me! I was just expecting a room with some music, but damn," Taif said as she tried desperately to shake Cherise's brother from her backside.

Both Lamya and Taif focused on a group of guys talking around a table food. As the girls approached the guys Eve's

"Shake it you Tail Feathers" blared through the speakers. While Mitch went to find Joint, wanting to hopefully be the first to suggest some music, Salem walked over and grabbed Cherise. By twelve midnight the place was packed. Mitch and Salem had at least three Hennessey's and Cherise was finishing up her second one. The environment was intense and as the sweat dripped from their heads down to the middle of their backs, hormones ran rapid as strange and familiar bodies rubbed against each other. In between the dancing Salem and Cherise talked. He found out that she would be definitely staying in New York after a short stint back home. At twelve fifteen a little swooned after having half of his fourth drink, Salem laid his head on Cherise's shoulder. Opening his eyes to scan the crowd, he spotted what looked like Jin about four people away, starring straight at him. Behind him waving their hands frantically were Renee and Alice. He was swaying to the music as the girls and others danced against him. His eyes surpassed their movements and only focused on Salem. His eyes had these perfect slits that when closed sat on his face like two perfect half moons draped with long black lashes. Strands of hair fell down both sides of his face caressing the height of his cheekbones. The rest of his hair was pulled back. Excusing himself from the ladies it seemed to Salem that he was headed toward him. He could see him completely, and though he was in all black, he had exchanged his gothic look for a matrix like suit. He was looking too much like a ladies' man as he ignored everyone who came up to him. Salem felt jittery again and as he looked through the

crowd, not only did he spot Jin, but also Erick. Like Jin he was in a black suit that screamed watch me. He was different than the last time he saw him. He knew that Salem had spotted him, but he didn't exactly look his way. Instead he turned his back on him and started dancing with another guy. Salem grabbed Cherise and held her tight, looked into her eyes and kissed her passionately. His kiss like his looks were extremely addictive, as she opened her eyes to acknowledge his efforts she stood on the tips of her toes and with a flirtatious smile returned his kiss passionately. She closed her eyes again, and he opened his. Jin walked right past them, smiled at Salem and moved on. Salem looked straight ahead and as he did he could see Taif and Lamya.

"Hey, why don't we grab some snacks," he said releasing himself from her.

As he rushed through the room of dancing drunks, Mitch reached his arm out through the crowd grabbing Salem by his collar.

"Man, can you believe this shit," he screamed.

Salem wanted to relax and have fun, but he found himself looking around the room. Baffled by his reaction to Jin, he felt that he needed his friends and family close by.

"Ha, ha, it's great. So what do you think we should do after this," he asked.

As he spoke Joint's voice went booming over the speakers.

"Ohhh, I think someone out there knows what time it is," Joint shouted.

"What, what, this is it. Let's see who goes home with the cash tonight," Cherise yelled.

She winked at the group, gave Salem a kiss on the cheek in front of his sister, and disappeared within the crowd heading toward the DJ's booth.

"Salem, I'm having so much fun! It's been so long, and having the freedom to do it in the open is even better than sneaking out with your brother hoping family wouldn't see you," she screamed.

"Wait a minute, so you're saying this is the first time that you have been out, what since you were a kid," Mitch yelled back.

Salem didn't hear another word. They were in the moment while he was feeling out of himself. He needed to get away from the crowd.

"Hey, I'll be back. Going to the bathroom," he yelled walking away.

As Salem headed back into the crowd, Jin had just fought his way through it, but caught glimpse of Salem as he disappeared around the corner. Salem had slipped out of the main room and into a back hall near the bathroom. Jin hesitated at first, but then decided to follow him. Almost hidden was a door to the left of Salem as he laid his back on the hallway wall. Seeing that it was unlocked he slipped inside gently closing the door behind him. There was a small conference table. He decided to take a seat and rested for a few. The alcohol rushed to his head as he tried to figure out why the sight of Jin the second time around seemed to fill him with fear. While Salem thought about Jin, Mitch kept eyeing Lamya.

"You know what? Tonight I'm gonna show you and your cousin how to do it up he yelled over the noise.

It was all or nothing that night and Lamya accepted his invitation without the slightest pause. Besides, she thought he was cute, cuter than any of Salem's friends in the past.

While Mitch tried to drag Taif along, she was too busy receiving a kiss from some guy named Blake. She just liked the blond hair and blue eyes. Alcohol always made Taif sexually aggressive even though the aggression usually led her know where but back home alone in her bed, in the next room next to her parents. Her plan was to change that for the night, she just needed Blane to stick with her long enough to make it happen. Her actions came soon after. Taking no more chances, she took him by the hand, grabbed the back of his neck and planted a rough one on his lips. He didn't back away. She was in control, and he didn't seem to mind at all. Mean while Salem noticed a mirror on the far end of the small room. Loosening his tie he reluctantly stood up and slowly walked over to it. The closer he got the younger he looked, until he was around the age of five he was back to one morning as his mother got him ready for school. Even then he was looking at his face in the mirror behind her. He was naked as he waited for his mother to sort out some underwear for him. His father walked in smiling, but when he saw Salem naked quickly changed his mood. Salem hid himself turning his back on his father and running to the other side of the bed where he couldn't be seen. After his father left slamming the door behind him, he remembered covering his face and crying because of the rejection. He could hear Lamya in the other room giggling because his father was picking her up and tossing her in the air playfully, as he did each morning. He had the practice of putting the pillow over his head before the morning reached that point, but on that morning he was made to wake up earlier. Alone in the office he looked around and took a step or two away from the mirror. His face seemed to change and instead of five years old, he looked more around the age fifteen. After the incident in the morning with his father years earlier, he decided from that point on to be up and ready before anyone else. He also had the habit of doing the same in the boy's locker room. It was his first year in the American International School, and

he wasn't used to having to change his clothes in front of

twenty other guys. He felt inadequate compared to the rest

of his class. His shoulders were narrower than the other

guys, and his jawbone seemed to lack any real structure. He

was like a pretty little boy, while his counter parts were

strong and beginning to get manly looking. Watching the

others he stood in the locker room with a towel over his

shoulder, a bar of soap in his right hand and basketball

shorts that covered at least a quarter lengths of his scrawny

legs. He showered always with his shorts on, and made sure

he was in and out before anyone could have the chance to

say a word. Closing his eyes he remembered how much he

loved school, but hated the fact that he didn't feel confident

enough to hang with the other guys. Closing his eyes he

wished things had been different. He could feel the warm

hands of someone caressing the tops of his shoulders.

Slowly the hands went from the shoulders, up the back of

his neck, to the back of his ears. Reaching up Salem put his hands on top of theirs, he thought it was Cherise, but the hands weren't soft like Cherise's. Opening his eyes he looked back into the mirror where Jin stared back at him. His eyes were enticing and Salem chose to follow them.

"Who am I Salem? You still don't remember," Jin asked.

He wasn't in the mood for games and Jin was beginning to try his patients.

"Don't you think by now if I knew who you were I would have told you," he rebutted.

Leaning over he moved his hands from the back of his ears and down towards the inside of the breast of his jacket, messaging Salem's chest. Jin seemed to finding great pleasure in Salem. Salem felt nothing he was too bothered by the alcohol, which had started to upset his stomach. He was nauseas, and as Jin went from his jacket to the inside of his shirt, his hands felt ruff, but soft as he massaged against his chest. The room began to spin round and round, making him feel heavy from within. Fed up he grabbed one of Jin's arms, nearly swinging him across the room. Angry, Jin stood up, ran across the room, and wrestled Salem to the floor.

"What the hell," Jin struggles to yell out.

"The rooms spinning and you're grabbing on me," Salem yelled back.

Pinning Salem down by the arms and knees, Jin's face turned red as he struggled.

"Even if you hadn't of called me, I would have known where you were tonight," Jin said.

Salem tried to fight back, but he was pinned hard and the alcohol didn't help the situation.
Wanting to finish his words Jin took his left hand shoving Salem's chin toward the ceiling. He wanted to make sure he could see his eyes.

"You're the one acting like a different person. Like you're not the "Sim Sim Let Me In" I met a couple of weeks ago. Come on man. Let's be real here, and if you can't be real I wonder if this will bring you back to reality. Let's see Sim Sim. Let's see if I were to do this what I would find," he replied agitated.

Opening Salem's jacket he then pulled at his shirt until the buttons popped. He let go of Salem's chin and just sat on top of him, waiting for a response.

"Well, come on man! I don't know about you, but I don't see many men wearing a bra and probably the match panties," Jin said struggling to take a breath.

Salem stopped struggling and Jin stood strattled across him. Buttoning up his shirt he did his best to hide the tethered shirt under his jacket his jacket.

"How did you know," Salem asked, ashamed to look Jin in the eyes.

"How did I know? You told me buddy. You even showed me. You said you started doing it after that incident with one of your cousins. You know rub a dub, dub, two boys in a tub thing," he replied.

Salem had never told anyone about the incident, only him and his cousin knew, at least that's what he thought. Jin didn't laugh nor smile in-fact his face seemed blank like a chalkboard ready for more knowledge to be written on it.

"I know this is strange man, but I thought we had a good conversation going on that night, but you disappeared. That girl out there, are you seriously with her? Does she even know you man," he asked.

Jin's questioning seemed to make time stand still for Salem. No reply came from his mouth. The music and the loud crowd all seemed to stand still with him. Cherise was the only girl he wanted since he first noticed her two years ago. She made him feel right for the first time in a long time. But Jin was right she knew nothing about him. His family was so indifferent to him that he wondered if they even knew him. Pretend is what he called it. There were a lot of things that the family pretended not to see. He had

been away so long that he'd forgotten. He looked back a Jin

who seemed to not have moved from his place. He was

asking the right questions, and because of this Salem knew

that he knew something. A stranger knew what others

didn't.

"Okay so tell me," Salem asked.

Motion came to Jin's body once more. Salem didn't

know what to do with himself, so he propped his back

against the mirror.

"The night you came in with my friend, I didn't pay any

attention to you, but when you started drinking, you

seemed to change. You were more relaxed, comfortable in

your skin. You started asking me about my face and

clothes, and why I was trying so hard to be different when

most people were trying all their lives just to fit in. Salem's head continued to spin as he took himself back to that night, back to the underground club. He remembered sitting at the table, and the more Jin talked the further his memory took him. It seemed that Jin was upset about something and jumped up from the place he was sitting.

"Wow, what did you say to him? We never get a reaction out him," Serene said knocking back the last of her drinks.

"Whoa man I didn't mean anything. I was just asking a question," Salem yelled.

"Then next time be sure to take the assumption out of your questions." Jin yelled back.

"What do you mean," Salem asked following behind

him.

Jumping up on the table he reached down and pulled Salem by his collar and jumping off he led Salem into another room. It was darker than the first and the music had gone from upbeat, to dark and pretentious. The people who inhabited the room were dressed similar to his new buddy. Unlike him the men painted their eyes in black eye liner adorned their lips with dark colors. White candles dripping of wax ran the length of an oblong table. Fake skulls with glowing eyes were placed at each end. Five people sat around the table holding hands, with their heads down. As the two watched one of the strangers gestured for them to join in. Moving to take a seat Jin grabbed him by the arm just shy of Salem sitting down.

"Not trying to be funny or anything, but I don't see you as being the type of person interested in this type of crowd," Jin replied.

He was right. Salem's only venture in their territory was watching old movies like the craft. The drink was beginning to make him light headed. His body seemed to have no weight, and he felt as if he could fly.

"So why did you bring me here," he asked.

His new buddy was starting to think he was a little stupid, or that the alcohol was a little too much for him.

"Look around you. They just want attention, now not all of them, but most. When they go out they want to make sure their seen. I'm not like them. I like black, simply because I wear it well. I look good in it. I have a few friends, and none of them are like me. There's not a gang of us hanging out anywhere, they do their thing and I do my mine because I and only I am happy with it," he said.

While Salem laughed, Jin didn't crack a smile. He was still a little iffy about the guy. The weightlessness that Salem felt turned into a tingle.

"And while their trying to show off something, it seems like your trying to hide something," Jin asked.

"Hah, you couldn't have my difference," Salem said stumbling over his words.

His forehead met Jin's as he said this, and Jin thought he knew what Salem was getting at. Even though they were in what Jin considered a dirty dark whole in the wall, the only glimmer of innocence he saw was in the face of Salem.

"I think I could handle any surprise you gave me man.

Yeah, I'm sure of that," he said as he leaned in closer to Salem and gave him a soft kiss on the lips.

"I don't go for men," Salem whispered still stumbling over his words as Jin let up to breath.
Neither of the men moved, they just stood there looking at each other as if something catastrophic was about to happen, and then Jin whispered into his ear.

"If that's true, then why haven't you moved," Jin asked.

Salem didn't move, nor did he look directly at Jin.

"To see how much of a difference my difference makes," he whispered back.

Drifting his eyes towards Jin his new buddy moved in once more to kiss him bringing him back to the present.

"Have you been listening to me at all," Jin asked.

He didn't have to hear it, he remembered. Sliding to the floor he began to cry.

"So what happened after the kiss," Salem quivered.

Jin knelt down beside him. He wanted to comfort him, but at the same time seemed to have no sympathy for him.

"What are you crying for? You made the choice to keep going," Jin replied.

Holding his head in between his legs he went back to that night as Cherise stood on stage collecting her winnings from her cousin. Taif looked on as she danced with her blonde god, while trying to get the attention of Lamya, who she just knew would be jealous. Lamya didn't notice Taif, because as Salem cried in another room and Taif batted her big eyes at blonde, Lamya was seeing something different in Mitch. The mood of the crowd smothered each of them like a baby in a blanket, and though they felt as if they needed to be freed the new comfort that they found in each other that night would not let them go. As they swooned in its trance Salem remembered swooning to the music and the people in the underground club as he received a third kiss from Jin.

"I told you, I don't like men," Salem said moving away from Jin.

"I'm not either. I just happened to like what my eyes are attracted to," Jin smiled.

Salem moved away further holding his hands out as if he wanted to be searched.

"So you think you like this, right? Do you even know what this is, what I am," he asked taunting Jin with a wicked smile.

Jin was confused and started to think Salem was a little off. He knew that what he was saying didn't register for Jin, but at that point he didn't want to keep quiet any longer. He figured if he had to tell anyone, a stranger would be his best bet. He could leave the club and know a hundred percent that he would never see the guy again.

Swaggering Salem had Jin follow him to a dark corner of the room. When he was sure no one was around. He clumsily unzipped his pants. Falling against the wall he accidentally knocked open a door. It was one of many private spaces the club provided if you had the money to spend on it. He felt as if the room had been awaiting him, and pulling Jin in behind him he made sure that the area was locked. Salem still struggled, but Jin had no shame in helping him out of his predicament. As the pants were dropped, Jin stepped back. He expected to see sexy male briefs or some fun boxers, but what he saw instead were black-laced panties, and the bra to match as Salem also pulled off his shirt.

"Okay, so it's a fetish. There's nothing really different about you man, a lot of guys have the same fetish," Jin smiled.

After the free viewing Jin believed that he would have a huge smile on his face for at least a week. As he enjoyed basking in visual bliss Salem starred hard at him, squinting his eyes as he focused.

"What if I told you that I could satisfy anyone willing to try," he asked sweating as he spoke.

"I'm not sure about that, but I'm quite sure you could satisfy me," Jin replied.

Salem didn't laugh. He didn't speak. He just stood watching Jin. He knew his next move would get a reaction, but he didn't know what kind. He shrugged his shoulder at Jin's boyish remark and as he did the Jin of the present snapped his fingers in front of the man holding his head between his legs.

"You remember now? You had something to tell me that night, but before you could get it out we ended up playing around, and talking," he laughed.

He wanted to see his buddies face and putting his hand under Salem's chin he held his head up so he could see his eyes.

"What's wrong? Are you ashamed of kissing another guy? You had fun that night. Tell me what you wanted to tell me the other night, come on," he pleaded yearning to see the same Salem he met some weeks ago.

There were no words left to speak. Jin gave him a kiss as Salem thought back to when he was just five. They were in Marina Mall at one of the children's clothing stores. He stood playing with a toy airplane as he watched his parents fighting over a cute summer dress. Mrs. Tamimi was trying to put it back on the rack, while Mr. Tamimi was trying his best to take it off. It ended with them settling on a pair of baby blue shorts and a t-shirt. He wore the over sized outfit to a walk on the cornish later in the month. Mr. Tamimi decided that it was time to mention the birds and the bees. Stopping to watch a boat race he picked his son up placing him to sit on some bars where he could view the race better. Salem sat close to him so Mr. Tamimi bent down and talked quietly in his ears while Salem listened. It was the closest that his father had ever been at that time, unless he was changing his clothes, which was very seldom.

"I don't know if we really could have changed anything, so I left it in Allah's care. Maybe I was right to do so, because you seem to be growing into such a good boy. You could be anything, but it seems that you're gonna become the son I always wanted," he smiled, while nodding his head for Salem to agree with him.

And that was it. That was the speech. His father didn't realize, but he gave his son a lot to think about, on that day the rest to come. In the other room while Salem regrettably reminisced, Cherise left the stage and was roaming through the crowd looking for him. Salem had forgotten about Cherise. Nothing else at that moment mattered to him, but to find his truth. The men had both stripped bare, and were entangled in an intense embrace. There would be few on earth that could experience what they would that night. Their moist bodies meshed together as if they were made for each other. Salem didn't want to let go and felt ashamed that he thought about Mitch at that moment. Cherise could find no sight of him in the crowd, deciding to make a pit stop to the bathroom. All the while Mitch had spent enough time with Lamya that he started to see something different in her, something that he admired too much to let go. He wanted to show off a little. Three weeks earlier he found a great place in Manhattan looking over the whole city. He hadn't even told Salem yet and it would be awesome if he could invite her and the rest of her family to come see the place. Pulling Lamya out of the crowd he to tell Salem right away. As Cherise left the bathroom she ran into Lamya and Mitch. As the three stood baffled by Salem's disappearance, they could hear what sounded like a loud thud down the hall from the bathroom. Playing three hours straight Joint decided the hand his turntables over to another DJ. His first stop was the bathroom. Realizing that the sound came from a private room, Mitch thought it would be funny to burst in on who was ever doing what in the room. Jin and Salem were still in their sacred position as Mitch slowly turned the knob. Lamya was just as curious as Mitch, and so she took charge bum rushing past Mitch into the room. Startled both men fell to the floor. Lamya screamed in disbelief, while Mitch tried to cover her eyes. Struggling to get up Salem grabbed his pants. He opened his mouth to speak, but wasn't able to say a word. Covering her mouth with her hands, Cherise fell to the floor. As he hurriedly dressed he couldn't force himself to look at the group, but out of the corner of his eye he could see that Limy and Mitch held each other tight, too tight. Rage filled within him faster than water nearing a damn. Forcing himself past people who began to feel like strangers, he ran into the crowd wanting to be lost, and hoping somehow just as quickly to be found again.

"Hey, what up man? What's your hurry," Joint yelled putting up his hand waiting for a high five.

Salem hid his dismay choosing not to exactly look Joint in the eyes.

"Now that you say something, I'm trying to surprise Cherise. Is it possible for me to borrow your car so I can pick up a little late night food and a good movie," Salem said laughing nervously as he spoke.

"No problem at all man. I'm not going home to at least the sun comes up. So have it your way. Just don't get know tickets," he said patting Salem on the back.

"Hey, I'm trying to emulate you. I'll make sure no

tickets are gotten," he said graciously taking the keys from Joint's hand.

"Alright, tell Cherise I said good night, because if I don't get to the bowl soon it will not be pretty," he smiled walking away quickly.

As the keys hit his hands he never looked back. Palms sweating and heart beating ferociously, he made his way out of the crowd and out the door. Jumping into Joint's car his stomach began to turn as his temperature rose. He drove fast in hopes of reaching his destination as soon as possible. He passed a corner store, several food places, one or two flower booths, and never looked their way. His only stop was at the record store. He remembered the psychedelic colored key that Cherise used to lock Joints door. Climbing the back steps, he unlocked it and went straight to Joint's roof. Though it was closed in completely there was single door on the corner of the roof leading to the ledge for maintenance. Salem stepped out to the very edge.

Looking down at the street he then turned looking over his left shoulder. Sheik stood behind him. He was smiling and with tears dripping from his eyes, Salem smiled back at him. He was back in Karama on the rooftop of Sheiks apartment building. Moments before guest arrived Sheik confessed that he had deep feelings for Salem. They were reminiscing about when they were boys thirty minutes earlier, and just like boys they wrestled one last time. Exhausted Sheik found himself on top of Salem resting his forehead on his chest. Slowly getting to his feet he found himself nose to nose with Salem. He was an old friend who with his head flat on the floor always looked like a girl to Sheik, and at that moment his emotions were in turmoil, knowing that his closest friend would be leaving for what he thought would be for good. He wanted a lasting goodbye, and so he lowered himself kissing Salem gently on the lips. Disgusted Salem pushed Sheik off of him on to the floor.

"What's that," Salem asked nervously.

"I don't know. I heard you weren't exactly a guy. Sometimes I see a guy sometimes a girl. Your parents were talking about it one night. I was up and," he said then pausing not sure if he should say anything at all.

A while ago Sheik saved Salem from drowning at a local beach in Dubai. He had lost his footing and somehow got his foot caught on some wiring beneath him. The wiring turned out to be part a small boat close by. As the boat moved the wire tightened around his ankle, pulling Salem out into the deep with no room to move. Seeing his distress Sheik swam to help, grabbed on to his body and locked on to his wire wrapped leg. Salem was out of breath and Sheik blew air into his mouth as he desperately struggled to unwind the wire. A freed Salem floated to the top, while it took a few minutes to retrieve Sheik. He was hospitalized for three days unconscious while Salem sat by his side night after night. He knew how Sheik felt; he felt the same, under the water as Sheik blew life into him. But like his father said he had grown into a man, no matter the situation. One man didn't kiss another no matter the feelings.

Turning his back on Sheik for the last time he stood on the corner of Joints roof and held his hands high in the air as if he were going to fly. Looking down he spotted a taxi. He could see Cherise and Joint getting out. She was beautiful he thought, but so was Sheik, Mitch and Jin, Jin being the loveliest of all, he had the courage to explore a stranger, tempt his senses, and awake him fully. They had lost their virginity together. Looking up to the dark sky

Salem felt that it was time to let go and with little effort at all for a moment he felt as if he were flying, flying like Sheik must have felt the night Salem said his goodbyes. Sheik was a brother that saved his life because of love, and took his own life that same night from the lack of it. Flight began to feel like falling and as he faced the sky he remembered covering both genitalia, as he stood bare-naked in the tub with Mohammed. Sensations over came him, and though Bakir didn't notice Mohammed did. For a second he could hear the wind pushing through his ears forcefully. He wanted to see himself positive at that age and changed the memory to suit his heart. He saw himself letting his hands go exposed, caring not a bit about who saw what. He smiled. The wind ceased. He had completed a life time from the first breath he took on the roof to the last breath on his way to rebirth.

Lamya and her parents were at Mitch's new place with

the rest of his family. Getting a call from Joint he decided to break the news to Lamya on the balcony. Earlier Taif received a text from Joint. She called Lamya's parents where they were informed in the living room of Mitch's place. Mrs. Tamimi immediately blamed her husband. Salem was loved and Mitch knew that Renee and the rest of the group would want to know right away. As the police surrounded the scene, Renee received the news. Sitting on her couch she took a puff of her cigarette and a sip of wine. The statue that Salem seemed to fancy so much sat in the middle of her living room, and looking over at Alice she could only conjure up these words.

"I guess the monkey king finally had to show his tale," she said trying to hold back her tears.